THE ONLY WAY?

A Novel by

Victor W Watton

DEDICATION

In loving memory of my darling daughter Abby, a wonderful Mummy and teacher.

And for my wife Jill, my children Simon, Rebecca, Tim and Peter, my grandchildren, Jasmine, Benjamin, Kisa, Phoebe, Thomas, Franky and Jacob.

Acknowledgements

This is a work of fiction and so, although most of the places referred to are real, the people are not. Any resemblances to actual people or situations are purely coincidental and totally unintended.

I would like to thank: Jill, my wife, for her love and support and for putting up with me being 'tied to the computer'; Jasmine, my granddaughter, for her interest, encouragement, and suggestions; Mark Earl from Cleveland Constabulary for his advice on police methods.

"Jesus answered, 'I am the way and the truth and the life. No one comes to the Father except through me.'"   John chapter 14 verse 6

"He (Saul) went to the high priest and asked him for letters to the synagogues in Damascus, so that if he any there who belonged to the Way, whether men or women, he might take them as prisoners"
Acts of the Apostles chapter 9 verses 1-2

CHAPTER ONE

How in the name of all that's holy (actually I used some four-letter words not becoming in a vicar) had I got myself into such an unbelievable mess? Here I was, a vicar who no longer believed in God, quite a difficult thing to be even in the Church of England, in a marriage to a woman I had never loved, on my way to an assignation with a beautiful woman who was not my wife, in order to break one of the Ten Commandments!

As I drove along the A61 from my home (for want of a better word) in Leeds, to my rendezvous in Ripon, I struggled to work it all out. What had put me in such a ridiculous predicament?

First and foremost was Sarah, my wife. Wife she certainly was, we had a certificate to prove that. Love of my life she definitely was not. In fact, I was on my way to meet the real love of my life, and she wasn't Sarah! As I thought about this, it suddenly dawned on me that maybe marrying Sarah was the reason for the state I was in. Indeed, marrying her was as likely as not the biggest mistake I had ever made. How the hell had it happened?

I suppose if I were to be totally honest with myself, I would have to admit that my marriage was the Church of England's equivalent of an arranged marriage. I had arrived at my first church in Redcar a shy, young, single curate, and as Jane Austen might have said, 'It is a truth universally acknowledged that a young man possessed of a dog collar must be in need of a wife'.

Sarah was certainly in need of a husband. The only child of doting pillars of the Church, she had done teacher training and was back living at home whilst teaching in a primary school in Middlesbrough. She had no boyfriend, and what social life she had revolved around the church and its middle-aged to elderly congregation. What her parents needed to make their lives complete was to fix Sarah up with a good marriage, and what better marriage partner could there be for a daughter like Sarah than a vicar?

Sarah's father, Trevor, was some sort of senior manager at the local steelworks (what had been British Steel before its various takeovers by Asian multi-nationals), and was church warden at my church. Sarah's mother, Christine, was a nurse and secretary of the Mothers' Union. Consequently, they were in an ideal position to make their plan come to fruition as they had no difficulty in ensuring that Sarah and I met frequently. I suppose that in many ways I was a willing accomplice in their devious scheme as Sarah was far from being unattractive. She was tall and slim with long, shiny, blonde hair and a very good fashion sense, all of which made her strikingly attractive, though the lack of emotion in her greyish blue eyes and the tendency for her mouth to turn down at the corners stopped her from being entirely beautiful. I can certainly remember being totally captivated by her appearance - the appearance of a woman totally out of my league.

Of course, a man in a dog-collar does not have much opportunity for the intimate side of courting (what a wonderful old-fashioned word) and none at all for living-together before marriage. Hence it was only after our marriage that I had the opportunity to get to know Sarah properly – insofar as it was possible to get to know Sarah at all.

I thought that real love, with all its passion and intoxication, would come after marriage, but Sarah thought differently; as far as she was concerned there was no need to know more than the external persona. Marriage for Sarah was not about love or passion, it was simply a status, a natural progression, not a deep relationship. Consequently, it was only after we were married that I discovered the emptiness lying beneath the bewitching exterior. Sarah was a mannequin rather than a person; someone devoid of all feelings, except those involved in maintaining the appearance of a well-dressed, well-coiffured Christian lady who could mouth all the platitudes of Evangelical Christianity without an ounce of real feeling or compassion.

Out of this maelstrom of thoughts, I suddenly noticed that I had reached Harrogate and soon found myself waiting in a queue of traffic on the way past Betty's tea rooms which, for some reason, made me think about the other big mistake of my life, right up there competing with Sarah to be the biggest – becoming a vicar.

Why had I left King's College, London with a history degree and suddenly become a vicar? Of course, it was, a bit like my marriage to Sarah, something I'd drifted into. But like most momentous decisions, there was a catalyst. For me it had been my parents' death. A tragic accident when they were mown down on the pavement one evening by a stupid drunken driver. Looking back, I must have had some sort of breakdown, though I didn't see it as such at the time. Now I realise that is exactly what my refusing the help of my university friends, including my girlfriend, and retreating into a lonely pit of despair was.

My parents had been nominal C of E, and the vicar who took the funeral befriended me and gradually led me out of the slough of despond into which I had descended. I had no idea what to do with my life, and when it was suggested I should be ordained, it seemed like a light at the end of the tunnel. At first it was a great success. I thoroughly enjoyed the theology in the training, and loved the opportunity to help people and share in the great moments of their lives after my ordination. But now after almost seventeen years as a vicar, it was all changed.

I was now driving past the huge hotel to which Agatha Christie had 'disappeared' in 1926. The imposing building from a bygone era focussed me on one of my many problems with the Church - the growth of the Evangelical Movement which was trying to take the Church back to the supposed certainties of the Victorian Age instead of coming to terms with the realities of the twenty first century.

I had become so involved in my thoughts that I hadn't noticed the music on the radio stopping to be replaced by the four o'clock news, but one announcement forced its way into my consciousness and made my heart sink at the same time, "The Reverend Timothy Harris, leader of the One-Way Christian Group, has just announced a campaign to bring Britain back to its Christian roots, including an attempt to reverse the law on same sex marriages. The Reverend Harris speaking at a One-Way meeting in Ripon Cathedral said,

'This land of ours is a Christian country and has been since its beginnings. Like you, I love this country and want it to regain its greatness, but we can only do that if we re-discover, and embrace, our Christian heritage. We could start by getting rid of the aberration of same-sex marriage. We all know that God created marriage for a man and a woman, indeed this was stated by our Lord Jesus Christ himself. Now ...' "

I cut Timothy Harris off in full flow by switching off the radio. I refused to call such an evil monster a reverend and had no intention of listening to his claptrap. Harris was the leader of a group who were convinced not only that they were right, but also that all atheists, agnostics, members of non-Christian religions and even non-Evangelical Christians were wrong and heading for hell. Perhaps the only good thing Timothy Harris had ever done was make me face up to the truth. Could I really stay in a Church which not only allowed such rubbish to be spoken in its name, but actually encouraged such people to meet in the cathedral church of my diocese?

I'd been a strong opponent of the One-Way group ever since its inception – which was another problem for my marriage since Sarah and her parents had been almost founder members of the group! To me any group claiming that Jews, Muslims, Hindus, Buddhists and non-believers must be told they are wrong and persuaded to turn to Christ is tremendously dangerous since it's not exactly the greatest way to promote community cohesion!

My outspoken opposition had caused much conflict with my superiors, especially the Bishop of Ripon and Leeds. He was a voluble supporter of One-Way since to him bringing lots of wealthy middle-class converts into the Church had to be a good thing. To me, on the other hand, any group that claimed Jesus was the only way to God had to be a bad thing in a multi-faith, multi-ethnic diverse society like Britain. Hence the bishop and I had a major impasse.

By now the twin towers of Ripon Cathedral had appeared on the horizon shifting my mind to another problem – my assignation with Jasmine. Jasmine had been my first love, in fact my only girlfriend before Sarah. Jasmine was the one whom I had treated so abominably in the depression that engulfed me after my parents' death. Jasmine was so normal, so communicative, so full of emotion, so wonderful! I'd never expected to meet her again after our break up over twenty years ago, but I had thought of her a lot during my marriage to Sarah. Time and again I'd regretted my cruelty and stupidity in ending our relationship. Then fate had taken a hand – or as my rational mind preferred to think of it - a serendipitous chance encounter occurred.

I saw a leaflet in the library about a public lecture at Leeds University on religion as a cause of conflict given by the Professor of War Studies from King's College, London. When I was at Kings, Michael had just begun as a history lecturer, now he was a professor, and I thought it would be good to see him again.

Seeing Jasmine in that lecture room, made my heart leap and my stomach churn like a lovesick teenager. She had changed so little: her face still full of life and laughs, her eyes still that deep liquid brown, still lively and inquisitive. I stammered my way through my initial expressions of surprise and joy at seeing her, and my contrition at my appalling treatment of her, before we began to catch up on the last twenty years. She was at the lecture to gain information for her A level students. I don't know whether she gained any information, but I certainly didn't. I hardly heard a word of the lecture as I kept gazing at Jasmine and thinking that I couldn't let her go again.

That was six months ago. We'd met regularly since in various locations in North Yorkshire (which I'd planned to be far enough away to ensure none of my parishioners from Leeds would see us) and our romance had blossomed. Jasmine had had a brief unhappy marriage and for the last few years had been working and living in the Stockton area teaching R.E. Now, at last, we were moving on to the next stage of our relationship: a night as Mr and Mrs Baker at the Old Deanery Hotel in Ripon. Now there was a problem for a married vicar!

Actually, it wasn't really a problem for me. I hadn't had sex for longer than I could remember and now I was about to spend a weekend of passion with a gorgeous woman. Where was the problem?

Well of course the problem was my job. Extra-marital affairs are not part of the job description for a vicar! But a more worrying problem to me was Jasmine Baker herself. I had no intention of this being a one night stand, but was Jasmine ready for moving on as deeply as I wanted? She'd told me that since the acrimonious ending of her two year marriage to Stephen, she had kept clear of men. Was she now ready to commit to me? Did she really want to hitch herself to a vicar whose frigid wife didn't understand him? Did she want to be the other woman? Did she want to be any man's woman? After all, Jasmine was a successful professional woman. She had a career, her own home and car; she had a good fulfilling life, she didn't need a no-hoper like me.

As I turned my silver Focus (typical vicar's car) into the town centre car park, I saw Jasmine get out of her car and walk towards me, and my doubts evaporated. Unlike my wife Sarah, she didn't look like she had just walked off the cover of Vogue. Jasmine went for casual comfort, but she looked stunning. As she approached, I involuntarily leapt out of the car, ran over to her and lifted her up in a passionate hug.

"I love you Jasmine. I want to marry you!" The words shocked me as much as they clearly did Jasmine. I was far too old to behave like a love-sick teenager, yet that was how Jasmine made me feel. The words themselves had come out without forethought, indeed almost without me realising that I was uttering them.

Jasmine stepped back, looked at me and said in a worryingly serious tone, "Come on Simon (she'd always called me Simon rather than the Si to which many people abbreviated my name without asking my permission – including Sarah). You don't really mean that do you? You're just saying it because you're here for a night of passion."

I looked into those beautiful, deep, brown eyes and wondered how I'd ever been attracted to anyone else, and why I'd ever let her go. This realisation made me reply, "I do mean it Jazz (I'd soon reverted to the abbreviation we both preferred and which, for me, summed up her personality). Maybe I've only just realised it, but I do want to marry you. I want to start a new life with you. Goodbye Church! Goodbye Sarah! Hello Jasmine! Hello the new me!"

This soppy speech provoked a decidedly sceptical look from Jasmine and a reply which hit me like a bucket of cold water. "Let's go into the hotel, have a drink and talk it over Simon," she said. "This is all too sudden. Put this parking ticket on your car. Put your luggage into my boot and I'll drive us round to the hotel just like we planned. Then we'll have a drink and a discussion before we check in. If we check in..."

Wow! Instant deflation! I searched for a smart reply and failed to find one. That 'if we check in' was far too worrying. So, I followed instructions with my head down. The idea had been that if I parked my car away from the hotel it would deflect suspicion.

We drove out of the car park, into the market place, down Kirkgate and then up Bedern Bank where we found ourselves at the magnificent west front of the cathedral. Ripon might be a small city, but its cathedral had been designed to impress. We turned into the car park of the Old Deanery Hotel and clearly the Deanery had also been designed to demonstrate the power of the Church to the hoi polloi. Compared with my semi-detached vicarage it was a stately home!

We got out of the car and gazed at the huge windows, the beautiful, mellow, Yorkshire stone, before walking through an ancient oak door into the reception area where we received a warm friendly welcome from a lady standing at the desk (who we later discovered was Linda, the owner). No doubt she was a little fazed when I paused before replying to her welcome. What to say? Were we checking in? Were we just having a drink? That 'if' was becoming a huge barrier which I had to break down. Finally, I spoke, "Hello. We're Jasmine and Simon Baker. We've a booked a room for tonight. Do you think we could have a pot of tea before we check in, we're desperate?"

I was quietly pleased with my response. It provided the space Jasmine had asked for, whilst almost precluding the possibility of us not checking in. I was also pleased that Jasmine had booked the room on her credit card. The hotel needed proof of identity, but as Mr Baker, I was anonymous!

Linda guided us past the great oak staircase and into a large sitting room. Despite the empty space next to Jasmine on the black leather sofa, I deliberately chose to sit on the opposite side of the large coffee table so that I could watch her face closely as I quizzed her about that 'if'.

Experience with Sarah had taught me not to leap straight in to tricky situations, so I steered the conversation to generalities as we waited for the tea to arrive.

"Look at the plasterwork on that ceiling. It's elegantly sumptuous isn't it?" I began, at the same time thinking to myself, Oh my God, I'm sounding like someone from the 'Antiques Roadshow'. "Do you think it's original Jazz?" I continued, making the questions rhetorical so I could move on before she had a chance to reply." It's certainly an up-market place for a Christian clergyman to have lived in. I've always wondered how our bishops and deans justify their splendiferous living quarters. What do they think when they read Jesus' words 'It is easier for a camel to go through the eye of a needle than for a rich man to enter the kingdom of heaven.'? Perhaps they think that because they're only living in the places and don't actually own the wealth, they don't count as rich men."

Jasmine raised her head and rolled her eyes at my inane babbling which was luckily cut short by the arrival of the tea delivered by a smartly dressed young waitress. I poured two cups before asking the question (the answer to which I had been dreading ever since we left the car park), "What's wrong?"

"What's wrong?" somehow she managed to keep her voice down as this exclamation burst from her lips. "What's wrong is that I don't have a good track record with marriage; plus, you have the added problems of already being married and being a vicar. How can you marry me? I was just about coping with re-discovering our relationship, though I have to admit I wasn't sure you were going to get any sex tonight, but I certainly can't cope with you telling me lies about marriage and new lives. That's why I think I might just go home."

As I looked across at that captivating brown face, I saw that it had tears welling up in its eyes. Her full lips were turned down at the corners and a deep sadness seemed to be smothering her normal exuberance. Like many men, I suppose, I'd been self-obsessed. I had been so busy thinking I was the only one with problems, when Jasmine clearly had just as many as me, if not more.

I thought carefully, knowing instinctively that my next words would make or break our relationship. I just had to get them right; I couldn't lose her again! "I've made many mistakes in my life Jazz," I began, "but by far the biggest was leaving you twenty-five years ago, and the next biggest ones were getting ordained and marrying Sarah. Since I met you again, I feel I've been given a chance to start over and when I saw you beside your car waiting to spend the night with me, I just knew I didn't want our relationship to be for one night, I wanted it to be for the rest of our lives. I don't want some casual, sordid affair meeting each other for the odd night in a hotel Jazz," I paused before continuing, " I want to spend my life with you. I want to be totally committed to you."

As I finished the speech, I looked at Jasmine and thought, 'Oh shit!' Strange, but all those years of wearing a dog collar haven't stopped that from being my automatic expletive when things go wrong. The questioning look on her face sent my heart to my boots. I was sure I'd been a bit too Mills and Boonish and that she was going to tell me to get lost. I waited with baited breath for her reply.

"That's easy enough to say Simon, but how are you actually going to put it into practice? You have a wife, a job in the Church and no alternative career. You can't just leave them!"

Her reply gave me the chance I'd hoped for! I'd been working on a game plan ever since reconnecting with Jasmine at that lecture.

"True my darling, I can't **just** leave them, but I can leave them. For a start I think the Church is already expecting me to leave."

"What do you mean?" Jasmine enquired sharply. Good I had her attention again.

"Have you heard of the One-Way Group?" She nodded and I continued. "Well, the Bishop has become a major supporter and I had a massive row with him about his views at the Diocesan Synod. I said one or two things which I shouldn't have said and now I have a meeting with Lord Jim on Saturday at which I think he's going to ask for my resignation."

"Lord Jim?"

"It's what some of us call our beloved bishop. It combines his Eton and Oxford origins with his feeble attempts to be a man of the people."

"No doubt also referring to the moral cowardice of Conrad's hero?"

"Come off it Jazz. Most of today's vicars don't even know Lord Jim is the title of a Conrad novel let alone that he was a moral coward! Certainly, our sainted bishop wouldn't sacrifice his life to make up for a cowardly act. That's far too Christian for a bishop."

"Wow! He has got you annoyed. What on earth did you say at the synod?"

"I only told them the truth about One Way."

"Yes?" she asked quizzically.

"Nothing much. Just that it's a group of upper middle-class twits who are either too thick or too lazy to think clearly about religion. I may also have said that they're extremely dangerous because they're trying to convince Britain that Christianity is the one true religion. And saying something like that implies that those many of our fellow citizens who have no religion, or follow another religion, are not only wrong, but are also working against God."

"So, you didn't say anything too bad then," Jasmine replied sarcastically.

I ignored the sarcasm as I continued, "Well, maybe not. But then I maybe went a little further than I should by telling them that the Reverend Timothy Harris had made me lose what little faith I had left because if he was inspired by God, then it was a God I didn't want to know. Unfortunately, I added that anyway I was no longer too sure about the existence of any such divine being, hence my summons to the meeting and the likely request for my resignation. But actually, I'm going to tell him where he can put his job before he asks for my resignation. I can't do a job I don't believe in."

"OK. Well that's sorted the job and the Church," Jasmine said with the beginnings of a grin. "Now what about the wife?"

I poured another cup of tea before replying, "I've already told you that Sarah has never been interested in the physical side of marriage and has never even given me a kiss since she discovered she's infertile, and since I met you at the lecture, we've scarcely even spoken to each other. I've consulted a solicitor and she reckons I have good grounds for a divorce because of Sarah's unreasonable behaviour. Grounds that Sarah's not likely to contest as she won't want people to know we haven't had sex for fifteen years! I've also been surfing the net to see what flats are available up in Stockton."

Jasmine's face was a picture as her emotions went from grinning, to questioning, to incredulity. When she spoke, it was in a disbelieving tone, "My God Simon! Are you really ready to give up everything and come to live near me? I don't know what to say. Let's check in and then I can try to get my head round it all."

I gave myself an inward high five and went back into reception. Twenty minutes later we were in the hotel's Room 4, a large room with two windows overlooking the garden and an enticing king-size bed. I went into the bathroom as a way of giving Jasmine the space she was bound to need to come to terms with the bombshell I'd just dropped on her.

Just because I was back in love and ready for a new life didn't mean she was. She must be thinking back to the way I betrayed her in the aftermath of my parents' deaths. She'd been ready and willing to help me through the grief and trauma, but I'd rejected her, retreating into my selfish grief and then, after our finals, simply disappearing into the arms of the Church. She had to be wondering if she could trust my words now.

Since our meeting up again at that lecture, I'd apologised several times for my appalling behaviour after Mum and Dad's deaths and offered garbled explanations of that weird decision to go into the Church, but had it been enough? True we had been getting it back together. In fact, we were behaving like two adolescents from the 1950's having a love affair without sex! I sat on the toilet seat hoping against hope that the sex was going to come to our love affair.

"Simon! Simon! Come here quickly!"

The shout from bedroom galvanized me into action. Surely she wasn't that desperate for sex! I shouted, "What is it?" and sprinted out of the bathroom.

Jasmine was standing at the window overlooking the garden. "Look down there Simon!" she said pointing down. "Please tell me it's not what I think it is."

I went to the other window and looked down towards the part of the garden at which Jasmine was pointing.

May is one of the most beautiful times of the year, and this year was no exception. The willows at the bottom of the garden were covered with a deliciously gentle spring green. Clumps of bluebells gave vibrant splashes of colour to the edges of the lawn. In the corner to which Jasmine was pointing, there was a tangle of overgrown grass and weeds, and something else.... something out of place... was it a coat? No, I could make out features. It was a man lying semi-covered by the undergrowth. A man so still, so lifeless, I was pretty sure we were looking at a dead body. Even though I was sure, I decided to play it cool and cautious with Jasmine.

"It looks like a bundle of rags to me," he said. "I thought at first it was a body, but I can't see any face. Let's go down and have a look. There's no point in making a big fuss if there's nothing there."

Jasmine took little persuading that it might not be a body, but she took a lot of persuading to go down to the garden with me. I felt a bit mean as I grabbed her hand and cajoled her into following me down the staircase and into the reception hall. Then I began to convince myself, I was mistaken. After all what would a dead body be doing in the garden of the best hotel in Ripon?

Having no real idea of how we could get into the garden, I decided we might as well off-load the responsibility and communicate what we'd seen to the management.

Linda was sitting at her desk puzzling over something on the PC, maybe a bill? I interrupted her in as non-alarmist a fashion as I could muster, "Excuse me, but we were looking into the garden from our room and we saw something which probably needs investigating."

Linda looked up with a smile, "Oh good! An excuse to get away from this blasted machine. What did you think you saw?"

I looked around, several guests were within earshot, having drinks in the lounge. I thought it might be a good idea if hotel guests were not aware of the possibility of a dead body in the garden. "It might be better if we talk in the garden," I replied.

Linda looked up with a conspiratorial gleam. "Follow me," she said and led us through the dining room, out of some French doors and into the garden. "Now what did you see, and where was it?"

"It was at the corner of the lawn where there's a tangle of overgrown grass and weeds, and we thought it was a body. A dead body."

CHAPTER TWO

Linda maintained her calm 'I'm-in-charge' mien, but walked rather quickly across the lawn. Only the tautness across her shoulders and the tightness of her lips betrayed the worry she had to be feeling. No hotelier wants guests to find a dead body on their property. When she arrived at the corner, she stopped and muttered, "Oh shit!!"

I took the expletive to mean that there was indeed a body there and shouted, "Don't touch anything. We'd better call the police and keep everyone away from here!"

"You're right," Linda replied her face now displaying the worry she had to be feeling. "I'll go and phone for the police, you two stay here and don't let anyone go near."

As Linda walked rapidly back to the hotel, we approached the body. It was clearly a man. He looked to be about our age and there was a slightly puzzled look on his pale face, and a brilliant red line round his neck. He was clean shaven, with receding brown hair cut short.

Jasmine peered over my shoulder, concentrating her gaze on the face of the dead man. Did she recognise him? To be honest at that moment I didn't actually care. I had a more urgent worry.

"Stop looking at him and start concentrating on what we're going to say to the police," I hissed. "We can't tell them that we're Mr and Mrs Baker. We're going to have to tell Linda the truth so that I can give the police my real name. Oh my God!" I groaned as the implications began to dawn on me. "The press'll have a field day when they discover a vicar having an affair. I'm so sorry Jazz. I never intended you to get caught up in something like this. What a mess! We won't be able to keep it quiet because there's always a policeman with a line to the tabloids, and they're always desperate for a story about a vicar and his mistress. I can just see the headline in 'The Sun'.."

Luckily Jasmine interrupted my babblings, "Calm down Simon. It needn't get to that. I'm sure Linda can help us out here. The police don't need to know that we're sharing a room here as Mr and Mrs Baker. We just tell them our real names and that we're staying here."

As Jazz was speaking, Linda came back into the garden. "The police are on their way," she said. "You were right Mr Baker, they want us to make sure that nothing is touched."

She smiled as she said, "Mr Baker" as if sharing a joke. The smile gave me the opportunity to make a heart-felt plea to Linda. "Actually, I'm not Mr Baker, I'm Simon Keep. Unfortunately, it's also the Reverend Simon Keep, and there is a Mrs Keep who is not Jasmine. We're going to have to give our real names to the police and if there is a hint that we're sharing a room, it could make the front pages. It's not as sordid as they'd make it appear and I don't suppose you'll believe me. But I am giving up my dog collar and getting a divorce, but.."

"Don't you worry," Linda cut in sympathetically. "Obviously I knew you two weren't married. And you're right. Finding a body here is going to be all the publicity we need. Lucky for you, I'm the sort of hotelier who believes it's my job to make my guests' stay as pleasant and trouble-free as possible, so I've brought you the key to room 7, Simon. Nip in now and take your case up there. Regrettably it's on the second floor, but it's the only empty room. Move quickly and get back here as soon as you can. We'll talk after the police have gone."

I took the key and rushed back into the hotel. As I raced up the stairs, I realised that I didn't give a toss about everyone finding out about my unfaithfulness, even if I hadn't actually been unfaithful yet! However, I did give a lot more than a toss about Jasmine and would do everything in my power to prevent her from being dragged through the trauma of a press mauling. I grabbed my case from room 4, took the stairs two at a time to room 7, dumped my case on the bed, locked the door and was back in the garden within three minutes.

When Linda saw me, she clasped Jasmine's shoulder in a re-assuring gesture and said, "Don't you worry. Your secret's safe with me. I don't suppose the police will be interested in you and Simon when they've got a mysterious death to investigate. We don't get much crime in Ripon. This'll add a bit of interest to their boring lives. Much better than the usual shoplifting and bicycle thefts."

"I think they might be interested in the two of us since we're the ones who found the murder victim," Jasmine replied, the troubled expression remaining on her face.

"What do you mean, murder victim?" asked Linda in a tone of voice mingling questioning with horrified.

"If you have a look at the body Linda, I think you'll agree he was strangled. I don't see how else he got that deep red line round his neck. And I don't think it will need CSI New York to work out that strangling means murder. And if he was murdered, the police are going to be interested in the people who found the body. And that means me and Simon."

"Bugger! Bugger! Bugger!" Linda exclaimed. "You're right again. That is going to make one hell of a difference. There was me assuming it was a tramp or a drunk who'd been sleeping in the garden and just died. Murder, on the other hand, will make all the difference in the world. It probably won't make any difference to you and Simon, but it will to me and the hotel. The police will be all over the place which will not please our guests. In fact, we might end up with no guests if they all leave."

Jasmine's brain was working faster than mine, perhaps because I was still recovering from the race up the stairs. "You've got no need to worry Linda. If it is a murder, the police won't let anyone leave," she reassured Linda. "Also they'll want food and drink, and when the news breaks you'll have a queue of journalists wanting rooms."

Before Linda could reply, the sound of police sirens filled the air, making her rush back into the hotel and Jasmine urgently whispered in my ear, "We're here for a discussion about RE teaching and whether you want it as your career after the ministry. That is unless you just want to tell them the truth."

I just had time to nod my agreement and understanding before four men, two in police uniform, the other two in plain clothes, appeared in the garden at a brisk walk. The plainclothes men headed straight for me and asked me where the body was. Clearly North Yorkshire police did not expect a woman, let alone a black woman, to be able to help them in their enquiries.

Jasmine soon disabused them of their stereotypical prejudice as she said, "Excuse me. I was the one who spotted the body when I looked out of my hotel room window. I then enlisted Simon's help to come down into the garden and establish that it was a body and its exact location, which is just over here." Jasmine indicated the overgrown area where the body was lying before adding, "We informed Linda, the owner, on our way to the garden. She came with us and when we confirmed it was a body, she went in to phone you whilst Simon and I stayed here to ensure no one touched anything."

The detectives called over the uniformed constabulary and instructed them which areas to tape off as the crime scene before escorting us back into the hotel and instructing Linda to gather all the guests in the lounge. Once gathered, we were instructed that no one would be allowed to leave until everyone had been interviewed. At the same time, Linda was asked to compile a list of all the guests who had been in the hotel over the past three days.

The detectives (at least I assumed they were detectives because of their plainclothes) left us in the lounge and went back into the garden. We helped ourselves to a cup of coffee which the unbelievably efficient Linda had had placed on the tables. We sat in a state of shock for a few moments as what had just happened sank in. Then, as we drank our extremely welcome coffee, the SOCOs arrived, donned their white suits, gloves and boots and went into the garden.

All the access routes to the garden were swiftly blocked off by police tape which the police doctor and senior detectives had to duck under when they arrived to take charge of the investigation and, presumably, make an estimate of the time and cause of death before the post-mortem.

Jasmine and I were of the same mind. We had to resist the urge to talk to Linda, as she was clearly busy with the guests and printing off lists of guests and their details, and concentrate on sorting out our responses to the police questions.

"Look Simon, all we need say is that as soon as I saw the body I phoned you in your room and you came straight down. Then we can just tell it as it happened. Okay?"

"Sounds good to me," I replied, but before I could say anything further, our discussion was interrupted by a tall distinguished-looking man of about fifty. His slightly bouffant black hair showed little sign of thinning or grey, but plenty of signs of an expensive hairdresser.

"Hello Simon. What are you doing here and do you know what's going on?" My stomach churned as I looked up past the black Armani suit and purple stock to see my boss, the Bishop of Ripon and Leeds. How stupid had I been in thinking it was possible to have a secret night away. Perhaps it was a good thing for me that there had been a murder!!
Deciding to pre-empt his questioning, I stood up and said, "Hello my Lord (I deliberately used the official form of address as I knew he professed to hate it, but really loved it). Fancy meeting you here."

"Come on Simon, you know I don't like using these pompous titles. How many times am I going to have to ask you to call me Jim?" The smile on the bishop's face revealed the insincerity of his words. He loved his title even more than he loved his Armani suits!

"Fine, Jim," I continued, "Do you know Jasmine Baker, she's an RE teacher in Stockton? We were at uni together and we're just having a meeting to discuss the possibility of my becoming an RE teacher."

Jasmine got up as I spoke and shook hands with the Right Reverend James Scott-Phillips, Bishop of Ripon and Leeds.

I could see from his reaction that Jasmine's idea of a meeting about a teaching career had been a brilliant one as Lord Jim was now puzzling about my leaving the ministry rather than about my relationship with Jasmine and, to keep him on the back-foot, I quickly continued, "And what are you doing here Jim?" I emphasised the Jim in such a way that it clearly indicated 'Your Lordship' rather than 'my mate'.

With a somewhat diffident expression, the Bishop simply explained that he was at the hotel for a meeting and ruled out any further questions by asking, "Have you any idea why we're being kept in the lounge to be interviewed by the police?"

I explained about Jasmine finding the dead body and was just about to question the Bishop further about his meeting when a detective came in and asked me to go into the dining room to make a statement. It seemed to me that Lord Jim was actually relieved by my exit. Strangely enough, it appeared he was just as discomfited by meeting me here as I was by meeting him.

The police questioning was a walk in the park. The detectives were not at all interested in my relationship with Jasmine. For the first time in several years, they had a murder on their hands, so all their quizzing was about our finding of the body and our reactions to it.

Nevertheless, they questioned us separately, presumably to ensure we were telling the same story and had not committed the murder ourselves – though even from our fairly cursory look at the body, it appeared he had been there at least overnight. So, when I returned to the lounge, Jasmine was ushered into the dining room for her questioning.

Left on my own, I surveyed the other guests who were chatting quietly as they sat waiting their turn to be questioned, and what a nauseating sight greeted me. Timothy Harris, as usual minus his dog-collar to show what an ordinary guy, man of the people he was, was talking to a florid faced, rotund gentleman dressed in a country gent Harris Tweed suit. Surely that was George Blenkinsop, the Conservative MP for some North Yorkshire rural seat. As I looked round I saw there were two more Tory MPs for Yorkshire rural constituencies. Was this why Lord Jim had been so lacking in transparency about the nature of his meeting? Was the Church of England becoming once more the Tory Party at prayer?

As we had been warned, guests and staff were stuck in the lounge and dining room until everyone had been questioned and the police were sure their enquiries were complete. This could have given Jasmine and me a good opportunity to talk about our relationship and where it was going, but the proximity of Lord Jim meant that we kept our discussions to RE teaching.

To be honest, I couldn't really see myself as a teacher. Keeping thirty unruly teenagers in order whilst trying to teach them things they didn't want to know was not my idea of a good time! Nevertheless, I was amazed to discover how much RE had changed and how much vicars, bishops and other high-up religious people were in the dark about it all. Of course, I'd read some of the press campaign about the Government downgrading RE by refusing to allow it as a subject for the EBacc, but really I had little idea of what was taught at GCSE. I was completely stunned to discover teenagers were tackling questions like whether God exists, what happens when you die, should abortion-on-demand be allowed, are inter-faith marriages a good idea. I wondered how on earth this was not as important as history and expressed this rather forcefully.

"Keep it down Simon," Jasmine's whisper accompanied by a kick on the shin stopped me in mid-flow and I realised that several people were listening to my anti-government rant.

Obviously, we had been providing a welcome break from the worried waiting to be questioned and the post-questioning gossip about who the victim might be. The police were showing everyone a photo of the victim, but the gossip was that no one had a clue who he was or why his body had ended up in the Old Deanery garden. I say no one had recognised him, but Jazz had confided to me that she had felt a jolt of recognition when she first looked at the body; a feeling of recognition that was reinforced when she saw the photos. However, as she had no idea who it was or why she felt she recognised him, she had not mentioned it to the police and would not do so until she had something more specific to tell them.

It was not until after dinner that the police gave permission for everyone to leave (presumably they had by this time verified everyone's identity). Before he left, the lead investigator, Inspector Byrom, gave me his card with the words, "If you think of anything that may help, give me a call."

Suitably wined and dined, the Bishop went with some of the other guests for his meeting in the Cathedral library. As they left, Jasmine tugged my arm and whispered, "Look over there. At least four of your bishop's friends are Conservative MP's as well as your friend Timothy Harris. I wonder what they're plotting."

"I thought I recognised some of them before?" I replied. "He must be having a meeting with One-Way Christians and Tory MP's. What an unholy mix! They're probably organising some sort of fund-raising campaign to support Harris's vision of re-Christianising Britain. I think we want to keep well away from them!"

"Hang on Simon! Isn't that Charles Matthews?"

I looked over at the medium height man chatting to George Blenkinsop. The signature tweed jacket, Tattersall shirt and maroon regimental tie were the giveaway. It was indeed Charles Matthews, ex-leader of the virulently anti-EU party which had driven the vote to leave the EU. What was he doing here? And weren't those Tory MPs some of the leading Brexiteers?

Our evening of passion had definitely been pushed onto the back burner, so I suggested we should explore the city. Although technically a city, Ripon is really a small market town (Wells, Ely and the City of London are the only English cities with a smaller population) and it didn't take long for us to explore it. Fortunately, it was nine o'clock when we returned to the market place, just in time to watch the Wakeman perform the ancient ceremony of blowing his horn at each corner to signify the start of the night watch.

The murder, the chance meeting with the odious Bishop and the unspoken, but ever present, concern about the postponed night of passion, meant we didn't want to return to the hotel, so we slipped into one of the many pubs on the market square. Ever since the death of my parents at the hands of the drunken driver, I have been teetotal and so don't often frequent drinking pubs. However, this pub suited me down-to-the-ground since it had a Costa coffee franchise, so I drank a medio Americano while Jasmine sipped a white wine and lemonade.

Twenty years is a long time, certainly long enough for me to have forgotten the furtive glances and whispered comments you arouse when you're in a predominantly white area with a beautiful black woman. Multi-ethnic Britain with its vibrant multi-culturalism had clearly not yet reached Ripon. I ignored the reactions of the locals and began to discuss the future.

"Horrible as it sounds, I'm glad about this murder," I led off. "I know it sounds terrible, to be glad about a murder, but it's true. I needed to do something about our future, and this has forced me into action."

My answer temporarily silenced Jazz, so I continued, "My life is going to change. I just hope and pray that you're going to be a major part of it. Everything that happened to me between leaving you in London and finding you again in Leeds was one ginormous mistake, the most enormous mistake of my life."

"So, are you going to tell her about me?" Jasmine interjected. I didn't need a first-class honours degree to know that 'her' meant

Sarah; and the tone of voice let me know that Sarah did not feature in Jasmine's list of favourite people.

"Why not?" I asked, suddenly realising how selfish I was being. I'd been thinking solely of me and what I wanted, I hadn't stopped for a moment to consider what effect my actions were likely to have on Jasmine.

"Plenty of reasons Simon," Jasmine replied almost before I'd finished enunciating the 'not'. "But the main one is that I don't want to be cast as the other woman. I don't want to be portrayed as the evil bitch who lured you away from your precious wife. So please keep me out of it."

I sipped my coffee and thought. I thought so hard that it must have seemed to Jazz that she could hear my brain cogs whirring. I realised it would be a major logistics exercise to work out how many lives my actions were going to have a considerable impact on. My first thoughts were for Jasmine. She was right. I needed to keep her right out of what was going on. It was essential that I deal with the problems of Sarah and the Church without involving Jazz before embarking on my new life with her and beginning whatever new career I could conjure up for myself.

As I made my decision, Jasmine spoke again, "This is going to sound ridiculous Simon because it's such a non-sequitur, but I'm seeing the face of the murder victim, and I'm thinking of it with a moustache, and I'm thinking of university. I do know him. Somehow, he's connected with King's College and with a moustache, but what's the connection Simon?"

CHAPTER THREE

On my way back to Leeds the next morning (I'd already stopped calling it home!), I tried to work out what I was going to say to my wife, or more correctly, I thought joyously, my soon-to-be ex-wife. I decided to begin by telling Sarah about my meeting tomorrow with Lord Jim and my decision to leave the Church.

"You evil, devious, bastard!" Sarah's response shook me. I don't know what I'd expected, but it wasn't this! I never knew she had so much emotion, let alone so much vitriol, within her. I'd never even known her to swear!

"You decide to give up being a vicar without even telling me, your wife, first!" she yelled and then began a series of vicious rhetorical questions. "Do you have no feelings for me at all? Where will we live? What will people say? How will I hold up my head in church ever again?" Sarah's normally pale, placid and emotionless face became red and ferocious with the anger seething inside her. "So, you've decided to go and see Bishop Jim tomorrow to tell him you're resigning. Tell me you're not serious. Tell me! Tell me! Tell me!"

I was about to say that I would love to tell her that I had no feelings for her, but she continued before I had a chance to get a word in, "You expect me to give up my home, my life, the position I've always wanted and you don't even consider that I might deserve some sort of say in such a momentous decision?"

So that's why she married me! She wanted to be a vicar's wife. What a career aim – to be a vicar's wife! I suppose I'd always known she had no feelings for me and it would have been easy for me to turn this conversation into a slanging match, but I didn't want that. If she started crying, I knew she'd make me feel sorry for her. Also, of course, I knew I was likely to say all sorts of things I might regret. I told myself to keep calm, to be apologetic, to attempt to get out of this emotive marital strife with as few hostages to fortune as possible.

"I'm so sorry Sarah. I never thought you'd react like this. I've known for years that you don't love me. Let's face it, our marriage has always been a loveless sham! I suppose I just thought my job was up to me. I didn't mean to hurt you."

I thought my description of our marriage would hurt her, but she ignored it as she replied, "Well you have hurt me. I can't believe you'd do such a nasty, deceitful, horrid thing. You know the Church is everything to me. What sort of a status will I have in the Church when I'm the wife of an ex-vicar? And of more immediate concern, where will we live? It's the Church you despise that provides us with a roof over our heads. Have you thought of that? We'll be homeless!"

"No, you won't. I might be, but you won't," I replied keeping my cool and using the opportunity she had unwittingly provided to start discussing how I intended leaving her.

"What do you mean by that?" she asked, picking up on my hint immediately despite her fury. "What are you going to do without me?"

I took the opportunity presented by her question to take the conversation onto a different tack as I replied, "I think we should split up Sarah. We don't love each other. Let's face it we've never really been in love. And now I don't even think you like me." She knew this was true, but would never want to admit it, so I continued quickly, "You know we've got enough money in the Building Society account for a decent house. You can have all of it to buy a house wherever you want. There's more than enough for you to buy a nice house in Redcar with no mortgage, near to your mother and father. I don't want any of it"

The combination of money and Redcar started to dissipate the rage and a thoughtful expression began to appear on her face. She'd never been happy about leaving her beloved Redcar to come to Leeds. Added to this, she'd recently given up her teaching post after a row with the Head and was now only doing supply teaching. She could leave Leeds whenever she wanted and there were probably teaching posts aplenty in the Teesside primary schools.

She was silent as she considered her options and I decided to press home my advantage as I continued, "And, don't forget, my actions won't affect your status at all Sarah. You'll be the injured party. The people in the church will love you because you'll be the faithful wronged wife. It'll be me they hate. Me, the apostate vicar who rejected his beliefs and his wife. Let's just calm down Sarah. I'll put the kettle on and make you a nice cuppa."

I moved into our pristine kitchen which seemed to sum up Sarah so well. The shiny white cupboards and sparkling black granite worktops were glamorous and attractive, but the kitchen had no heart. Nothing was allowed to be out of place. There were no coffee jars on the worktop, no dirty pots in the sink. I switched on the gleaming steel kettle (no finger marks allowed) and got the china teapot and china mugs out of a cupboard (no teabag in the mug for Sarah, no pot always china – indeed I'd never really understood why she didn't insist on cups and saucers rather than mugs).

As the kettle boiled and I filled the teapot, Sarah came into the kitchen. I couldn't stop myself from flinching as she put her hand on my shoulder.

"Can't I even touch you now?" Sarah reacted immediately to my involuntary wince. "You've pestered me enough for touches and more in the past. Anyway, I'm not going to sit and have a cup of tea with you as if nothing has happened. You've ruined my life, Simon Keep, and I'm going to phone Daddy for advice on what to do," and with that she flounced out of the kitchen.

What sort of a woman reaches the age of forty and still calls her parents mummy and daddy? Of course, I knew how the phone conversation would go. Trevor and Christine would do all they could to protect their darling daughter. They would also be incandescent with rage at me. Not only for rejecting their little girl, but also for rejecting their beloved Church and, perhaps more tellingly, I thought cynically, leaving all the alterations to the vicarage which they had funded at Sarah's request. I was pretty sure they would suggest Sarah should return home to the bosom of the family for comfort and protection. I was shocked to realise that that would suit me fine. Fifteen years of marriage and all Sarah was to me now was an encumbrance. I have to admit I felt guilty at my feelings, but I also felt joy. If she returned to Redcar, I would be free to do what I wanted with my life.

As I sat drinking my china mug of tea, I heard Sarah put the phone down and rush into the garage. She came back into the house with a large cardboard box of the type used by removal firms, then went round the house putting into the box anything that caught her eye. Probably I thought, as I became more and more cynical, she was putting in anything she thought valuable or attractive. All the ornaments went in. All the pictures hanging on the walls went in. She returned to the garage for another box. More ornaments and more pictures. She returned for another box and continued the process. The boxes appeared to be brand new and there were masses of them. They had not been in the garage the last time I was in there. Admittedly that was a couple of weeks ago as we used the garage for storing things rather than for garaging the cars. Nevertheless, this was clearly not the unexpected shock I had expected it to be. Had she actually been preparing to leave me?! Was that anger just a put-up show?

"Mummy and Daddy will be here in a couple of hours to take me home," were her first words. There was an extreme emphasis on the word 'home' to which she gave a quick follow-up, "This has never really been my home, and I assume the floozie you were with in Ripon will suit you better. As you no longer want me, I'm leaving. I'm taking some of my things now. Daddy will be back with a hire van tomorrow for the rest. You'll be hearing from my solicitor tomorrow as well."

Sarah then retreated into her bedroom (we'd been in separate rooms ever since sex was banned). As I listened to her packing clothes into suitcases, I pondered on what she'd just said. I knew she'd never regarded the vicarage in Leeds as home, but how on earth did she know I'd been in Ripon with Jasmine – who was definitely not a floozie. Hell's teeth (being a vicar had taught me some polite swear words) it must have been my lord bishop. No, it couldn't have been. He could never have guessed I was in a relationship with Jasmine from what he'd seen, could he? And if he had, why on earth did he immediately tell Sarah?

Jasmine Baker was also involved in making a hot drink in her flat in Yarm. She looked across from the flat's second-floor window to the vibrant and varied spring greens on the opposite bank of the Tees. It was the flat's location in the centre of the small Georgian market town, yet on the banks of a lovely river with a view across into countryside, which had persuaded her to put her name down for a flat whilst the block was being built. Other people soon came to the same realisation, but too late for the cheap offer and so her investment had rocketed in value to a price she could never have afforded. As she waited for the coffee to brew before pressing the plunger into the cafetiere, she looked yet again at the front page of the Northern Echo with its headline 'Murder victim found at Ripon Hotel'. She knew him. She knew she knew him. But from where and who was he?

She plunged the cafetiere and thought of King's College London. The poor dead man was definitely something to do with her undergraduate days in that college on the Strand. She poured the coffee into her favourite mug and thought again. As she sipped her favourite brew of Taylor's Cafe Imperial, she suddenly thought: College photos! Of course, she might actually have a photo of him. She went into the spare bedroom, opened the wardrobe and pulled down the holdall containing her memorabilia. She was sure there had been a photo of the Theology and Religious Studies Department. She found the old photos folder and took it back to the kitchen.

There it was. Kings College 1984. And there he was sitting next to Guy Prentice. Yes, he had a moustache, but what was his name? She tried taking a gulp of the coffee to jerk her memory, but all she got was - 'gay'. That was it. Whatever his name was, he was part of the gay community of Kings.

*   *   *   *

I felt it prudent to leave the house so Sarah could do whatever she wanted on her own. I walked up to Street Lane knowing I would find somewhere in café culture land where I could drink a coffee and read a paper. As I walked, I thought about what had just happened:

'Mummy and Daddy' coming straightaway; a solicitor contacting me tomorrow, even though we'd never had a solicitor; all the boxes ready for a move. It didn't need an Einstein to know that divorce, separation, call it what you will, had been as much Sarah's idea as mine. Indeed, more so. To have all this prepared, she must have been thinking about it for a while. Had she told the bishop what she was thinking? Had he been looking for easy evidence to get rid of me? An affair is all that's needed for a priest-in-charge to be sacked. Had she known about Jasmine long before Ripon, even though we'd been so careful?

Street Lane had a wide choice of coffee shops, delis and eateries to choose from. Not feeling up to choosing, I simply walked into the first one and ordered a large Americano, black. I had discovered long ago that although an Americano was a black coffee, a jug of milk would come with it unless, and often even if, you asked for it black.

One great advantage of cafe culture is the fact that the inflated price of a coffee gives you a free read of newspapers. I picked up a copy of the Yorkshire Post. The murder was the main feature of the front page. I was immediately struck by the fact that there was no photo of the victim. The police had made it clear that they had no idea who he was, so why wasn't the front page emblazoned with photos of the victim appealing for identification? This led me to think about why he had seemed familiar to Jazz and whether she'd got any further with her search for who he was. Of course, thinking of Jazz made me feel good. Really and truly, I didn't care that Sarah hated me. In fact, I didn't care about Sarah at all, not even that I'd clearly hurt her! I was in love with my black beauty.

Turning over the page I discovered a news article about the meeting the Bishop had been attending in Ripon. The headline said it all–'One Way Group Plans Campaign to Restore Christian Values'. I knew even without reading the article that the values would not be any that I would recognise as Christian.

Needless to say, I ended up reading the article and discovered that my boss, my supposed to be father-in-God, had been part of a group drawing up plans for a massive campaign to re-Christianise Britain. The article emphasised the fact that One Way referred to the statement of Jesus in St John's Gospel, "I am the way, and the truth and the life. No one comes to the Father except through me."

How I had come to hate that verse and the way it was misrepresented by people like Harris and the Bishop. Anyone who knew anything about New Testament research knew that John's Gospel was far from being the gospel truth. It was the most argued about of the Gospels and most scholars agreed that, as the latest of the four gospels it was the one most likely to have had words put into the mouth of Jesus by the author; words which reflected arguments taking place at the end of the first century rather than actual words of Jesus. Yet here was Harris using this verse as a proof text for Christianity being the only true religion.

The article got worse with Harris claiming that the growth of homosexuality, abortion, cohabitation and divorce were the cause of all the troubles in the world (I wasn't aware that any of these featured prominently in Syria, Afghanistan or Iraq!). The campaign they were planning would focus on these evils and show people how living according to the Christian values of respect for life, marriage and the family would make Britain great again (did they really have no idea of the Trumpic irony of this?). No wonder the Bishop had not wanted to give me any details about the meeting he was attending!

As I finished reading, I realised that it might not have just been the theology he wanted to keep quiet. There was no mention of Tory MP's and nothing at all about Charles Matthews and GBnotEU. Presumably the political connections were to be kept totally secret, though I couldn't help wondering what politics had to do with a campaign to re-Christianise Britain.

I sipped my coffee and debated what to do next. Did I want to go back to the vicarage and meet the in-laws? Should I phone Jasmine to let her know what was going on? What was I going to do about the vicarage if Sarah was removing so much stuff?

The last question was the easiest to deal with. Sarah's attitude and preparations could well mean I would be left with only the study fit to live in. Did I want to live in the vicarage anyway? I guessed I would be alright tonight as 'daddy's' removal van wouldn't be there until during or after my meeting with the Bishop which would probably result in my being asked to vacate Church premises anyway.

Surprisingly it was the second question that was dealt with first when my mobile rang and I saw that it was Jazz.

"Hi love," I answered, still amazed at how much easier, indeed more normal and natural, I found it to express endearments to Jazz than I ever had with Sarah. "Have I got news for you!"

"Me too."

"OK. You first."

"Well, I've partially identified the guy who was murdered. He was at Kings on my course and he was part of the gay community. Did you know any of them?"

"What are you implying Jazz? Sorry. Didn't mean to be facetious. Let me think a minute. Er... Yes! Andy... Andy Rogers. Remember him?"

I was pretty sure she would. Andy had been an immaculately dressed, unbelievably handsome young man who most of the female students regarded as a challenge since they thought he was too lush to be gay.

"Vaguely! (the exclamation mark is mine, but I was fairly certain she had more than a vague memory of him). Do you have any contact details Simon?"

"Ah. Now there's where I need to tell you my news."

And off I went with a graphic description of Sarah's reaction to my news: the way she had immediately started clearing the house; her mother and father starting to drive to Leeds to pick her up almost before I'd finished telling her our marriage was over; the plans for a removal van to arrive tomorrow to clear the house. Then came the awkward bit, "There's just one problem darling.. Erm Andy's address is at the vicarage and I'm in a coffee shop. I really don't want go back there until there's no chance of meeting her mother and father."

Before I had chance to justify my cowardice Jazz retorted, "Are you a man or a mouse Simon? Get out of that cafe now and find that address for me. We're talking about a murder victim here and I'm sure Andy will know who he is, or more accurately was."

I replied in the only way a man in love could. I paid for my coffee and set off for the vicarage. I had to face up to the angry parents of my angry wife because the woman I loved needed to know exactly whose dead body it was that she had discovered.

CHAPTER FOUR

Whatever Sarah knew, or suspected about my relationship with Jasmine, I needed to make sure that Jasmine herself was kept totally out of the picture so that I kept that so important promise. That meant I had to make sure that Sarah did not find out anything about the murder, and therefore nothing about me coming back to search for Andy's address. So, when I got back to the vicarage and Sarah asked me why I'd come back, I simply said I'd come to say goodbye to her parents.

Luckily they were not long in arriving, as I was forced to stand in silence waiting for them – admittedly frosty silences had become quite a normal part of our relationship, but not usually standing up! Her parents soon arrived, they must have set off straight after Sarah's phone-call and really motored down the A19 and A1 to rescue their little darling. Dismissing these feelings, I tried my best to be friendly when they came through the door.

"Hello, Trevor. Hello Christine." I'd never been able to call them Mum and Dad, as they'd often requested. My Mum and Dad were wonderful people who could never be replaced by cold-hearted robots like Sarah's parents.

"I'm sorry we have to meet up like this. It was not what I ever intended when we got married," I rambled on with my apologies, but they cut no ice. Indeed, it would have taken an ice saw at the very least to cut the arctic atmosphere emanating from Trevor and Christine. The frosty, monosyllabic responses which met my attempts to express regret simply confirmed my previous suspicion that the state of our marriage, and my ministry, had been discussed and a plan of action put in place to be activated as soon as I made myself the perpetrator of the breakdown.

I left them to get on with packing the cars and went into the study. Not surprisingly, it was untouched. Sarah had little interest in me as a person, and so she had no interest in my personal possessions. As I thought, the address book was in my desk drawer. I flicked through to Rogers. There it was: Andy Rogers 238, Africa Drive, Brockley, London. There was no phone number. We didn't even exchange Christmas cards any more. Sarah had not been at all keen on my having a gay friend. She was definitely on the 'One Way' side of the Church divide and didn't want her husband to be in any form of contact with a gay man, unless it was to cure him of his illness!

I looked out of the window to see the state of play. There was no way I was going to phone Jazz whilst Sarah was around. Luckily, the boot lids were being closed so I made my way outside. Apologising and smoothing the waters are second nature to a vicar, and so I made a final attempt, "Well goodbye then, I'm sorry it's ending like this. I never meant to hurt you." As I looked at their faces, I stopped my spiel before I could dig an even bigger hole for myself.

"I don't believe you. I'll never forgive you, and I'll make you pay." Sarah's parting words gave me little in the way of comfort. It looked like breaking up with Sarah was not going to be an easy process.

"And we'll help her make you pay!" my ex-father-in-law (I'd never thought two letters could make you feel so good, but e and x certainly did in this case) shouted from the car window. Although his parting words gave me pause for thought, the sight of their car disappearing round the corner at the end of the street gave me an immense feeling of relief.

As I dialled Jazz's number, two thoughts struck me: firstly, that I needed to put her number in a speed dial; secondly that I didn't care what problems ending my marriage and my career might bring, I just wanted to be with Jasmine.

She must have been waiting for my call as she picked up at the first ring. I jumped in first to avoid any discussion of Sarah and her parents, "Hi babe, Andy lives at 238 Africa Drive, Brockley, but I don't have a phone number for him."

"Not to worry Simon. Some of us are computer literate. If you have a name and an address, Google will do the rest you know. I'll phone you back as soon as I get any results."

I found it impossible to settle down as I waited for Jasmine to ring back. I walked round the study looking at its contents: the piles of orders of service for weddings and funerals; the proofs for the church magazines; the reminders for PCC meetings, for confirmation classes, for marriage interviews. How had I got into a life like this? It was not what I'd intended when I was talked into being a vicar all those years ago. I was suddenly conscious of the fact that I really did want a new life. It wasn't just that I was in love with Jazz, it was that I wanted to do something completely different with my life. Appalling as it might sound, this murder had given me a chance for something different, some private investigation work!

I wasn't sure whether Jasmine had had long enough to find Andy's number and talk to him, but I decided to phone her anyway. I was raring to go and spoke as soon as she answered, "How did it go? Have you identified him?"

"Not yet Simon," she replied. Then she began to explain how Andy was not at home, but she'd spoken to his partner and discovered he was away on business and would phone her in the morning. What happened next was truly amazing, upsetting, but amazing. Jazz began to cry down the phone. "I miss you Simon. I want you near me. Can I come down to Leeds?"

The tears and the pleading in her voice produced two conflicting emotions in me. I was upset by her tears, but, on the other hand, I found it hard to control my joy as it registered that my feelings for Jazz were being fully reciprocated. Without a second thought, I replied, "Don't worry babe. I'll come up to Stockton right away, this very minute. The vicarage is empty, what's to stop me?"

"Your appointment with the bishop tomorrow?"

Jazz's reply felt like rain on my parade.

"Oh hell! I'd forgotten all about that," I replied before recovering my wits sufficiently to continue, "But it's not till eleven o'clock. There'll be plenty of time for me to drive down in the morning. I'm coming up now." I was thinking on my feet, or rather on the phone. "I'm not going to stay with you though because I don't know whether Sarah's got anyone following me. I think she and her parents are going to be looking for anything they can use to hurt us. I'll book myself into the Premier Inn. I love you babe, don't worry. By this time tomorrow everything will be fine."

After a few lovey-dovey farewells that felt so good and so normal, I switched on my laptop and booked a room in the hotel which I knew was just a couple of miles down the road from Jasmine's flat. I booked it for three nights, as I knew that after my meeting with the Bishop there would be little chance of my returning to stay in the Leeds vicarage. Then I packed an overnight bag, got into the car and drove onto the A61 heading for Stockton-on-Tees.

When I woke up the following morning to be faced by a large mirror reflecting a purplish abstract painting, I was totally disoriented. It took me a few seconds to realise I was in a hotel room in Stockton. I crawled out of bed, put on the kettle and prepared to make a mug of tea (hooray, there was no china teapot). I took the tea and the TV remote back into bed and switched on the news.

'North Yorkshire Police announced this morning that they have solved the murder of the mystery man found dead in Ripon on Thursday. Over to Amanda Fotheringay with the latest news from police headquarters in Newby Wiske.'

'Good morning. I'm standing outside the North Yorkshire Police Headquarters where Chief Superintendent Colin Major made this statement a few minutes ago.' The picture changed to a recording of a tall, plainclothes officer of about 50 who announced, 'On Thursday afternoon the body of an unknown man was found in the gardens of the Old Deanery Hotel, Ripon. It was clear from the strangulation marks on his neck that he had been murdered and this was confirmed by the pathologist yesterday. In a dramatic development early this morning, one of our officers discovered a thirty-five-year-old man hanging from a tree near to the village of Sandhutton, a few miles south of here. Letters found at the site have enabled us to identify both the murder victim and his killer. I can confirm that as a result of this discovery the Ripon murder investigation has been closed and that a fuller explanation will be given in a press release later today.'

The picture went back to the reporter outside police headquarters, 'No further details have been forthcoming, but I can assure viewers that we will be here for the press release when we will give you more details of this development.'

I switched off the television, took a gulp of my tea, disconnected my mobile from its charger and phoned Jazz, "Have you seen the news?"

"I was just going to phone you about it. The police have identified him far more quickly than I could. It sounds very weird. And why was there no photo in the paper?" Not surprisingly, her questions came thick and fast. "Have you got time for breakfast somewhere before you head back to your meeting?"

"Of course. Where do you suggest? They do breakfast in the restaurant here until 10.30, though I should really set off by 9.30 if I'm not to be late." I sensed unease coming down the phone, so quickly continued, "But it's only just gone eight now, so we've got plenty of time for breakfast."

"Brill. It's only a five-minute drive, add ten for me to get ready, so I'll see you in fifteen minutes."

I shaved, showered and brushed my teeth, all necessary manoeuvres for someone like me to feel human. I then dressed, very deliberately, in T-shirt, jeans and trainers. I wanted even my dress to make a statement to Lord Jim. Whatever the Bishop might want or believe, I no longer regarded myself as a vicar.

I rushed through the passageway to the restaurant next door to book us a table for breakfast and by the time I'd paid, I saw Jasmine coming through the door and signalled her over to the table.

Given the time factor and the dinner we'd eaten last night, I'd ordered continental breakfasts. We went over to the buffet table, helped ourselves to a glass of pomegranate juice and a bowl of cereal and returned to our table. As we began to eat, Jazz's mobile rang; she looked at the number, gave me a thumbs up and answered.

"Hi. Yes, this is Jasmine Baker... Oh hi Andy. Yes, it is a long time since we were at King's ... What do I want? Well this is going to sound very strange. Do you remember Simon Keep? Well he and I met at a hotel in Ripon and discovered a dead body... Yeah very creepy and yeah, he is still married to Sarah, but... OK we can talk about that later! The thing is, I recognised the body but can't put a name to him... Yeah, he was murdered and he was unidentified. Anyway, think back to a medium height, very good-looking, gay guy with a moustache. He was doing a BA in Religious Studies, an absolute super brain... That's him, of course, Mark Greenwood. Poor guy... According to the local news, the police have his murderer.

They've only just announced it so there are no details yet and Mark's name has not been mentioned. Of course I'll keep in touch. I'll let you know as soon as we have some more information..."

I signalled that I wanted to speak and Jazz handed me the phone, "Hi Andy. It's Simon. Yes, it is a long time. OK. OK. No, I'm not having an extra-marital with Jasmine, at least not yet! But my wife has left me and my life is in a bit of turmoil. Good to speak to you again. We'll be in touch as soon as the police tell us more. Cheers."

"Mark Greenwood. He was such a nice chap. I wonder what he was doing in Ripon?" Jazz asked.

"Can't imagine. I don't think he can have been at the One Way thing, unless he'd changed his sexual orientation," I replied. The clock above the bar reminded me that my date with the bishop was due soon, so I continued, "I suppose I'd better be getting off to see Lord Jim and tell our sainted bishop exactly what I think about him and his far from Christian Church!"

"My God Simon, are you really so annoyed still. What on earth happened at that synod?"

"Not much. I just told them the truth about One Way i.e. that it's a group of upper middle-class twits who are either too thick or too lazy to think clearly about religion. I said that no intelligent theologian could accept the divine inspiration of a book whose words and origins are so shrouded in argument and mystery. I also said that they are an extremely dangerous group because they are trying to convince Britain that Christianity is the one true way. This implies that anyone who follows another religion, or has no religion, is not only wrong, but is also working against God and the truth. I then went a little further than I should have by saying that the Reverend Timothy Harris had made me lose what little faith I had left because, if he was inspired by God, then it was a God I didn't want to know. Unfortunately, I added that anyway I was no longer too sure about the existence of any divine being and no doubt that's why I've been summoned to the meeting. I don't think the Church is too keen on having vicars who don't believe in God; which is why I'm expecting the bishop to ask for my resignation. But more importantly, I'm coming back here as soon as the meeting's over. What do you think about me renting a flat up here?"

"We'll sort that out later cos you can always share my flat, but you'd better not keep your bishop waiting. Get yourself off and see him because I'd rather share my flat with an ex-vicar than a real vicar. You tell him what to do with his job and then get back to me babe. We have a murder to solve."

Jazz's words made my heart sing. She really did care about me! But I could not let myself get carried away. Jazz was too precious and Sarah and her parents were too vicious for that. "I will babe," I replied, "but I'll get a flat up here. I'm not moving in with you until I get things sorted out with Sarah. I'm not going to let Sarah, or her parents, get you involved in their threat to make me pay."

With those words, I gave her a huge hug, a passionate kiss and set off for Leeds.

CHAPTER FIVE

I had tuned the car radio into BBC York so I would get the local news, and, sure enough, just as I hit the Harrogate by-pass the local news came on. I turned up the volume.

'North Yorkshire Police have just released a statement about the Ripon murder. Apparently the victim has been identified as Paul Williams, an unemployed homeless man who had been living in a hostel in the Ripon area. The man found hanging in Sandhutton was Michael Brown, a teacher from London. According to the police, he admitted the murder in a suicide note found beside his body. In the note, Brown claimed that the murder was the result of a lover's quarrel and that he could no longer live with himself after killing the man he loved. Now, if you're interested in gardening, you should go the RHS show at Harlow Carr today..'

I almost crashed into the Knaresborough roundabout as the shock of the words hit me. Just managing to get round the roundabout, I pulled into the side of the road and put on my hazards. Who on earth was Paul Williams? Had Jasmine and Andy really been wrong in identifying him as Mark Greenwood. As I began to ponder the implications, my phone rang.

"Simon are you driving?" Jazz asked anxiously.

"I've just pulled over. I take it you heard the news bulletin?"

"That's why I'm phoning. I'm sure the dead man I saw in the Old Deanery gardens was Mark Greenwood. I'm sure, sure, sure. What do you think it means?"

"I have no idea what it means, but whatever it means it's extremely weird. Why would you think it was Mark if it wasn't? And why would the body be in the Old Deanery garden? I don't want to seem ghoulish, but you have a good think about the body and whether you could have been mistaken in thinking it was Mark. I've got to get to this meeting and get my old job out of the way. Then my time's my own and I'm all yours!"

Half an hour later, I was sitting in the office of the Bishop of Ripon and Leeds. The fact that I was in the office and not the house meant either that I'd been downgraded in the ranks of vicars, or the bishop had already decided I was on my way out and did not want me polluting his residence. I was pretty sure I was being regarded as a pollutant!

As I looked round the converted coach house which had been made into offices when the bishop's residence had been moved from Ripon to the population centre of the diocese, I was pretty sure Lord Jim referred to this suburban complex as his palace. I had intended to put myself in control and start off with questions that would wrong foot Lord Jim, but, thanks to the shock of the police statement and Jazz's phone call, I just sat there like the underling he regarded me as when he came in.

"Good morning Simon," began the Bishop, "Thanks for coming."

Thanks for coming I thought. Did you give me a choice? Could I have said that I had a prior engagement?

"Well now," he continued. "Why have you got such a bee in your bonnet about Tim Harris? He's a good guy who's managing to get a lot of financial backing for his campaign to re-Christianise the UK.

This campaign is really going to raise the Church's profile here, apart," he added, very much as an after-thought, "from obeying Christ's command to preach the word. You really need to get onside with this Simon. And you've got to moderate your language if you want to keep your job. You just can't go around calling some of the most senior and influential Christians in the UK 'upper middle-class twits'."

Who did he think he was talking to? His pompous and condescending manner roused me from the shock of the police statement, and I jumped in with both feet, "You mean that as I'm an Anglican vicar, I can only tell the truth as long as it doesn't upset people?"

That made me feel better, and I followed up with the attack I'd prepared. "Tell me Jim," I continued loading his name with as much irony as I could, "what makes you think Christianity is the one true way?"

"What do you mean?" he spluttered. "It's what the Church and the Bible teach and we, as Christ's priests, follow the teachings of the Bible and the Church because they are the truth."

"Fair enough, my Lord," I said, adding even more irony to the title I knew he really preferred. "In that case, what does the Bible mean when it says, 'In my Father's house are many rooms'? And, more appositely, how come you as a bishop don't follow the teachings of the Bible?"

My questions clearly flustered him and he used a delaying tactic as he worked out an answer. "We're not here for a theological debate Simon. We're here to discuss your future in the Church," he said in his most authoritative episcopal tone before slyly adding, "If you have one of course."

He'd now worked out his answers and continued, "Now I'll answer your questions one at a time. Firstly, I think the many rooms means that different faiths can get to heaven. Secondly.." I tried to interrupt at this point, but Jim refused to break off. "Secondly, you know I follow the teachings of the Bible to the best of my ability. We all fall short, that 's why St Paul asked us to show Christian love."

He was now struggling and was forced to pause giving me the chance to interrupt, "Well Jim your first answer tells me a lot. You and Tim Harris keep saying Jesus is the only way, but you also accept that Jesus believed there are other ways to get to heaven. You can't believe both! Either Jesus contradicted himself or he's not the only way to heaven."

I had to feel a bit sorry for a bishop who was nonplussed by such a thought, but I didn't let this hold back my attack, and continued, "As for your second answer, it looks to me like you're not trying very hard to follow the Bible because I can see you're wearing a polycotton episcopal shirt when the Bible clearly states in Leviticus that you should not wear clothes made of two fibres. Now as for my attitude to the One Way Group, I might not feel quite so angry about them if they showed even an atom of Christian love for gay Christians. Can't you see that they're just the same as groups like the American Tea Party? Next they'll be attacking abortion clinics and denying evolution."

That felt better. I sat back knowing that my Lord Bishop would try to take the interview onto a different tack to avoid having to face the truth of my statements.

"Be that as it may Simon," the Bishop replied neatly sidestepping all the points I had made. "I've called you in here at the request of some of your congregation. Apparently, you've been making statements, from the pulpit, casting doubt on basic doctrines such as the Trinity and the divinity of Jesus. We can't have our priests preaching doubt. I've been consulting some other bishops and we've agreed that you can say things like that at discussion groups and Bible study, but from the pulpit you must avoid expressing any of your personal beliefs that contradict the creeds."

Oh dear! What a typical C of E compromise. You can believe what you like as long as you don't say it officially! Fortunately or unfortunately, I was in no mood for compromises and offered my bishop a direct challenge, "And what if I refuse to compromise my beliefs and insist on using the pulpit to tell the truth?"

The look on his face indicated that the Bishop's Christian love for me was wearing decidedly thin, "Get real Simon! We have responsibilities. We can't upset the beliefs that keep our congregations going (and keep the collection plates full I thought cynically). We also have a responsibility to our families. Heresy can still get you dismissed from the ministry and that means not only no stipend, but also no home and no pension rights. Is that what you want?"

"No, your Lordship," I spat out the title in such a way as to indicate not only that I did not think of him as a Lord, but also that I though clerical titles were absurd to people who believed in the brotherhood of Christ. "I just want to get out of this hypocrisy. I don't want my stipend. I don't want my house. I don't want my pension. I don't want to be involved with people who are prepared to jeopardise the social cohesion of this country because they think a nutter like Timothy Harris can bring converts and money into the Church. So, Jim I'm off. My wife has a furniture van coming tomorrow. I'll leave my keys to the vicarage in the hall and ask her to post her keys through the letter box when she leaves."

Jim, I was pleased to see, was visibly shocked, his normal verbosity momentarily reduced to spluttering, "But... but... You can't... And what about this affair you're having?"

Ah. So it had been the Right Reverend who'd shopped me to Sarah. I studiously ignored his question and continued, "Sorry my Lord, I'm off and I can't say it's been a pleasure knowing you, because it hasn't. If you want to give me a leaving present, then stand up to Timothy Harris and his financial investors and show some Christian love to the gays, and the desperate women seeking an abortion, and the Muslims and Sikhs and Jews and Hindus they so despise." With these words I walked out, hoping that I was leaving a more thoughtful bishop in my wake, though I very much doubted it.

*   *   *   *

Jasmine came off the phone and switched on her PC. She was determined to do some investigating before she accepted the police statement that the murdered man she had discovered was not Mark Greenwood. She went straight onto Google and typed in Mark Greenwood. Up came several Mark Greenwoods on linkedin.com, even more on www.192.com, a few on en-gbfacebook.com/people, then came up one that leapt out at her – abdn.ac.uk/religiousstudies/people/mark greenwood.

Clicking on this website took her to the Department of Divinity and Religious Studies at Aberdeen University where she discovered that Mark Greenwood was the Senior Lecturer in Contemporary Religion having previously lectured at St Andrews and Stirling Universities. He had graduated from King's College London in 1986 and gained his PhD from St Andrews. Clearly, he was the Mark she had known. Another click took her to staff news. This told her that Mark had the summer term off to complete a research project for the Institute for Community Cohesion.

Jasmine then surfed the site till she found the staff directory, clicked on Mark Greenwood and up came his profile with a photo. "Bingo!" she exclaimed. The photo was that of the dead man she had last seen in the Old Deanery gardens at Ripon. What on earth were the police playing at?

CHAPTER SIX

I felt a strange sense of satisfaction as I drove to the Leeds vicarage to collect my belongings. I no longer felt I was a clergyman. I was no longer the Reverend Simon, vicar of souls and defender of the true faith! I was plain Simon, secular agnostic, an ordinary person.

I'd spent some time on the phone to the church warden and the secretary of the PCC explaining the situation. Their reaction told me that my leaving the ministry was not a shock to them, indeed they seemed to have been expecting it. Nigella, the secretary of the PCC, was also the parish lay reader and she would look after the services for this week.

It was hard to believe, but it already seemed that the last twenty years were not only a mistake, but also another life. I should have had this meeting with the bishop many years ago. I shouted an inward hooray as I turned into the road and saw no removal van and no car outside the vicarage. Perhaps if I just threw everything into the car, I could be up and away before they arrived.

As soon as I walked into the hall however, I realised that they had been and gone. But not only had they been, they had also stripped the house! No telephone table or pictures in the hall; no suite, television, radio/CD player, coffee table, CD collection nor pictures in the sitting room; no table nor sideboard in the dining room; the kitchen cupboards bare except for a mug with 'Simon's mug' printed on it; electric kettle, toaster etc all gone. How had she managed it so quickly?

The only room that had been spared was the study. Surprisingly, it looked as if she had not touched a thing in there, but of course there was nothing there she might want. Books had never been her thing. Computers on the other hand... Yes, the PC and printer were gone. Thank goodness I'd kept my laptop in the car.

Upstairs was just the same except that here my clothes were in heaps – not neat heaps either – on the floor, as all the furniture was gone. That meant, of course, that the cases and holdalls were gone as well. How was I going to get my clothes out of the house? However, this internal debate was ended when my phone rang.

"Hello. Oh, hi babe. You won't believe what she's done."

"Simon, I don't care what she's done. I'm caring about the fact that it was Mark Greenwood."

"What do you mean it was Mark Greenwood?" I asked. "You know you were mistaken, the police have identified the body as Paul Williams. They must know who it was."

"Simon, trust me, I know who it was," Jasmine answered firmly, "and it wasn't any Paul Williams, whoever he may be. It was Mark Greenwood, I've just found a photo of him on the Aberdeen University staff site, and the body we found was definitely Mark Greenwood."

"Are you sure?"

"Of course I'm bloody well sure. Check it for yourself, darling. I'll text you the website to make it easier for you darling."

The use of darling rather than babe, and the way she enunciated its syllables with great deliberation rang alarm bells. Jazz was clearly very upset. I needed to tread very, very carefully here.

"OK babe," I replied in as non-confrontational a way as was possible. "You do that and I'll look it up straight away."

I went out to the car, opened my laptop and switched it on. I found the text just arrived on my phone and copied the website into Google. As the website opened up and the photo emerged, I could not help gasping. There was no doubt about it. The body we'd found at the Old Deanery was Mark Greenwood, senior lecturer in Religious Studies at Aberdeen University. I went back onto my mobile straight away.

"I'm so sorry babe. I should have believed you straight away. That body was Mark Greenwood. I don't know what the hell is happening, but we're going to find out. I'm available full-time now. I've just told the bishop what to do with his job."

Of course, she wanted the details of the meeting and after I'd given them, I told her what Sarah had done to the vicarage which caused her to say some very unkind, but very true, words about my ex wife. Then we sorted out a plan of action. First off, I would nip up to the supermarket and buy some heavy-duty long-life bags to put my clothes in now Sarah had taken all the hold-alls and cases. The books could go in any left-over bags, or in piles in the car. Once the car was loaded, I would leave Leeds and my old life and speed up to Stockton and my new life and new love.

I told Jazz that on my way through Ripon, I would call in at the police station, and see if I could find out anything more about this weird misidentification of the body. I hoped to be with her in a couple of hours. In the meantime, she was not to worry. As I said this, I cursed myself for my nascent male chauvinism, and blamed it on my life with Sarah who expected men to protect her.

*   *   *   *   *

Jasmine put the phone down and thought carefully about what to do. She was no little woman type to be told not to worry whilst a man sorted things out. She was quite capable of sorting things out herself. After the initial shock of seeing Mark's photo on the Aberdeen University website, she had had a little time to think things through. She was pretty sure Ripon police station would be back to being a minor incident office with restricted opening hours now that the murder enquiry had been closed down (like most police stations in these days of austerity). Any information would have to be sought from the North Yorkshire Police HQ at Newby Wiske.

For some reason which she could not fathom at the time, but for which she was most grateful at a later date, Jasmine decided to keep her enquiries anonymous. She walked into town and found one of the few remaining (and working) public phone boxes. She phoned the police HQ and told the receptionist that she was a reporter with the London Evening Standard wanting information about the suicide of Michael Brown because of his London connections. She was put through to the press office and identified herself as Alice Connolly, a reporter on the Standard whose by-line Jasmine remembered reading on her last visit to her mother's.

Jasmine was amazed that no more identification was required before her questions were answered. Michael Brown had been identified by his head teacher in London. Paul Williams had been identified by the director of the homeless shelter which had been named as his home in Brown's suicide note. On Jasmine asking for more details, she discovered that Williams had been a resident in the Saviour's Hostel in Ripon. As the police had already announced, Brown's suicide note contained a confession to the murder of Williams, so that the murder enquiry was now closed as the murderer had been found and the victim identified. Jasmine thanked them for their help and put the phone down.

She went straight back onto her laptop and straight back onto the Aberdeen University site. As she looked again at the staff photo of Mark, any doubts put in her mind by the information she had been given by the police disappeared. There was absolutely no doubt about it. The body she had found was the body of Mark Greenwood, not Paul Williams and that raised a huge problem. Either the police were telling lies or the director of Saviour's Hostel was telling lies. That in itself was worrying enough, but behind that was an even bigger problem why had they identified the body as someone it was not?

* * * * *

It didn't take me long to load the car. Large heavy-duty supermarket bags are easily filled, hold a substantial amount and take up much less space in a car than suitcases. As I drove out of Leeds, I waved a figurative goodbye to my old life. I had no idea what my new one was going to be except that it was going to be with Jazz and would begin by me finding out more about this murder.

As I approached Ripon, I realised I had no idea where the police station was, so I pulled into Morrison's supermarket car park to look it up. A quick Google showed me that I needed to keep off the by-pass, drive through the town centre, or city centre as it boasted on the signposts, and onto the road out to the North. For the first time since the murder, I suddenly felt hungry and decided to fortify myself with a coffee and a sandwich before beginning the investigation. Morrison's now provided freshly ground coffee and their egg mayonnaise on wholemeal was not only good, but also cheap!

I'd just had time to eat half the sandwich when my phone rang, "Simon, have you been to the police station yet?"

Jazz sounded agitated, so I replied in what I thought was a soothing tone, "Calm down babe, I'm just having a coffee. I'll be there in about ten minutes."

"Don't you talk to me as if I were a female Labour MP, and you were David Cameron. You'd be as flustered as I am if you'd just had the phone call I've had with North Yorkshire Police HQ."

I apologised profusely whilst Jazz gave me the details of her call and suggested that rather than visiting the police to be given less information than she had already received, I should see if I could find out anything about Saviour's Hostel whose director was the one who appeared to have misidentified the body. Of course, I agreed, using some more of the endearments which were becoming more and more a part of our conversations. It felt so good to be talking to a partner who was a real person, maybe Sarah had just been a life-size Barbie doll!

Tracking down the homeless hostel proved to be much more difficult than finding the police station. Putting Saviour's Hostel into Google brought no hits. Putting homeless hostels into Google only produced sites requiring me to sign up to gain any information. This was rather puzzling as it seemed unlikely that anyone requiring help in finding a bed for the night would have the sophisticated phone or lap-top needed to access that help. After a fruitless thirty minutes, I decided to go to the police station whose whereabouts I had discovered. The police station was empty, but following the advice to ring the indicated bell brought a young policewoman to the desk. She quickly and efficiently directed me to a large, scruffy Victorian house in a street behind the market square. Next to the porticoed front door was a discreet sign saying, 'Saviour's Hostel'.

I'd found the hostel, but could I find out anything about its ownership? Yes. There next to the paint peeling pillar of the portico was a very small company notice stating that Saviour's was part of the Fishermen Group whose registered office was an address in

London WC1. There was no mention of a director and the place was clearly in a fairly run-down condition.

As I wrote down the office address, a couple of residents emerged from the front door – at least I assumed they were residents from their shabby clothes and down-at-heel footwear. I'd enjoyed chatting with and helping the homeless at various points in my pastoral work and had no problem in striking up a conversation.

"Nice day. You staying here? Is it a decent place?"

The men were clearly unused to being addressed by what they might have thought of as respectable people, but the smaller of the two replied, "Yeah we live here and it's okay. Why you asking?"

"Oh, I've had to use these hostels once or twice to get myself an address so I could get a job. I was on the streets of London at the time. The hostels I was in were always run by holy Joes. You know the type, give you a night's kip as long as they can sit with their Bibles and tell you that Jesus loves you. Is this one like that?"

I was amazed at how easily the lies came to me now I'd thrown off the dog collar.

This time the taller one answered. He shot the cuffs of his threadbare houndstooth check sports jacket and adjusted the stained tie onto the frayed collar of his blue shirt. Clearly, he had been used to better things before he hit the bottle, a surmise backed up by the educated voice which said, "They're never as obvious as that sir. This establishment appears to be run by some very intelligent members of the Lord's army. They let us know who the saviour refers to and what he means to them, but, no doubt as you did, we just go along with it for what we can get out of it."

I decided to push my luck, "Do you fancy a coffee and a bite to eat? I was always ready for some decent grub when I was living rough."

Not surprisingly, they both agreed with alacrity, and I took them round the corner to a Caffe Nero I'd seen. A toasted vine tomato and mozzarella panini each, accompanied by a grande latte, seemed to lubricate their throats well enough for a considerable conversation during which I learned that a 'boss' (the word director was never used) had come up from London and been in charge for the last week, but the warden had returned last night, and the boss had gone.

John and Dave, it hadn't taken long for first names to be exchanged (never surnames with those who'd lost their respectability), had clearly reached the stage where they were looking to drag themselves out of the hole that drink and family problems had thrown them into. I thought I might be able to throw them a lifeline. This was what I, unlike Lord Jim, meant by Christian love. I told them about a factory in north Leeds that was looking for workers (it was run by one of my parishioners) and gave them sixty pounds to buy a season ticket each on the 36 bus so they could get transport to the factory for a week. I didn't really mean to bribe them, but within seconds of my offer I had the name of the disappeared director, Samuel Watkinson. I also knew that they had never met Paul Williams and that no one in the hostel knew anything about him being the murder victim.

CHAPTER SEVEN

Within an hour of leaving Ripon, I was back in Stockton drinking yet another cup of coffee, but this time in Jazz's sitting room in Yarm, enjoying her flat's panoramic vistas over the River Tees. Jazz, however, was not interested in the view.

"So," she began, "let's get this straight Simon: you're an atheist Christian vicar whose marriage is over; you've given up your job and moved out of the home the Church provided. What are you going to do? And with what financial resources?"

Put like that it sounded a bit of a downer, if not a disaster, but I was feeling far from down. In fact, I was feeling on top of the world because I had news for Jazz.

"Well," I answered. "Do you remember that my Dad was running a bookshop when he died?"

"Of course, he was. I'd forgotten all about that. You used to get us cheap books. Whatever happened to the shop?"

"There's the surprise babe," I replied. "I was so traumatised by my parents' deaths that I just handed the shop over to Pete Jenkins – do you remember him from Kings? Computer mad, but failed his degree. Well, he's managed the shop ever since, and although I've never asked for any money, I know he's been putting 'rent', as he calls it, into an account for me.

Sarah hates Pete so I've never told her anything about it. Indeed, I'd never really thought about the money until I fell back in love with you," I leaned across and squeezed her hands. "But now I want to make a new life with you, it's going to come in very handy. Twenty years of rent must be a tidy sum by now. So, I don't think there's any need to worry about financial resources. My life is going to change babe, and you're going to be the centre of it."

Jazz smiled, but it was clear that she was worried about more than my financial future.

"Fair enough," she said. "You're not going to be penniless, but what are you going to do? You've no job and no home," she paused and grinned at me, "Unless you want to change your mind about moving in with me?"

"I would love to babe, but not until I've sorted things out with Sarah," I replied. "She and her parents sounded pretty vicious, and I want to keep you well away from that. I'm sure I'll be able to rent a little flat somewhere near here. As far as a job's concerned, I was thinking of private detective work and this murder.."

"Yes, Simon, this murder! It is so weird. Not that I've had any experience of non-weird murders, but there are so many questions Simon. Like we know the victim was Mark Greenwood, but the police say it was someone called Paul Williams, why are they saying that? Then there's the question of who Paul Williams is or was, and even more so, who was Michael Brown, and did he really murder Mark Greenwood, and why would Michael Brown admit to the murder of Paul Williams when the body was Mark Greenwood? Then there's the question of who was Samuel Watkinson and why would he identify Mark Greenwood's body as that of Paul Williams?

Then comes the biggest question of all – What is it to do with us, and shouldn't we just hand it all over to the police?"

I stood up and looked down at the river flowing past. Two swans were sailing downstream majestically, going with the flow. As I watched them, I knew that I didn't want to go with the flow.

"It is to do with us babe," I replied, "because we found the body, and you recognised him. You actually knew him, and he was not who the police say he was. That's why we can't just hand it over to them."

"You're right," Jazz replied. "Maybe it was a while ago, but I knew him. I found his body so I am involved, and I'm not prepared to let poor Mark's death go unacknowledged. We can't let Mark Greenwood just disappear, we've got to find out what happened."

Jazz's words made me feel better. They confirmed my decision not to take the easy way out. I crossed the room, sat beside her and put my arm round her.

"You're right babe," I said. "Plus, we have a duty as the finders of the body to make sure that it's the right body that gets buried, or cremated, and the right murderer who gets blamed. But how do we do that?"

I was rather hoping Jazz would say we should do some investigating ourselves. As I'd just intimated, a spot of private detective work would give me something to do. However, Jazz promptly scuppered these plans when she pulled out from her jeans' pocket the card the inspector had given us and said, "Here's our answer Simon. We get the professionals involved. We've got the boss's phone number here!"

Although thwarted in my unspoken ambition to emulate Hercule Poirot, and worried that the police were maybe a part of the problem, I had to agree that this was what we should do. After all what did I know about murders and false identities?

Jazz was soon talking to the inspector we'd last seen at the Old Deanery. After identifying herself, she quickly managed to explain to him how we'd identified the murder victim as Mark Greenwood and our consequent puzzlement at his being identified as someone else. I heard the inspector ask her to hold the line whilst he logged onto the Aberdeen University website. There was a loud gasp, presumably when he saw the photos, followed by an immediate request to come up and see us.

I grabbed the phone from Jazz before she could reply. It didn't seem like a good idea for Jazz's neighbours to see policemen arriving at her flat. "Hi inspector, this is Simon Keep. We're at the Stockton West Premier Inn at the moment, perhaps you could meet us at Stockton Police Station?"

The inspector said he would prefer to meet us at the Premier Inn, and I said we would meet him in the bar. As I put the phone down, I wondered why the inspector didn't want to meet us in the police station. After all it would be a more formal setting, and there would be access to information, computers and such like. But I didn't worry too much, after all it might simply be because Stockton was in Cleveland Constabulary, a different force, and a force with various question marks against it? I dismissed my misgivings without even communicating them to Jazz and we left for the hotel.

Whitbread pubs are ideal for me as they all serve Costa coffee. This one had a machine for you to serve yourself with unlimited access for a very reasonable fee. I made an Americano for myself and Jasmine opted for cappuccino. The bar was quiet on Saturday teatime as most of the hotel guests were either out or not yet arrived. We chose a corner table in the window overlooking the path to the entrance so we would see Inspector Byrom as he arrived. We were both fairly sure we would recognise him, but neither of us knew his first name as his card simply said, 'Inspector D. Byrom, North Yorkshire Police'.

As we waited, we composed a statement for Nigella to read out at Matins the next day. I just wanted to forget about the Church, but

Jazz insisted that I had a duty to explain myself to my congregation. With Jazz's assistance, I composed this statement:

Dear friends,
Sadly, I have to leave the parish. The Bishop does not feel that you need a vicar who no longer believes in God. Please remember me as a vicar who sought the truth and who tried to follow Christ's teachings which he took to mean that we should love and respect everyone whatever their faith, gender, ethnicity or sexual orientation. That was the basis of my ministry, and will still be the basis of my life. You don't need to believe in God to do that. After all, as Jesus' beloved apostle said in 1 John 4, 'anyone who does not love his brother, whom he has seen, cannot love God, whom he has not seen'.
Good luck to you all,
Simon

I e-mailed the statement to Nigella, hoping she would read it out without seeking the bishop's permission, which I was sure would not be given, and a few minutes later we spotted a tall, fair-haired man getting out of a very classy black BMW 3 series coupe. We immediately recognised him as the inspector from the Old Deanery. He was immaculately dressed in a charcoal grey, pin-stripe suit, mid-blue dress shirt and a multi-coloured striped tie. Perhaps I needn't have worried about him calling at Jazz's flat, he looked more like a lawyer or an accountant than a policeman. I went to meet him at the door, escorted him over to our table, ascertained his choice of coffee, went to get his latte and came back to sit down.

"Hello again you two. I think we can dispense with formalities, I'm David Byrom, but please call me Dave," as he spoke he looked around the bar area. He appeared to be checking that there was no one within hearing distance before he continued, "Well now, this is a bit of a rum do isn't it?" We nodded in agreement." When I saw that photo from Aberdeen University, I knew it was the same guy you found in the Old Deanery garden," he paused and looked round again, "Is there anywhere a bit more private for us to talk? I don't want anyone hearing what I have to say."

"Of course, "I said, thinking that police in your hotel room is totally different from police in your flat. "We can go up to my room, bring your coffee with you."

I led them up to my room, hoping I'd left it looking tidy. Of course, I needn't have worried, the cleaners had been in, and it looked immaculate. I offered the inspector the chair next to the counter which acted as a table, a shelf and a desk, Jazz sat herself on the bed settee and I sat on the bed, no need to reveal our relationship yet. Both Jazz and I sat in nervous anticipation for the announcement which could not be made in a quiet area of a quiet bar.

"Can I trust you not to divulge anything I say?" Dave began. "And can I also trust that you two want to do all you can to get to the bottom of this murder?"

Since that was what we'd just been discussing, we had no hesitation in giving a rapid affirmative to both these questions.

Dave gave us a constabulary looking inspection before he spoke again, "And can I also rely on you to help me solve this case no matter what?"

What on earth did he mean by that? He was the police. It was his job to solve the murder, not ours. Plus, the police had already announced that the case had been solved. Jazz expressed my thoughts before I could, "Why do you say, no matter what? What can go wrong if you're in charge?"

"That's the problem," answered Dave, "I'm not in charge. I was taken off the case within a couple of hours of sending my initial report to HQ, and it was taken over by the head of CID. I found that a bit upsetting, as I'd had no time to start investigating my first murder case, but it was also a little disturbing because it was so unusual. Normally, the first investigating officer would be given a chance to make some headway before media, or political, pressure forced the top brass to demonstrate how seriously they were taking it by putting a top-ranking officer in charge. Your phone call, however, raised lots more worries for me.

As soon as I saw the Aberdeen photo, I realised that was the man whose body you found in the Old Deanery garden, and it didn't take a mastermind to work out that there was something weird about a murder being solved by wrongly identifying the murder victim. This was confirmed by the fact that," Dave paused, whether for effect or because he'd run out of breath wasn't clear.

Jazz broke the silence, "The fact that what Dave? Come on let us know!"

"I've got to be absolutely sure I can trust you before I give you this fact. That's why I'm hesitating. You're both religious, aren't you? Can I trust you to be like Trappist monks with this one?"

"Yes, you can," our reply was so as one that it was like synchronised swimming. "We will say nothing because we want to ensure that Mark's murderer is brought to justice."

"Good. You may soon regret that promise, but here goes. When I phoned in after our phone call and reported that evidence had emerged that the murder victim had been wrongly identified – thank goodness I mentioned neither names nor witnesses –I was told in no uncertain terms to keep out of the case. As far as the top brass is concerned, the murder victim was Paul Williams, the murderer was Michael Brown, the case is closed and will not be re-opened. Interestingly enough, I was given two new cases on my way up here. Evidently, I'm to be kept too busy on other things to keep sticking my nose into the Old Deanery murder case. This case is beginning to smell like Whitby quayside and I don't like being used, anymore than I like the thought that someone might, quite literally, be getting away with murder. What I was hoping was, will you have, or make, the time to help me?"

His words should have worried me because of their revelation of top-level police corruption, but all I heard was the realisation of my Poirot dreams. Of course, Jazz had her feet much more firmly on the ground as she replied, "Are you actually saying you want us to find out some serious wrongdoing in the North Yorkshire police and report it to you, so that you can keep your nose clean, but also keep your conscience clean because you're not letting the crooked cops get away with it?"

"I suppose it could seem that way from your point of view," Dave replied. "But that's not the whole picture," he continued rapidly. "There's something very strange going on here, and it's coming from very high up. I don't know what this Mark chap knew, but he clearly knew something which these high-ups don't want to come out. I'm still just a plain, ordinary inspector because I've always been seen as a policeman who was never prepared to toe the party line. As soon as I phoned up about the wrong identification, I became a marked man. They'll be watching what I do and if I disobey orders and continue this investigation when I should be investigating the cases I've been given, the least that will happen will be my suspension, and then we'd get nowhere."

Here was my chance and I spoke without really thinking, "I've got the time Dave. I'm at a loose end as I quit my job this morning and helping you would give me something to do as well as making sure that Mark's death doesn't go unrecorded."

"Hang on a minute Simon," Jazz intervened her feet ever more firmly anchored to the ground. "We've got three dead people here and you're going to investigate someone with the power to influence things at the top of the police force?" she turned to the inspector, "And why should we trust you? We know nothing about you. Why should Simon help you? Indeed, should Simon help you? That's what I'm asking myself?"

I'd forgotten how feisty Jazz could be, it was over twenty years since I'd seen this side of her! Part of me was embarrassed for the way she was speaking to a police inspector, the part that had been too influenced by the 'little Miss Perfect' Sarah, the other part of me was proud of her spirited performance. Unfortunately for my ambitions, I also had to agree that she had a point.

"Yes. Why should we trust you?" I said backing up Jazz. "How do we know you're not a part of this police cover-up?"

Dave appeared nonplussed by the barrage of questions. He shifted nervously on his seat and coughed before saying, "The main reason you should trust me is that I'm here. If I was part of this thing you call a cover-up, I would either have fobbed you off when you phoned, or sent a squad of uniforms to arrest you on some trumped-up charge. But there are other reasons why you should trust me. If you Google my name, you'll find newspaper reports of cases I've solved. Several of them will refer to me as 'the maverick police officer' because of the way I refused to be held back from discovering the truth by police red tape."

"And why should that make us trust you?" Jasmine cut in.

"Because it shows I'm not part of the police establishment. It shows that I care more about justice than following the rules and obeying orders from on high."

This speech put an end to the confrontation, and before long we were discussing strategy. We decided that I would be the investigator, Jazz (or Jasmine to Inspector Byrom of course) would be the co-ordinator and Dave would do any searches better done using police facilities (but try to keep it off the radar in case his work was being checked).

It was decided that I would kick-start it by going down to London to try to find Samuel Watkinson so I could ask him about his identification of the body. Whilst there, I should also be able to find out more about the Fishermen's Group by visiting the address given as their registered office in Judd Street WC1. I don't know why, but for some reason I didn't mention that the trip would also give me a chance to see my old friend Pete to sort out the bookshop money. I was to be very grateful about that omission.

We decided it would be best for me to go down on Monday as the people I needed to see might be out of town for the weekend. This would also leave me Sunday to sort out whatever I would need for my new life as a private investigator.

I was feeling somewhat euphoric about the new life beckoning me, but this soon dissipated with Dave's farewell gesture. He gave me the number of his private mobile with the words, "Don't use the number on my business card, you never know who might be listening in to those calls!"

CHAPTER EIGHT

Sunday was a busy day. My phone was hot as news of my resignation spread through the parish after Nigella read out my announcement. The first few messages were supportive, but then I started getting some very abusive ones from fine Christian members of the parish! I decided that the best thing I could do was put a new message on my answer phone thanking people for their kind messages of support and explaining that I was very busy with my new life. Then I only needed to answer callers I wanted to speak to.

First priority for my new life was to find somewhere to live, somewhere I could dump all the bags which at the moment were making my car a magnet for car thieves. So, Jazz and I toured the estate agents and letting agents. I was surprised to see that several of the offices were closed on Sunday. This seemed odd to me since Sunday is surely the most free day of the week for most people (and for me now I thought), indeed it was almost a vicar's mantra that dwindling congregations were caused by Sunday trading, never anything to do with what vicars were doing wrong.

Despite having to skip several closed offices, within an hour we had secured me a modern one-bedroomed flat in a newish development just round the corner from the hotel. A substantial deposit (bond), and signing all sorts of documents promising to make good any damage I might inflict, secured me the keys to move in straight away. £495 per calendar month seemed a very reasonable rent to a man who had no idea of the cost of housing. Though when I thought about it, that would be almost half my stipend! Then I thought again and realised I would now have no stipend. I hoped I was right about what Pete had saved up for me.

We went straight from the estate agents to the flat to see what was needed by way of kitchen equipment, bedding, towels etc. Between the large Wilkinson's at one end of the stupendously wide High Street and the Debenhams at the other we soon had what I needed. On top of all my bags from Leeds, the car was now looking like a removal van, so we returned to the new flat and unloaded. I was ready to sit down with a cup of tea, but Jazz was made of stronger stuff. She drove me the short distance down the A66 to Stockton's retail park where Marks and Spencers, Next and River Island provided me with a wardrobe suitable for a modern forty-five-year-old man at ease with the second decade of the twenty-first century, rather than a Church of England vicar.

When I was living on Teesside, all rail trips to London began at Darlington. Since then the Grand Central Railway had been established and, on Jazz's advice, I was on Eaglescliffe station the next morning, my car parked in the large car park, awaiting the arrival of the 7.30 Grand Central train to Kings Cross. I would have been amazed at how many people were on the platform had Jazz not told me that the cost of a return anytime ticket was over a hundred pounds cheaper than on the Virgin East Coast main line (the privatised competitor to Virgin West Coast!!). As the train pulled in, I realised that it was not only the company that sounded like New York, the sleek black and yellow train looked very U.S. of A.

When the train came to a halt, there was a scramble for seats between those looking for an empty seat and those looking for their seat reservation. I stood back to avoid the bun fight and walked towards the back of the train, hoping it might be quieter there. My hopes were realised when I reached the last carriage and found several empty double seats. I sat down in one, plugged in my laptop and sat back to think.

Leaving the Church, leaving Sarah, starting a permanent relationship with Jazz, they were things that had been planned, but even so had happened far more rapidly than expected. However, the murder, and our part in it, had been totally unexpected and part of me was feeling in a state of shock. But another part of me was feeling liberated. I'd never really felt like a reverend, and the way people reacted to my dog collar had often got on my nerves. Even the most irreligious people moderated their language and seemed to think I was not interested in sport or sex. More particularly, I'd never been happy toeing the party line. That's why Lord Jim annoyed me so much. I was pretty sure that his life was an act, always saying what he thought he ought to say rather than what he actually believed.

As I listened to the sounds of the train, I became conscious of the fact that while many men harbour a secret dream of being a train driver, my secret dream had always been to become a private detective, a dream that was now on the point of coming true. I began to think about the case, and what I would need to do in London

Before I knew it, the train was pulling into York, from where it was direct to London. Many people departed and boarded at York, but few came into the last carriage and so I kept the double seat to myself. I texted Jazz to let her know I was safely on the train, then made my way to the buffet car. It took a while and was at times precarious as the train reached its maximum speed, but I arrived back with a ham sandwich and an Americano, thankful to see my laptop still there, still plugged in and hopefully well-charged.

I logged onto the Grand Central Wi-fi site to get an internet connection and searched for Samuel Watkinson – forcing myself not to waste time by exploring irrelevant websites. He was obviously not the Mayor of Nottingham in 1700 nor was he a Liberal councillor in York from 1850 to 1856. However, he surely had to be the Reverend Samuel Watkinson mentioned in a Guardian news article as a chaplain to the Archbishop of Canterbury who was out helping the homeless who were sleeping rough. The train slowed down going through Peterborough station and I broke off to check in with Pete by texting him.

"Hi Pete we seem to be running on time. Just going through Peterborough. I'll get the train from Kings Cross up to Hornsey, then walk up Tottenham Lane to Crouch End. I reckon I should be at the shop in an hour and a half to two hours. It'll be great to see you again after so long."

I put my mobile back in my pocket. It would indeed be good to see Pete again. I had so much to share with my old friend.

*   *   *   *   *

When Jasmine arrived at work, she found a message from the Head in her pigeonhole asking her to see him as soon as possible. In the first few years of teaching, such a message would have made her wonder what she had done wrong, but now she simply wondered what it could be about. Trouble with her tutor group? A need for an extra member of staff to accompany a weekend trip. These thoughts flashed through her mind as she walked down the corridor to the Head's office, then knocked and entered after a voice told her to come in.

"Hello Jasmine, had a good holiday?"

"Curate's eggish," she replied ambiguously.

"Did any of the bad parts get you into trouble with the law?"

"What do you mean?" she could not help a note of nervousness and apprehension entering her voice as she thought about what had happened since she set off for her intended naughty trip to Ripon.

"Well I've had this solicitor on the phone wanting to know whether we had an employee called Jasmine Baker."

"Are you sure it was a solicitor and not a journalist?" she asked and then told Howard (he was the sort of authoritarian head who tried to appear trendy by encouraging senior staff to address him by his first name) about her discovery of the murder victim. Naturally she made no mention of her developing relationship with Simon, nor the mystery of the misidentification of the body.

"So, you were the guest referred to in the news programme I saw it on. That must have been quite an experience. What exactly happened?"

"I think you'd call it disturbing, Howard. I booked into the hotel, went up to my room and looked out of the window. I reckon that if I'd looked out at a different angle, I wouldn't have seen it, but as it was I could see a body in the bushes. I called my friend and we went down to check, and it was a body with what looked like strangulation marks round the throat. Of course, all hell then broke out as the police were called and arrived to question everyone. I assume that's what they were after.."

"No, it really was a solicitor Jasmine. He gave a name and I've checked it, Humble and Lewis in Redcar. Any idea why he wants to contact you? I told him you'd phone him. Here's the number," he handed over a slip of paper before continuing, "I hope this isn't trouble, Jasmine. You know that I don't like any bad publicity for the school and I certainly don't like the office staff being pestered by teachers' private business."

It was incredible how Howard could tell you off, command you not to do something and make you feel guilty whilst making a statement which did not specifically refer to you. Jasmine resisted the urge to tell her head to 'piss off' and instead sought to justify her innocence as she said, "I'm sorry Howard. I have no idea who this solicitor is or why he phoned the school. Rest assured I'll tell him not to contact me via the school ever again when I speak to him. Was that all?"

On receiving an affirmative response, Jasmine left the Head's office. Although she was desperate to phone the solicitor's, she knew she had better see her tutor group and teach her lessons first. Break would be soon enough to phone unless she wanted an even frostier meeting with the head who had an uncanny sense of choosing the exact moment you had popped out for a moment to walk past your classroom.

The tutor group was a lively Year 9 glad to be back after half-term and desperate to catch up with the goss. The clamour soon ceased when the students became aware of the expression on Jasmine's face and the mood it implied. Jasmine checked their attendance, read the Head's daily bulletin and sent everyone off to their lessons. Her Y12 class was more attentive as it was only a week to their mock exam. Luckily her revision class was on the arguments for God's existence which she could now teach blindfolded. As she taught, she thought about this strange phone call. Why was a Redcar solicitor looking for her, and could it have anything but bad consequences?

Several students lingered at the end of the lesson to ask questions about their imminent exam, but Jasmine shooed them out and as soon as the room was empty, she phoned the number on the sheet given her by the head. When she had identified herself to the receptionist (why, she thought, are receptionists always young women and not young men?), she was put through to Mr Lewis.

"Why are you looking for me at my place of work?" she asked with a belligerence that was far from put on. "Indeed, why are you looking for me at all? I don't know you. I can't even say I would like to know you and I certainly don't want to be hounded by a.."

Mr Lewis interrupted her flow, "Excuse me madam." The use of the formal courtesy title had the desired effect and Jasmine remained silent whilst he continued, "I am merely following the instructions of my client. She did not know any details about you except that you taught at a school in Stockton. I was merely trying to find a contact address."

Polite formality only defused Jasmine for a brief time, "So who is this client of yours who is so desperate to get in touch with me that she's prepared to pay the exorbitant hourly rates I'm sure you're charging her?"

"I'm afraid I cannot tell you madam as that is part of client confidentiality. Can you confirm that..."

Unfortunately for Mr Lewis, this was not the type of response to gain Jasmine's cooperation, "You can tell your idiot of a client that I don't speak to anonymous people even if they are represented by devious, dishonest, legal creeps like you," and with that she broke the connection.

She immediately dialled Simon's number and reached him just as his train got into Kings Cross.

*   *   *   *   *   *

As I got off the train my mobile rang and I saw it was Jazz. I had no chance even to say hello before a furious voice shouted in my ear, "Simon have you heard of a firm of Redcar solicitors called Humble and Lewis? Because I've just had a most infuriating phone conversation with Mr Lewis who was trying to find my contact address for a client whose identity he won't reveal. He phoned school asking for me early this morning, thereby getting me into trouble with the Head. I only know one person from Redcar - your bloody wife! What the hell have you got me into?"

Oh my God – was this a way of making me pay? Both Sarah and her father had said I would be hearing from their lawyer, but they hadn't said Jazz would hear first. Anyway, how did they know Jazz's name? Eventually I managed to get a word in edgeways, "Calm down Jazz. You say a Redcar firm of solicitors. Yes, it could be Sarah's, but where would she have got your name? She knows nothing about you. I've never even mentioned your name to her or to anyone she knows."

"Well somebody in Redcar knows about me. I'm not a happy bunny Simon. It feels like I'm being followed. You don't think it could have anything to do with finding Mark's body, do you?"

I was making my way from the new platform 0 at King's Cross to the suburban platforms to catch the train to Hornsey. Of course, platform 9 ¾ was where Harry Potter caught the Hogwarts Express and this somewhat coloured my reply to Jazz, "Let's not get melodramatic Jazz. I would guess that somehow Sarah got hold of your name and the fact that you taught in Stockton and decided to use it as part of her revenge. Her last words to me were, 'I'll never forgive you, and I'll make you pay'. I'm sure this will have something to do with making me pay."

"Well Simon your pretty, but stupid and sexless, wife has picked on the wrong one here."

"Now don't be hasty Jazz.." My words fell on deaf ears as Jazz had rung off.

Jasmine was re-ringing Mr Lewis almost before her call to Simon was complete, "Good morning, could I speak to Mr Lewis please? This is Jasmine Baker. Yes, I'm sure he'll want to speak to me. Good morning again Mr Lewis," Jasmine's fury was now totally controlled. "Lovely to speak to you again. I have a message for your anonymous client. Just tell her that if she, or you, make any more attempts to contact me, the fact that she refused her husband sex for eighteen years will be plastered all over the tabloids. Good morning."

CHAPTER NINE

As I boarded the somewhat geriatric train heading for Welwyn Garden City, I thought about Jazz. What a difference from Sarah!

Jazz was a real woman. She had no need to prove she was as good as a man, it just came naturally to her. I also thought about the phone call from the solicitors. They had to be Sarah's lawyers, but from where had she got hold of Jazz's name and employer?

I was thinking about the very few people who knew about Jazz when it hit me like a sledgehammer – Old Deanery Hotel, this is Jasmine Baker, she teaches RE, at a school in Stockton. I had been right; when Sarah talked about my floozie in Ripon, Lord Jim had told her. The realisation made me shudder. The Bishop didn't really know Sarah, so he must have deliberately sent her the information, it couldn't have come up in conversation. But for what reason? Why did he want to cause me trouble even before that disastrous interview?

I was pulled from my reverie by the train stopping at Hornsey. Walking up the steps to the ticket office and then down the old Victorian stairway to the street took me back to my childhood and gave me that buzz of excitement I'd always felt when Mum and Dad brought me here to go up to town. However, the buzz soon dissipated as I trudged up the hill to Crouch End and thought again about Jazz's phone call and just what we were going to be made to pay by Sarah, her parents and now the Bishop.

As I came up the hill and approached the Broadway, the area of my youth brought more memories of my parents. They had been my rock: dependable, supportive, always there for me. My Dad, full of humour, always with a new joke – from what supply I never discovered – my Mum, always full-square with reality, provider of wonderful food and clean, ironed clothes. Of course, that was why I didn't visit the bookshop. Their sudden death all those years ago still hurt, consequently visits to Pete in the bookshop had been very few; he was living in the flat above the shop which had been our home till they bought the house. I realised just how few visits I'd made when I approached the Broadway and saw how much it had changed. Wine bars, restaurants and coffee shops had replaced the tired old pubs, greengrocers and Woolworths I remembered. Clearly Crouch End was now one of the up-and-coming places of North London.

The old family bookshop had also been transformed. The original nameplate, 'The Crouch End Bookstore', was still there, but otherwise this was a bookshop for the metro middle-class consumer. There was now a Starbucks on the first floor in the area where Dad had had shelves of second-hand books. The ground-floor had tables of 3 for 2's; booksellers' choices with summaries of why the staff enjoyed these books; display shelves of the top twenty paperbacks, top twenty hardbacks, new releases. There were plenty of customers both browsing and buying, and it took me a few moments to spot Pete, despite the bulk which usually made him unmissable.

It was an incredible pleasure to see my old friend again, all eighteen stones of him. After I married Sarah, our communication had been e-mail, texts and the odd phone call, not the same as a physical face-to-face. Pete caught sight of me and a path opened up for him to rush through and grab me in his trademark bear hug. I felt the breath being squeezed out of me at the same time as I realised that Pete was still immersing himself in Ralph Lauren Polo every morning.
"Well bugger me! I've just been talking about you, and here you are. How bloody amazing to see you," Pete's language had always been colourful, but never too earthy. "Come on me old mate, let's go and get a coffee and find out what brings you back to the old family homestead."

Pete went over to the tills, whispered something in the ear of the sophisticated young lady working there and then led me up the stairs. He ascertained what type of coffee I wanted, ordered and led me to a table in the far corner. Obviously, the manager didn't have to stand waiting at the end of the counter whilst the baristas performed their magic, he had his coffee brought over to the table.

"What a transformation Pete." I said, looking around.

"Does the man from Del Monte like it?" Pete asked.

"He say , 'Yes' Pete. It's wonderful. Dad would be thrilled at what you've done, but how did you manage it?"

"Contacts in the trade mate. You can't beat having the right bloody contacts; that got me the right wholesalers at the right discounts. Then there was my obsession with computers and computer games. They might have been responsible for my BA failed at Kings, but they got me a bleeding computerised ordering and accounts system before the local bookshops had learned how to use a Spectrum. The Starbucks came because I offered them a bloody cheaper rent than anyone else on the Broadway. I suppose my best wheeze for getting the punters in was my 3 for 2 scam."

"That really has me puzzled Pete? You're running schemes like Waterstones and Smiths, but you're a sole independent. You can't get the same discounts as them, can you?"

"Course I can't, but I don't need to. I can go to the supermarkets. Asda and Tesco, sell the bestsellers at 2 for £7, Sainsburys often have them for £2.99 each. I go round and buy from there – like that's less than four quid each - then sell them at 3 for 2. So, I charge the cover price for two books - £16 - and make more than £5 on each three I sell. It's not a big bloody profit, but it brings people in and when they see what else we've got, they buy something else to boost the profits. It all helps you mate."

"What do you mean, 'it all helps me'?"

"It helps you because you get half the bleeding profits, and I think that's something you need to be worrying about."

"I don't mind if there's no money for me Pete, as long as you're making a living out of all this work."

"That's not what I meant. There's plenty of money for you, Si, but you know I said I'd just been talking about you. Well guess who I was talking to?"

I thought about which of my friends knew Pete, but could think of no one who might have just been talking to him. "Not a clue," I replied. Then waited expectantly to hear which of my friends from long ago had been talking about me.

"Your bloody wife, Sarah!"

I spluttered into my coffee and my heart quickly descended to my boots. I'd never talked about Pete to Sarah, except when I introduced them at our wedding and told her that Pete had taken over Dad's bookshop. She'd only been with me on one of my visits and had not just been disinterested in Pete, she'd told me in no uncertain terms that Peter (she did not shorten his name) was not the type of person a vicar should have as a best friend. Pete was well aware of her attitude to him and she'd scarcely been mentioned in our phone calls and the odd visit I'd made since I got married. I was sure I hadn't mentioned any financial arrangements and I certainly hadn't given her the phone number of the shop.

"What on earth did she want?" I eventually managed to ask.

"Well that's the odd thing. I think she was after finding out what our financial arrangement was and what money you might have made from the shop. I know she's your bloody wife Si, but she sounded like a right bleeding bitch."

We were onto our second cup of coffee by the time I'd finished explaining the nature of my marriage, my relationship with Jazz, my resignation from the priesthood, the ending of the marriage, Sarah's swift exit from the marital home and her parting words that she would make me pay.

"Ah," said Pete, "that explains a lot. She kept saying it was a wife's right to know about her husband's financial dealings. She bloody well badgered me about ownership of the shop, who got the profits, how well the shop was doing. Lucky for you I never took to her. When you brought her down on that first, and only, visit, she struck me as a cold fish. I remember thinking when I saw her hold your arm, 'That looks like bleeding possession not passion'."

This was presumably the way she was going to make me pay, financially of course. Evangelical Christians always seem to like to have plenty of money and material possessions. Unlike Jesus, they have no problem in loving God and money.

"I take it you've given her my share of the profits then," I said dismally, seeing my dreams of financial security swirl down the plughole.

"Don't be bloody daft Si. We're mates, have been since we were kids, haven't we? She doesn't know there are any profits. She thinks I'm a grasping mercenary bastard who took advantage of a friend's grief and depression to cheat him out of his inheritance. I gave her to believe that you gave me the shop, all bleeding legal and above-board, and now you have no claim to it."

"Thanks Pete." I involuntarily gave my old friend a bear hug. "I've got no job. I've given my soon-to-be-ex-wife all our savings, so a share of a bit of profit to start me on my new life with Jasmine would be brill, but I wonder how she found out about you and the shop?"

"No bloody idea how she found me, but she found out nothing from me! And sounds like a bleeding good job too. Anyway, you've got no worries about money mate. Just let me check your accounts on my lap-top, and I'll give you your latest financial situation. Let's go into the office."

In the office, he switched on the laptop and informed me that I had an ISA account that had started off as a TESSA which now had close to £100,000 having received £3,000 a year over twenty years and averaging 5% interest. Apparently, I also had a building society account whose income had fluctuated with the shop's profits, but the current balance was over £350,000! Tax had been paid at source on the interest from the building society and tax had been paid on the profits by the bookshop.

I was stunned, no I was totally gobsmacked. I could vaguely remember signing the forms to set up the accounts, but I had no idea they would contain so much money. Twenty thousand or so was what I was hoping for, and that would have been fine. Clearly, I had no immediate financial worries despite losing my vicar's income! However, as soon as I recovered from the shock, I asked Pete the question that was still worrying me, "Do you really have no idea how she obtained your contact details?"

"I haven't a bloody clue. As far as I'm aware none of my friends have any sort of contact with her. And even if they did, they wouldn't be able to tell her about the shop because no one, but no bleeding one, knows what you did for me. Everyone thinks I got a loan or something to buy the business. Only I know that you provided a wonderful career, and flat, for a man with no hope after failing his finals. I still owe you bloody massively Si."

"You must be joking Pete. Given the way you've handled this shop, and the money you've put away for me, I'm in your debt big time. But if she didn't learn it from me, and she didn't learn it from you, there's only one way she could have found you – the Church!"

"Jesus, Mary and Joseph! Sorry Si couldn't help myself," Pete apologised clearly thinking that even an ex-vicar would object to the use of religious names as swear words. "I've just come across that brilliant Catholic swear word, or should I say phrase, and it just seemed so right for what you said. How in God's name would the bleeding Church know about me? And perhaps more pertinently, why, would the bloody Church want to tell your wife about me?"

"The how is easy to answer. When I applied for ordination, I was living here, so the address and phone number will be on my file. The Bishop must have my file, and I know he contacted Sarah to tell her about meeting me with another woman. I guess he also looked up your address for her. The Bishop is extremely miffed by my resignation."

"You're bloody joking me Si! You can't have a bleeding bishop being such a petty, small-minded, vicious prick, can you?"

"Oh yes you can Pete. The Lord Bishop of Ripon and Leeds is not used to being rejected, and I would guess he thought telling Sarah about you would cause me a lot of trouble. People like you, who're outside the Church, aren't always aware of the politics, and nastiness, that goes on, especially in the hallowed confines of a cathedral!"

"Maybe I don't know about the bloody Church Si, I've been an atheist most of my life, but it seems to me that this is more than a bit of nastiness. It seems more like, er more like something that's part of a plan. Are you sure there's nothing else?"

Of course, that was when I told him about our intended naughty trip to Ripon and Jasmine finding the body. He thought it hilarious that I got a dead body instead of a night of passion. However, the wrong identification of Mark Greenwood (who Pete remembered from King's), the detective seeking our help, and Samuel Watkinson probably being connected with the Church soon stopped the hilarity.

"Well bugger me!" exclaimed Pete. "Now that sounds more like a bleeding reason for my details being leaked to your wife. They would think that if you were worrying about Sarah causing you trouble, you wouldn't want to get involved in any form of investigation, and might even go back to your wife. Are you going back to your darling wife?"

"Don't be daft Pete. Not only do I hate her, but now I am head over heels in love with Jazz. Mate it feels so good, especially after twenty years with the ice maiden. What's more I absolutely hate the bishop; and that feeling has almost doubled after what you've told me. There is no way I'm letting these people, whoever they are, get away with murder! I'm making my life with Jazz and I'm going to find out about this Samuel Watkinson!"

CHAPTER TEN

The search for Samuel Watkinson did not begin immediately. Pete knew much more about the ways of the modern world than I did and suggested that it might be a good idea to get some cash from some of the savings to fund my investigation.

"Look Si. You're obviously involved with some pretty nasty, but powerful people. People who can get away with murder. People who can plant bodies. People who can influence police investigations. Bastards like that can use card transactions to check your movements and even to bloody pinpoint where you are. If you're sodding serious about exposing what's happened, I think you should bloody well stop using cards, credit or debit, and start using cash. Also, we'll get you a cheap pay-as-you-go phone and I'll get some of my computer-whizz friends working on this Samuel Watkinson."

"Do you really think I should? And how on earth do you know all this sort of thing, Pete?" I asked in an awestruck tone as I tried to get my head round the idea of people tracking my movements from my use of plastic. Pete was talking about a world I didn't know existed.

"Yes, I do think you should bloody well do all these things because you're dealing with bleeding murderers! I know these things because of the type of books I read and because I'm still the computer geek you knew at college. My friends on the net share all sorts of tricks and gizmos. Give me five minutes and I'll show you what can be done."

In fact, it was only two minutes later that Pete informed me that I had bought a return ticket to London from Eaglescliffe station that morning, withdrawn £50 from the cash machine at the shop next to the station and bought a sandwich and coffee on the train. Not surprisingly, this demonstration totally spooked me and within an hour I had two hundred and fifty £20 notes in my pocket and a brand-new Nokia 1800 with £30 top-up. I immediately texted Jazz to tell her she should use this new number for me and to take care.

While Pete got his friends to work on the internet to find Samuel Watkinson and the Fishermen's Group, I walked back to Hornsey station in a very different frame of mind from when I'd left. I found it impossible not to keep looking behind to see if I was being followed. After all, if these people were as organised and evil as Pete seemed to think they were, then they might want to stop me getting to Judd Street. The Nokia call sign frightened the wits out of me until I remembered my new phone and answered it.

"Simon, it's me," the sound of Jazz's voice calmed me down. "What's happening? Why have you got a new phone? Where are you?"

"Hi babe. I love you," these heartfelt words halted the barrage of questions. "Is it your lunch hour?"

When she answered in the affirmative, I began to fill her in on what had happened since my arrival at the bookshop – the shop itself, the amount of the nest egg, Pete's worries and his advice about keeping a low profile.

"Well, I think he's right and I'm glad you're following his advice. It spooked me when that lawyer had found out my name and workplace. You be extremely careful babe, and don't go asking people questions. Remember the words 'low profile' and remember that I love you too and want you back safely tonight."

Three of Jazz's words stuck in my head, 'I love you'. Somehow they made all the problems, worries and fears worthwhile. They also made me determined that I would follow Jazz's advice and keep a low profile. I was going to restrict myself to looking for signs of the group's ownership rather than just barging in and asking questions. I scoured the platform checking the other passengers. I wasn't sure what I was expecting to see. This, after all, was the twenty first century, anyone following me would not going to stand out with an eye-patch and a crutch like Blind Pew in 'Treasure Island'.

I made a careful note of all the waiting people, then alighted from the train at Finsbury Park rather than Kings Cross and made another careful survey as I waited for the next train to Kings Cross which was coming from Cambridge and so would not have stopped at Hornsey. Only one person from Hornsey was on the platform, and they didn't get on the Kings Cross train giving me reason to hope I was not being followed. Despite this, I couldn't help checking again when I got off at King's Cross.

A crowd of people was using the pedestrian crossing over Euston Road and I tried to scrutinise each one to see if any looked familiar, but none did. To check further, I decided to walk past Camden Town Hall and down Argyle Street. As I turned into Argyle Walk past McGlyn's pub, I saw I was actually the only person in the Walk. I continued down Whidbourne Street and studied the Victorian edifice of Holy Cross Church as if I were a student of late Victorian church architecture. Indeed, to complete the impression and fool anyone looking, I pretended to take photos with my new phone (though Pete had made sure it was so lacking in technology, it didn't even have a camera!), all the while looking around at the passers-by.

It seemed strange to be back in this part of central London where several of my college mates had been in halls of residence. I turned the corner from Cromer Street into Judd Street and there staring me in the face was a plaque saying – Fishermen's Group Registered Office. I looked around again before crossing the street to investigate the old London regency style town house. The display window was full of popular style religious books published by One Way Publications with prominent use of its logo. Clearly there had to be a connection between the hostel and the Reverend Timothy Harris.

*   *   *   *   *

"Of course, you'll agree with this One-Way chap, won't you Jasmine?"

The question roused Jasmine from her daydream of being attacked by a gang of clergymen. It had been asked by a grey-haired, slightly overweight man in his fifties. He was wearing pale blue Farah trousers and a bluish Harris Tweed jacket with leather elbow patches. On a younger man it could have been designer trendy, but on Colin Taylor, Physics teacher, it was more like the uniform of boring teachers from way back when.

"What do you mean Colin?" Jasmine asked.

Colin showed her the headline on the front of that morning's Daily Telegraph:
'Christians Declare War on Gay Marriage' under which she read, 'Exclusive interview with Rev Timothy Harris leader of the influential One Way Christian movement'

"I'm not sure," she prevaricated, not wishing to get into an argument with such an obnoxious colleague. "What's it about?"

"Well this chap Harris reckons the government is going to betray all the Christians of the UK by changing these civil partnerships into full gay marriage, and making the good old C of E give a wedding service to any gay couple who want one. He claims that would destroy the whole basis of marriage which is the union of a man and a woman under God. And I think he's right Jasmine. We've had far too much of this moral surrender to current fashions. It's no wonder this country's in such a mess when the Government won't even preserve basic morality."

"Are you telling me you agree with him?" Jasmine had to struggle to use the word 'him' rather than 'raving nutter' which had first come to her lips. "Do you think many people actually agree with his ideas?"

"Course they do Jasmine. You know how many of our problem kids come from broken homes. They have no proper family, no stability and hence no chance of a decent future. Lots of people think that if we got back to proper families, a man and a woman getting married, not just living together, and raising a Christian family, this country would be a much better place. Rev Harris struck a chord with me when he said that God created Adam and Eve not Adam and Steve. We've gone too far with this idea that anything goes."

Jasmine was amazed and yet not amazed. It was generally agreed in the staffroom that Colin was out of touch with reality and yet he was an intelligent person. Surely you had to be to teach A level Physics! He was also a member of the local Conservative Association and active in his local C of E church. He had connections and he sounded like a member of the One Way Group.

"Sorry Colin, I have to make a phone call before my next class." True it was the coward's way out, but she didn't want to start a full-blown row in the staffroom which would draw unnecessary attention to herself, and probably lead to another interview with the Head. She went to her classroom and phoned Simon.

*   *   *   *   *

"Hi babe," Jazz's voice saying such a wonderful greeting of endearment more than made up for the shock of my new mobile ringing for the second time. "Have you seen this morning's Daily Telegraph?"

"You don't really expect me to have started reading the Tory press do you, babe? I've left the C of E not joined it!"

That got a chuckle from Jazz. "No. It's not the paper, it's an article that's in it this morning. I've just struggled to stop myself having a blazing row in the staffroom with one of our old brigade staff who thinks Timothy Harris should be running the country. Apparently, Harris has written a big article in today's Telegraph. I thought you might want to see it."

"Good thinking batgirl," all the phrases that should come naturally between lovers, but which I would never have dared use with Sarah, were certainly flowing with Jazz. "I'm standing in Judd Street looking at the Fishermen's Group registered office plaque and guess what the office is?" I was, of course, asking a rhetorical question. There was no way she could guess; anymore than it was likely I'd been reading the Daily Telegraph that morning.

"I've no idea Simon, but I'm assuming there's some sort of connection with the One Way group" she replied.

"Right first time babe. It's the office of One Way Publications. The window's full of books and pamphlets by the Reverend Timothy Harris and his friends."

As I said these words, I looked in the window and read out a few of the titles, "You'd love these babe. There's 'Closer to God', 'Fruits of the Spirit', 'God's Dangerous Book' and guess what? There's even a little book by Lord Jim called 'Living in God's Way'. I don't think he knows much about that!"

"So, there is a connection Simon?"

"There is indeed, and I'm going to see what else I can find out. I'll buy a copy of the Telegraph and read the article on the way home."

"Be careful Simon!" were Jazz's final words.

I was surprised that describing Stockton as home had come out automatically without any thought process at all. I was also very pleased to be feeling that way. Evidently I already felt a harmony with Jazz that I'd never experienced with Sarah.

A small bistro/deli –according to its signage, but greasy spoon according to its looks – afforded an opportunity to think about what to do. I'd had enough coffee and opted for a cup of tea and a pain au raisin covered in sticky icing and cherries to aid the cogitation. Thought processes were definitely going to be needed to find the whereabouts of Samuel Watkinson, but any attempt to ask questions about him in a place that was clearly only a convenience address for the hostel's holding company would certainly not be in line with keeping a low profile!

A sign informed me that five pounds would give me an hour's wi-fi access, accordingly I offered a five pound note and was given the log-in details. I took my drink and bun to an out of the way corner table, switched on my laptop and logged on to the bistro's wi-fi connection. I had not yet looked for the Fishermen's Group website and now when I did, up came a list of hostels around the country. The men in Ripon claimed Watkinson had said he was going to London, so I copied out the addresses of the three hostels in London: one in Cleveland Street, Fitzrovia, one in Southwark and one in Holloway Road.

I had no idea where Fitzrovia was, so I googled Cleveland Street and discovered it was just behind Goodge Street tube station. Apparently Fitzrovia was a name given to the area in the 1930's when writers such as Virginia Wolf and Dylan Thomas lived there and drank in the Fitzroy Tavern. It was only a short walk from Judd Street and so I determined to walk there to see if the same ploy I'd used to discover information from the homeless in Ripon would work in the more bohemian area of Fitzrovia.

I walked down Judd Street, once more keeping an eye on the people around me even though I was not quite sure what I should look for in a stalker. I went through the Brunswick shopping centre (much improved since my student days especially now Safeway had become Waitrose) past the tube station and into Russell Square where I sat on a bench, ostensibly watching the fountains. My position enabled me to scrutinise most of the people in the park. As I perused people, something struck me about a man who had just bought a coffee from the garden cafe.

Most of him was nondescript: medium height, medium build, mousey hair cut fairly short, dark clothes. What stood out was his nose, large and protuberant, rather like an eagle's beak, and I'd seen it before today. Yes, the man drinking a coffee in Russell Square Gardens had been waiting on the platform at Kings Cross as I got off the train from Finsbury Park. Was it just coincidence that he was here?

CHAPTER ELEVEN

Given the warnings I'd received from everyone, and more particularly my promise to Jazz to be careful, I decided to take no chances. Abandoning my plan to walk through Senate House to Goodge Street, I walked over to the cafe, bought a coffee and sat down just a couple of tables away from birdman (it seemed a good identifier for someone whose name I did not know!).

Maybe it was something I'd read in a Lee Child thriller, I don't know, but I felt that doing the unexpected might upset this man who, I was use, was watching me. Anyway, nearly twenty years in the North had given me a rather different attitude to chatting to strangers from the normal Londoner.

"Nice day isn't it?" I commented to the birdman. He was totally startled at being addressed by me and didn't seem at all sure how to react, so I continued, "I've just finished my business down here and I'm on my way back north. I was just enjoying these beautiful gardens before going to King's Cross to catch my train. When I saw you enjoying a coffee here, I thought I might as well have one rather than getting to the station too early."

Birdman studied his coffee and tried to ignore me, but I was determined not to let him. "Do you know anything about these gardens?" I asked. "I think I heard they were something to do with the family of the philosopher Bertrand Russell. Is that right?"

Birdman was clearly discomfited, and, like any true Londoner, had no qualms about appearing extremely rude. Consequently, my words, rather than encouraging him to join in the conversation, made him get up and leave. I continued to drink my coffee whilst watching birdman disappear in the direction of the British Museum. I gave him time to get out of sight, left my unfinished coffee on the table and made my way as quickly as I could, without appearing to hurry, out of the Gardens via the opposite corner from where birdman had left.

There was no way birdman had seen me go to Hornsey. I was sure of it. The station had been too quiet and I had been ultra observant. Maybe he had been sent to King's Cross to meet my train from the North and arrived too late? Thinking back, I remembered that we had arrived a few minutes early, Whatever, I was now working to a plan to make it very hard for anyone to follow my next move!

I crossed Southampton Row, went into Russell Square tube station and bought a day travelcard for Zones 1 and 2, remembering to use cash. After what Pete had told me, I wasn't sure whether even an Oyster Card would allow me to be tracked! I then bought a single ticket to King's Cross, hoping anyone seeing me arrive at Kings Cross would see my ticket disappear and not be aware that I had a travel card.

The notice confronting me as I approached the lift was like a slap in the face. It informed me that the lifts were being re-furbished and that as only one lift was operating, there would be delays. The last thing I wanted was to be trapped by birdman in the station entrance. Luckily, as I was searching for the entrance to the stairs, the lift arrived and swiftly transported me down to the line. I didn't have to wait long for a train for Cockfosters, but even so it was a tense wait as I kept my eyes peeled for birdman arriving. I hurried off the tube at King's Cross, and exited from the top of the escalator using my single ticket, and climbed the stairs to the rail station. This time I had a chance to gaze in awe at the vast new canopy (supposedly the largest station canopy in Europe), then boarded the train on platform 8 which was leaving for Aberdeen in five minutes.

My hope was that if anyone had managed to follow me, or was even waiting and watching at the station, they would assume that I was going back up north on this train as it called at Darlington. I walked down the inside of the train till I was opposite the passageway through to the suburban station. I alighted and walked quickly through the suburban station and across the road to St Pancras where I walked back down to the underground by a different entrance. Then I walked through the maze of passages to the Metropolitan and Circle line using my travel card and caught a train to Great Portland Street. I was pretty sure no one could have followed me this time.

However, I was still taking no chances. Jazz's final words were ringing a loud and clear warning in my head. So, rather than approaching Cleveland Street from the northern end, I took a circuitous route to give myself time to check whether I'd lost any followers. As I walked down Great Portland Street, I tapped the number given me by the inspector into my new phone. When Inspector Byrom answered, I told him most of what had been happening to me in London, but again omitted all mention of Pete and the money, whether because I didn't completely trust him or simply because I thought it was nothing to do with him, I'm not sure. I ended by asking him what was happening up in Yorkshire.

"All sorts, Simon," the inspector replied. "They're obviously trying to keep me away from the murder case because I've never had such a massive amount of inconsequential work dumped on my plate. I'm in Pateley Bridge at the moment investigating the theft of a bloody dog from some television personality who lives here. I've never heard of her, but believe me she has one big mouth! Anyway Simon, I don't like what you're telling me about being followed."

"Haven't you heard anything about the murder?" I asked in a somewhat harsh tone, not liking the way he was taking as much information from me as he could, whilst giving me virtually nothing in return.

"I've heard that inquests are to be held tomorrow with no jury and all the paperwork given to the coroner enabling her to rubber stamp a suicide verdict on Michael Brown and a verdict of unlawful killing on Paul Williams with Michael Brown named as the killer. When once the inquests reach those verdicts, the case will be officially closed and the bodies released for burial or cremation, even though we know that Paul Williams' body is not Paul Williams!"

Chatting on the phone gave me the chance to keep looking around without appearing suspicious. I saw no sign of anyone following me and certainly no sign of the birdman. As I thought about what he had just said about cremating the body immediately after the inquests, I felt I had to ask, "Is there any chance of holding back the inquests so that Mark's body isn't cremated until we've had a chance to prove it's him?"

"Not a chance Simon," he answered and immediately changed the topic. "By the way Simon, have you found anything out about this Samuel Watkinson?"

"Not yet. But I have discovered a connection between the One Way Group and the Fishermen's Group. Any thoughts on that?"

"Take great care is my thought. It sounds just as fishy as the name suggests."

I turned into Cleveland Street and decided to terminate the conversation so I could concentrate on the task ahead. "OK Dave. Will do. I'm just approaching a hostel Samuel Watkinson might be at so I'll sign off. I'll keep in touch."

Half-way up the street a few men were standing smoking outside a scruffy Victorian building. They were not well dressed and seemed to be aged from about twenty-five to seventy, though of course they could be much younger, life on the streets aged people rapidly. I was fairly sure I'd found the hostel and said a quiet thank you for the smoking ban sending smokers out into the open air.

I slipped into a corner shop before approaching the hostel. Experience had taught me that it was always useful to have cigarettes with you when talking to the homeless, especially if you wanted information! The cigarettes were in a cupboard, their names hidden from view. I couldn't just ask for twenty cigarettes and I was pretty sure that the brands of my youth were no more! Luckily there was a man in front of me who asked for ten Regal; I asked for two packs of twenty. That should be enough to lubricate, if not irritate, some throats.

As I approached the group of smokers, they seemed to shrink against the wall. Of course, in an area of London so close to the tourist hotspot of Oxford Street, a smartly dressed man was going to represent authority, especially the authority of the Met. During Boris Johnson's mayoralty, the Met had been under instructions to clear the streets of beggars and the homeless, so these men would be far more used to being moved on than being stopped for information. I tried to think of an opening gambit that might make them less antagonistic. Nothing came, but I was now level with them and had to say something.

"Hi lads. Is this the Fishermen's Group hostel?"

It was not a Peter Kay opener, but it actually had the desired effect.

"Yeah," said a haggard looking, sandy haired man of indeterminate age. "What's it to you?"

His bloodshot brown eyes were looking me up and down, clearly taking in my smart new clothes.

One of his friends broke in even more belligerently, "What's a man like you want with a place like this? This is for people like us, not people like you."

I took in his shabby suit jacket and the mismatched trousers frayed where they dragged along the ground at his heels. The filthy, one-time white Adidas trainers set off an outfit which cried out to having come from an outlet way below Oxfam. These guys were a totally different breed from those in Ripon. I wasn't sure that my experience with, what I began to realise was the more respectable class of down and out in the North, would get me very far with these London men who seemed so hard and, to be honest with myself, frighteningly dangerous. I needed a different approach.

"I'm looking for a vicar called Samuel Watkinson," I said as aggressively as I could.

"What makes you think we might want to help you?" the haggard man replied with even more aggression, and two of his stronger looking mates came alongside him to eyeball me.

I tried not to let my fear show and came up with my cunning plan which I hoped would rival one of Baldrick's. "Because he knows where the vicar is who's been interfering with my twelve-year-old daughter," I said trying to emulate, or even better, their confrontational aggression. "And I want to make sure that that fucking scumbag gets what he deserves. "

I looked from one to the other of the group, making deliberate eye contact with each one. I knew that even the most depraved of men regard child-molesters as the lowest of the low and hoped that with the current climate of clerical abuse, these men would be sufficiently aware of the news to find my accusation believable. Incredibly, I was even beginning to believe it myself!

"They all protect each other don't they, just like the fucking Catholic bishops! Where did this happen then?" a more respectable looking, older man asked as he came into the foreground.

"At her confirmation class in Ripon. How could a vicar do that after a confirmation class? I'll bloody show him about Jesus loving him when I get my hands on him. The bastard's disappeared from Ripon, but word is that he came down here with this Watkinson guy." My belligerence was building up and I realised I was channelling all my fears and frustrations from the last couple of days onto a man I'd never even met and onto another man who didn't even exist because I'd just made him up!

"Of course, the little fucking git went up to Ripon a couple of weeks ago," one of the stronger-looking men piped up, inadvertently giving me the information that Samuel Watkinson was of small stature.

I was about to seek further information when the second stronger looking guy butted in, "He told us he was going up to Ripon to look after a hostel up there, but from what you say, he probably went up there cos his fucking mate needed some help."

There was menace in his tone and I realised I was losing the advantage of my initial shock treatment. I needed to rekindle it, and quickly. "I wouldn't care, I don't even believe in God," I continued, "but she goes to a church school and all her friends were getting confirmed. I thought these fucking paedophile priests were all Catholics but I've had to think again, and now I just want to make sure he doesn't ruin any other young girls' lives. Can you help me?" I was amazed at how easily lies start to flow once you get into the swing of it, especially if you start with a bit of truth.

"Any of you lads want a fag?" I asked opening up one of the new packs of Regal. They crowded round me seeking not only a free fag, but also offering information. It turned out that Samuel had come back on Friday night and was met by 'that anti-gay bloke who's always on the telly', I assumed by this they meant Tim Harris. He had then left with Harris and hadn't been seen since. They offered to come with me to help find him, so they could deal with his mate in a much better way than the law would. I demurred, claiming I needed to deal with Watkinson personally, so that I was sure I was getting the truth from him about the paedo's whereabouts. I thanked them profusely for their help and gave them all the cigarettes I had bought and a twenty-pound note from my wallet (not from the pocket with all the cash in) as a thank you and made my way down to Goodge Street.

I walked slowly back towards Judd Street. I thought it might be possible Watkinson was there in its rather more salubrious surroundings, but I also thought it might not be a good idea to hang around outside the One Way office looking suspicious. Looking in the window of a shop I was passing gave me an idea. I went in and bought a pair of very weak reading glasses, a Billabong cap, a London Transport hooded top and a carrier bag. I put my jacket in the shop's carrier bag and then donned my disguise. It was very simple, but quite effective – I had to look in the window twice before I recognised myself!

When I arrived back at Judd Street, I went straight into the bistro I'd been in before, ordered a coffee and another sticky bun and positioned myself so that I had a good view of the entrance to the Fishermen's Group office without being too easily seen from the other side of the road. I kept a hundred percent observation of the entrance until I noticed that my cup and plate were both empty and I was attracting stares from the Italian looking guy behind the counter (who was probably Romanian!). I bought another coffee and five pounds' worth of Wi-fi access. Although I opened my computer and logged onto the internet, I was only pretending. In reality I was still giving that entrance my complete attention.

As I watched the entrance, I thought about what I had done and began to have major regrets. I had no idea what sort of a man Samuel Watkinson was, yet I'd just convinced some shady looking characters that he was probably helping a paedophile escape justice. I shouldn't have done that! After all, the Cleveland Street men might even now be plotting to attack him whilst I sat in this bistro drinking coffee, and, if they did, it would all be my fault.

I was just about to order yet another coffee when I saw something that made me bury my head in the computer and then use the laptop to justify turning round so I could not be seen at all from the street. The Rev Samuel Watkinson whose photo I had seen on the internet that morning, had just walked out of the office, and he was accompanied by someone I knew only too well. Someone walking with a rather episcopal gait even though (for the first time since I'd known him) he was dressed casually, but oh so smart casual, in a pair of jeans, a pair of expensive looking loafers, and a Ralph Lauren Oxford shirt with a navy blue cashmere sweater draped over his shoulders. Not a vestige of episcopal status in sight. It was Lord Jim.

My regrets about Samuel Watkinson disappeared. The Rev Samuel and the Right Rev Jim were clearly into something very dodgy even if it was nothing like as bad as paedophilia.

CHAPTER TWELVE

I was really spooked by what I had just seen and determined to get home as quickly as I could, and yes, I was still thinking of Jazz as home. I determined to use a more circuitous route to get back as I wanted to keep birdman and any of his friends well away from my Jasmine. I also thought that a long journey would give me time to think and plan our next moves. I used my laptop to find out some train times, and to give the bishop and his friend plenty of time to leave the area, before I set off for the station.

Although it was only a short distance, I decided to take a cab, just to confuse anyone who might be following me. I asked the driver to take me to St Pancras rather than Kings Cross to further confuse, but now had to decide which way to return back north. I had googled a variety of routes whilst waiting for Samuel and the bishop to disappear and knew I had several options. I could simply go to Kings Cross and return on the Grand Central, or I could go up to Leeds on an East Coast train and come up to Stockton on a Trans-Pennine, or I could use Midland Mainline to go from St Pancras to Sheffield where I could catch a Cross-Country to Darlington and a local train to Eaglecliffe.

I paid off the driver at St Pancras and instead of going into the station, walked over to Kings Cross. I had made my decision. If anyone saw me catch a train to Leeds, they would assume I was going back to the vicarage. That would be the best way to keep them away from Jazz So I walked down Pancras Road and went into the new Kings Cross ticket office where I bought a first-class ticket to Leeds on my credit card. I had decided to use my credit card since it would convince anyone who might be following, or tracking, me that I was going back to Leeds. I'd decided on first class for two reasons: firstly, so there would not be many people for me to check on for potential followers; secondly to have enough space and quiet to sort out the situation and decide what to do next. I knew first class would be expensive, but I was amazed to find the cost of the ticket was a gobsmacking one hundred and seventy-six pounds single (how on earth was Virgin losing money on this line?). Surely the first-class carriages would be empty at prices like that?

What an eye-opener I received when I boarded the train and almost had to fight to get myself a seat. Clearly austerity was not biting too hard amongst the moneyed classes. Though looking around I saw that virtually everyone, both men and women, was in business suits and carrying laptops and briefcases. Maybe everyone had been at business meetings with their tickets paid for by the business. There was clearly money to be made from a train franchise, no wonder there were so many bidders for them.

I managed to find myself one of the single seats so that no one would be able to look at my laptop screen. I stood up to put my hoodie and cap on the luggage rack and took the opportunity to survey the rest of coach K. There was no sign of birdman and no one appeared to match any of the faces I had scanned during this eventful day. I sat down and texted Jazz – I'd already decided that phone conversations were too easy to overhear on a train – telling her to check her e-mails. By the time I'd plugged in and switched on my laptop, we were out of London and passing though the countryside north of Potters Bar.

The internet connection was not the speediest, and whilst I was waiting for it to download, I texted Jazz again to explain my travel plans and tell her I would ring from Leeds station. I was now connected to the internet, so I e-mailed Pete to tell him what I'd found out about Samuel Watkinson and about seeing him with my old friend the bishop. By this time, I'd been served tea and sandwiches (at least you got some free food for that exorbitant fare!) and unplugged the laptop to make room to eat, but was careful to leave it switched on and connected to the internet, I didn't want to wait for another slow download.

I was surprised at how hungry I was considering the number of sticky buns I'd eaten. As I ate, I thought about what I'd just seen in Judd Street. Clearly the bishop was at the heart of what was going on. But what was going on, and why on earth was a bishop involved in it?
As soon as I'd finished my cup of tea, I plugged the laptop back in and went straight to my e-mails. Pete was obviously one of those people who always know when they have received an e-mail because he had already replied to mine. I suppose there is something you can do that alerts you in some way to the fact that you have an e-mail without you having to keep looking at your computer, but if so I'd never mastered it. Then I realised that, unlike me, Pete would not be working with an old Nokia. He was always a techno-geek and so he would have the latest Apple i-phone and would be able to check and answer e-mails on that.

Evidently Pete and his friends had been very busy and as I read what they had discovered, my jaw must have dropped.

Pete's e-mail told me that Samuel Watkinson had been educated at Eton and was a contemporary there of Jim Scott-Phillips, my Lord the Bishop (so there was a long-time connection with Lord Jim). He was the younger son of the Earl of Dawlish whose family owned a merchant bank. Samuel had been a leading light in the Conservative Association at Oxford, and after graduating in PPE, became an ordinand of the Church of England and trained at Wycliffe Hall Oxford, a college well known for producing some of the leading Anglican Evangelicals. Apparently, his career in the Church was much more difficult to follow, but he had had two spells as chaplain to the Archbishop of Canterbury and one as the Church's media spokesperson. His current official position was CEO of the Fishermen's Group which would obviously have given him the opportunity to act as the warden in Ripon, but didn't explain why he had done so.

I e-mailed Pete back to thank him for the info and then settled back to read the Daily Telegraph I had bought on Jazz's instructions.

*   *   *   *   *
*

Jasmine Baker's life had been turned upside down by the events of the last few days. There were all sorts of things for her to worry about. There was the rapid change in her relationship with Simon from his leaving his wife and job, to moving to Stockton. There was the whole unbelievable thing of poor Mark Greenwood's murder, the police cover-up and Simon's chase off to London to investigate. But the thing that was really bugging her was Simon's wife, and in particular Simon's wife's solicitor. How dare they cause her trouble at work without so much as a by-your-leave!

Jasmine had never been one to let the grass grow under her feet, so as soon as lessons ended she got in the car and set off down the A66 for Redcar. It was a quick drive along the dual carriageway past Middlesbrough's Riverside Stadium and the semi-redundant Teesside Steelworks and she was soon searching for a parking space. She managed to find one on the sea-front near the ex-hotel which had featured as Dunkirk in the film version of 'Atonement'. Only the semi-derelict cinema remained of the film-set, the rest of the sea-front had been transformed by the new sea defences and the vertical pier known as the Redcar Beacon. Jasmine had little time for these, or for the sounds of the sea and the fresh sea breeze in her hair. She was on a mission and rapidly made her way to the High Street to find the offices of Humble and Lewis. She was determined not only to give the solicitor a piece of her mind, but also to find out the address of Sarah's parents so that she could tackle the cold bitch who had made her lover's life so miserable (strange that she thought of him as her lover even though they had never made love, though she had already determined that that would shortly change).

Full of aggro, she marched down the High Street until she found the solicitor's office next door to a betting shop (the High Street seemed full of betting shops, pound shops and pay-day loan companies). The door was locked. After rattling it viciously, Jasmine looked in the window next to the door and there were displayed the hours of opening – Monday 10.00 a.m. to 4.00 p.m. Unbelievable! And people like solicitors complained about teachers' hours! Somewhat deflated, she began a memory scan. What had Simon called her parents, apart from the swear words. Trevor that was the father, but what was his surname? Thompson, that was it. Trevor Thompson, but how to track him down? The library, they would have phone books, electoral registers etc. But where was the library?

It was no problem with a smart phone. There was a lovely map on the website she googled, and Jasmine was soon walking past the station and through the automatic doors into what looked like a fairly new library building. A couple of questions to a librarian, a quick scan of the phonebook, an even quicker walk back to the car and Jasmine was on her way to her confrontation with the 'other woman'. A bit of thought made her realise that actually she was 'the other woman' which made her wonder what better descriptor she should use for herself: perhaps 'the new woman'.

As she turned into Uttoxeter Road, she saw something that nearly made her crash the car. A black BMW was parked outside the house she was sure was the Thompsons. However, it wasn't just a black BMW; it looked to be an awfully familiar black BMW. Jasmine drove slowly past trying to see who was there whilst at the same time trying to look like a disinterested passing motorist. She could see nothing so she drove round the corner and parked. She had noticed that the BMW was parked facing the same direction as her, so it would not pass her if it set off.

Jasmine sat in her car puzzling over what to do. If the owner of the BMW was who she thought it was, she didn't want him to see her. On the other hand, she needed to check whether her suspicions about the owner were correct. If they were, the confrontation she had planned with the ex-wife was not going to happen, unless things went wrong and a very different confrontation ensued. Unobtrusiveness is hard to achieve when you are a black woman in a white area, and Jasmine decided that her best tactic would be to drive round the block with the hope that someone would emerge from the detached Sixties house for her to check without being noticed herself.

She stayed where she was for a few minutes looking, with what she hoped appeared to be concentration mingled with puzzlement, at a map she'd taken out of the glove compartment. Jasmine then put the map away, pretended she now knew where she was heading and set off down the road.

It was easy enough to drive round the block and Jasmine was soon driving down Uttoxeter Road again. This time she hit the jackpot. The BMW's owner was the person she'd thought it was. There was Inspector Byrom walking down the drive with a smartly dressed blonde haired woman of about forty, presumably the soon to be ex-Mrs Keep. Jasmine would have loved to stop and get a good look at the evil Sarah, but she didn't want the inspector to see her and so she drove straight past with her eyes fixed on the road ahead. She drove down to the Coast Road and parked in one of the empty car parks on the Stray to look at the sea and think about what she had just seen. She knew that even if the inspector had seen her, there was no chance of him returning to his base via the Stray.

*   *   *   *   *

*

I can't say I was riveted by Harris's article in the Telegraph. It contained all his familiar pathetic arguments. How the sinfulness of the present world was caused by a lack of religion (i.e. Protestant Christianity not religion in general) and could be cured by a return to the faith and morality of Bible based Christianity. Of course, chief among the examples of sinfulness he referred to were homosexuality, abortion and sexual promiscuity. Surprisingly enough, there were no references to bankers' bonuses, tax evasion and declining revenues for charities!! This was all standard stuff, but more worrying, to someone like me at least, were the references to the need for red lines in our negotiations for leaving the EU juxtaposed with references the sinfulness of EU policies of free access for Muslims and other unwelcome migrants. Also worrying were the veiled hints that the answers to our problems were not only to be found in the Bible and the Gospel, but also in the policies of European anti-Muslim groups. Then there was a large chunk about how the Conservative Party had lost all legitimacy as a Christian party by its legislation making civil partnerships into same sex marriage and of how it would only be a government committed to the principles of Bible-based Christianity that could save Great Britain from its slide into sin and irrelevance. There was a definite implication there that the One Way Group might be trying to start a British Tea Party by leading right wing Tories into a new right wing Christian group. I began to speculate about that meeting in Ripon and those Tory MPs.

My theories were interrupted by a phone ringing. It took some time for me to realise that the Nokia tune was not ringing for someone else in the carriage, it was my new phone with its factory set call sign. By the time I got the phone out of my pocket, it was indicating a missed call. I looked at the number and realised it was Jazz. Why was she phoning when I'd told her not to? I went into the passage-way between the coaches so there would be some privacy when I phoned her back. She knew why I'd asked her not to phone, so this must be something serious.

"Hi Jazz babe," I said cheerfully hoping to calm down whatever crisis she was in. "You rang?"

"Oh babe, you're just so not going to believe this." Worry was bringing out the London girl in Jazz's voice.

"Calm down babe," I answered in a soothing voice which belied the worries that were now assailing me. "Stop worrying. It can't be that bad."

"It can babe. This is a genuine emergency! Guess who I've just seen at your ex-wife's parents' house?"

"What on earth are you doing in Redcar?" I exclaimed. I now had even more cause to worry as I envisaged a meeting not only between Jazz and Sarah, but also between Jazz and the Thompsons.

I soon had more than that to worry about as Jazz replied, "Well I came to have it out with those bloody solicitors for phoning the school, but they were shut, so I found out where her parents lived and went round there to give them a piece of my mind and guess who I saw?"

Jazz asked me the question as if I was bound to know, but of course I didn't have a clue. I racked my brains as to who it might have been. Sarah? Trevor? Christine? Would they merit an emergency phone call?

"Inspector Byrom was there."

At that juncture the train went over some points at a hundred miles an hour and I was thrown against the toilet door. Physical events which mirrored my thought processes – shock and a fear that we were about to be plunged into the mire.

"I don't believe it?" I exclaimed in what must have sounded like a Victor Meldrew impression. Then after a pause, I managed to ask in a rather panic-stricken tone, "What the hell was he doing there?" Then, in even more panic as I began to realise the implications, I asked," Did he see you?"

"No way babe. Luckily I recognised his car outside the house and just drove past."

"So, it might not have been him, just a similar car?"

"Sorry Simon it was him. I drove past again and saw him in the drive with someone I took to be your ex-wife. I did it quickly and made sure he didn't see me."

"Where are you now?" I asked anxiously, afraid that she might now be under as much threat as the birdman had put me.

"I'm parked on the Stray looking out to sea and feeling scared."

"Stay there then and give me a chance to think about this and I'll phone you back shortly. I'm going to get some advice from Pete, then phone you from the station at Leeds. I'm coming home the long way round to fool anyone shadowing me. We'll be in Leeds soon. Look after yourself babe. Love you."

I rang off and returned pensively to my seat. Things were happening so rapidly that I was finding great difficulty in keeping up. We now knew that there was a close connection between the man who had misidentified Mark Greenwood's body and the Lord Bishop of Ripon and Leeds. I knew that I had been followed by someone in London. Now the police inspector, whom I was supposed to be helping and who knew I was going to London, turned out to have some sort of connection with my ex-wife and her family. I needed to talk to Pete, but not on the train. The sound of the train changed and I realised we were slowing down for our penultimate stop at Wakefield Westgate. I decided to email Pete an account of what Jazz had just told me, and then phone him from Leeds station in a place where I could not be overheard.

Five minutes after the train pulled into Leeds I was in one of the station toilets with the seat down and the door locked, on the phone to Pete. My first question was about Jazz's bombshell, "What do you make of Inspector Byrom being at Sarah's parents' house?"

"It makes bloody good sense of a few things Si. For a start we now know who tipped Sarah off so that she could set solicitors onto Jasmine. We also know how the bugger who followed you in London knew you were there. Did you mention me to this fucking inspector when you told him you were coming to London?"

That question gave me a shock, and I had to rack my brains to search for an answer. Pete must have been able to hear the relief in my voice as I answered, "It's OK Pete. I don't know why, but I decided not to mention either you or the money on any of the occasions I've spoken to him. But it's weird Pete. Why do you think he let me go to London if he was part of the plot? Wouldn't he have wanted to get rid of me straight away?"

There was a pause as Pete gave himself time to think about that one; then he answered, "I'm buggered if I know Si, but it could be that they wanted to get you out of their area before they did something. It may be that it was extremely lucky for your health that you spotted that bastard in Russell Square and managed to lose him. Do you bloody well realise that only you and Jasmine know about Mark Greenwood. By coming up on his own to see you in Stockton, Byrom has kept it that way. He's the only police officer who definitely knows that the body was misidentified. I think whoever he's working for may well have been intending an accidental death in London for you my friend."

"What do you mean working for? Isn't there a plot in the North Yorkshire Police Force?"

I could hear Pete laughing as he said, "You're still a bit of a bloody vicar Si – naive and trusting! I think you can forget every bloody thing Byrom said on that bleeding issue. I reckon he's the only police connection in the plot. He's the only fucker who knows about Mark Greenwood and the only police person who knows that you and Jasmine know. I guess it threw all their plans out when the people who discovered the body actually bloody well knew Mark. If they'd been anyone but you two, the finders of the body would just have assumed that the body was who Byrom said it was."

Pete paused and then continued, "Bloody hell Si, I'm worrying about Jasmine now. If they wanted you dead, they'll want her dead as well. I think you need to get her out of that fucking area pdq."

My blood ran cold at Pete's words. Was Byrom up in Redcar to organise another suicide or accident which could be connected with my wife and girlfriend meeting each other? I was sure Sarah wouldn't mind helping him get rid of my lover! I had to get in touch with Jazz now.

As I was reaching for my mobile, another dreadful thought struck me. Sarah had contacted Pete and if she knew about Pete so did Byrom and indeed the whole cabal involved in the plot, "Pete hadn't you better do something as well. Don't you remember that Sarah contacted you?"

"Don't you bloody well worry about me Si. I'm now an alter ego in a different place. Your bleeding 'friends' (I could hear the inverted commas round that word) won't find me. But what about Jasmine?"

What about Jasmine indeed? As Pete had said, we needed her out of Teesside pretty damn quick. And that was what I was thinking about rather than what on earth Pete might mean by being his alter ego. It didn't take long for me to respond as, I suppose, I'd already had most of it planned.

"Don't you worry about Jazz, Pete, I've got a plan. I'll keep in touch and thanks for everything."

CHAPTER THIRTEEN

Sitting on the loo was where I had often had my best thoughts and, fortunately this was one of those occasions. By the time I got back onto the station platform, the plan had been shared with, and agreed to by, Jazz.

I walked out of the station via the taxi stand exit, went over to a taxi and asked the driver to take me to the nearest Avis depot. I suppose I chose Avis because it was the first to come up when I googled car hire in Leeds. I was sure there was a more convenient car hire firm at the station, but I didn't want to make it easy for anyone following me. I calculated that Byrom would only have quick access to things in the North Yorkshire police area, and Leeds was in West Yorkshire so he'd have much more difficulty tracking me anyway.

However, things became much less easy when I arrived at the Avis car hire reception. Cash was not acceptable. I had to pay by credit card and have my driving licence photocopied. I trusted I would have sufficient time to use the car as a decoy for it not to matter. I got into the Vauxhall Corsa they had given me and checked where everything was. There were only slight differences from the Ford I was used to, and I was soon heading out of Leeds for Yeadon and the Leeds/Bradford Airport.

*　　*　　*　　*　　*
*

Jasmine was feeling slightly less scared as she burst into action and the adrenaline began to flow. The anger which had brought her to the solicitors in Redcar was also returning. How dare a police officer, indeed a police inspector, abuse his position in such a way? She would have loved to confront both him, and Simon's sleaze-bag of a wife, but if Pete thought whoever was behind this might have been trying to kill Simon, and Simon thought her life might be in danger, she needed to get away as quickly as possible. The image in her mind of Mark's dead body lying in the shrubbery reminded her that these people were not playing games. This whole bizarre situation had started off with a murder.

She was soon driving down the A19. No one but the library man knew she'd been in Redcar, so even if they had watchers on her flat, they could have no idea where she was. Rather than make her feel good and safe, this simply made her feel stupid. She felt she was behaving like someone in an action movie. Consequently, as she passed the signs for Yarm, she was tempted to divert to call at her flat for clothes, wash-things and make-up, but Simon's warning and the picture she had in her mind of Mark's murdered body kept her heading for the airport.

*　　*　　*　　*　　*
*

I dropped the car off at the Avis depot next to Leeds/Bradford airport and walked over to the Yeadon Stoop pub where I'd arranged to meet Jazz. My hope was that I'd left a not too easy to follow trail to an airport so that 'the plotters' (I had to give some sort of a name to the people organising this) might waste time trying to find me on a flight out of the country. I ordered a coffee and sat down to wait for Jazz.

As in many such pubs, Sky News was on. Unbelievably, it was showing Tim Harris leading a huge congregation in the chorus: 'Who put the colours in the rainbow? Who put the salt into the sea? Who put the cold into the snowflake? Who made you and me?' Such words had always made me cringe because they were so unscientific and anti-evolution, and they implied an omnipotent God who could do anything and make anything. One of the reasons my belief in God had dwindled away was that he so clearly could do very little. And of course, other words could have been added after all who put the Huntington's chorea in the genes and so on.

The sounds of the singing muted, though the film of the singing continued, as the newscaster's voice announced, "The Reverend Tim Harris announced today that his One Way Group is seeking an alliance with a group of Brexiteer Tory MPs and candidates to support them in their campaign to bring moral values back to the government of the United Kingdom, beginning with their campaign to reverse the law on same sex marriage. This is putting the Prime Minister in a very difficult position as many Conservative donors are part of the One Way Group and many Brexiteer Conservative MPs were vehemently opposed to the legislation on same sex marriage, which only became law because of the support of Labour MPs."

Wow! What an unholy alliance this was likely to be – nutcases united! I had been very concerned about the way the Church of England had reacted to the issue of gay marriage, and had had my wrist slapped when I preached a sermon explaining why it made theological sense for vicars to be allowed to officiate at and celebrate same sex marriages in church. But this was going even further than anything the Church had so far done. It was uniting right wing politics with Evangelical Christianity in a way very reminiscent of the Tea Party politics of US Republicanism. Even more alarming was the idea of them teaming up with the extreme right Nazis of Europe.

As I thought about this, an even more alarming idea sprang into my mind: was all of this somehow connected with 'the plotters'?

These thoughts instantly disappeared, however, when I spotted Jazz walking through the entrance and looking so gorgeous that I couldn't stop myself from running across the front of the bar, picking her up in my arms and giving her a passionate kiss. I just couldn't help myself. Perhaps it was relief that she had got here safe and sound, perhaps it was just a reaction to the danger we had so unexpectedly found ourselves in. Whatever the cause, it was wonderful and feeling her body melding into mine, I just didn't want it to stop.

"Put me down babe, everyone's looking at us," she whispered in my ear in a tone of voice which, whilst gently admonishing me, made me realise that she'd been enjoying it just as much as I had.

I put her down reluctantly and walked her back to my table holding her hand with the feeling of pride that can only come from knowing you are loved by a woman who is far better than you deserve. I could feel people looking at us, much more than the usual 'black girl/white man' looks, and had to admit to myself that maybe my reaction to Jazz's arrival had not quite been the right way to keep an inconspicuous low profile!

I bought Jazz a glass of white wine and lemonade to go with my half drunk cup of coffee and we sat down at the table to discuss our next moves. The discussion didn't take long, indeed it couldn't take long, as our first task was to buy clothes, suitcases, toiletries etc to last for a few days or even more. Pete had been adamant that neither of us should return home until both he and we were sure that we were no longer in danger from whoever 'the plotters' might be. Needless to say, ever since Jazz saw Inspector Byrom at my ex-in-laws, and my own experiences with birdman, I was not inclined to argue with him!

I finished my coffee and persuaded Jazz to leave half of her drink to ensure she was not under the influence, then we jumped into her car and turned left out of the pub heading for Harrogate.

The cream Mini Cooper with black roof was a typical career girl's car and she drove it with panache. It certainly had style and a fair amount of pace. I'd never been driven by Jazz before and it was an exhilarating experience. I watched her long-fingered graceful hands confidently change gear and move the steering wheel just sufficiently to head where she wanted. Her whole body was at one with the car. Watching her out of the corner of my eye, I soon discovered that, despite the danger, despite all the things we needed to do rushing through my mind, driving with Jazz was proving a sensual experience. Indeed, I was soon aware that the sexual excitement that had almost overwhelmed me when I picked her up in the pub was now building up in the car.

I struggled to concentrate on the more immediate issues and directed Jazz onto the Wetherby Road and into the huge Sainsbury's next to the Yorkshire Showground in Harrogate. I was sure that Tu was not a label that featured prominently in Jazz's wardrobe, anymore than it did in mine, but they were open, had a car park outside and we could find all we needed in one stop. In fact, within thirty minutes we had everything we needed, including two wheelie cases. I packed our purchases into the cases, removed the Sainsbury's labels from the cases and put one in the boot and one on the back seat. Another ten minutes and we were heading North on the A1, and now the questions began.

"Where are we going Simon?" she asked. "You may not have noticed, but I'm not the sort of woman who enjoys being told what to do. I'm used to being in control of my life and at the moment, even though I'm driving and so may appear in control, I'm not. You said there's a plan, what is it?"

I squeezed her knee and a jolt like an electric shock went through me (and from the swerve of the car through Jazz as well). "I'm sorry babe, we just haven't had the opportunity. I'm not keeping anything from you. Pete's given me all sorts of warnings about the type of people these plotters are likely to be. We need to keep vigilant and watch out for anyone who might be listening. I never thought that slogan from the Second World War – 'Walls have ears' – would apply to us, but it does!"

"Okay Simon. Cut the waffle," Jazz had a knack of getting to the heart of things. "No one can be listening in the car. Now what's the plan?"

I went through the plan which had essentially been organised by Pete, "We spend the night in a hotel in Newcastle. Then we drive to Newcastle airport and leave your car in the long stay car park. We catch the Metro back to Newcastle station and catch a train to Aberdeen where we try to find out whatever we can about Mark. Hopefully my hire car having been left at Leeds/Bradford airport and yours at Newcastle airport will make anyone who traces them think we have fled the country. "

I couldn't let Jazz think this was all my plan, so I confessed, "Don't think I came up with such a brilliant plan by myself babe, it was mainly Pete's ideas."

"I'm not so sure it is a brilliant plan Simon," she replied making me think that maybe Jazz also specialised in instant deflation of the male ego. "If we stay in a hotel we'll have to give our correct names, or at least one of our correct names, because we'll have to give some form of identification, then they'll be able to trace us, won't they?"

She was sounding as paranoid as I was feeling, so I squeezed her knee again and hoped my answer would re-assure her, "That's why I can't claim the credit babe. Pete has friends. He booked the room with a bogus credit card so that we are now Mr and Mrs Turner."

"What do you mean a bogus credit card?"

"I'm not exactly sure babe," I replied. "But Pete has a friend who can give you a credit card in a name of your choice, and Pete keeps a couple for use on the internet. One of them is in the name of Simon Turner, so we are Mr and Mrs Turner with no means of our real identities being traced. I didn't enquire about the legalities and methodologies of obtaining such cards, I was just grateful that Pete had the means to get us into hotels without anyone knowing that it's us. The only problem is that he'll have to book them online for us."

By this time, we were on the A19 heading for the Tyne Tunnel. I hadn't been through the tunnel since the new second tunnel was built and was astonished by the lack of queues. The toll sign sent me digging in my pocket for change. A toll of £1.40 with no change given set me giggling as I recalled the scene from Gavin and Stacey where Smithy physically raises the barrier of the Severn Bridge as they are 10p short and he has to be in Wales for the birth of his son. My giggling had to be explained to Jasmine and we spent the rest of the journey talking about the programme which we had both loved (Sarah, of course, wouldn't watch such 'muck'!).

Talking of Gavin and Stacey, Nessa and Smithy in the confines of a Mini increased the sexual tension; and after a quick book-in, we dashed to our room. Like sex-starved teenagers, we tore off our clothes and leapt into the king-sized bed.

CHAPTER FOURTEEN

Suffice to say that the reality far exceeded the expectations and we went down to breakfast the next morning holding hands and with big grins on our faces. We were also starving as we had only eaten on the food of love the previous night. A Premier Inn all-you-can-eat breakfast was the perfect remedy, but even as we ate, we couldn't keep our hands off each other. When we got to the toast, marmalade and coffee part, however, we became more serious and started to discuss the day ahead.

Whilst I used my phone to Google Newcastle Airport, Jazz used hers to phone school and tell them that a domestic crisis meant she would not be in for a couple of days. I could hear her being quizzed by the Head, and she was forced to explain that her neighbour had been rushed into hospital and that she had to look after the children to avoid them going into care. She set work for her classes and agreed to her leave of absence being unpaid. I found it hard to concentrate whilst being so impressed by Jasmine's mix of efficiency and ingenuity, but managed to discover that the airport car parks were bookable on-line and after some discussion we decided to park Jazz's car in the secure long-stay for 14 days. We both hoped that within that time this nightmare would be over.

Pete had had the credit card couriered to the hotel so I was able to book on-line for only £58 rather than the £128 I would have had to pay at the airport. Before we left, we packed all we would need from Jasmine's car into the cases we had bought at Sainsbury's ready to be taken with us on the train.

The drive to the airport caused no problems, nor did the parking. We walked briskly to the terminal building – we had decided it might look odd to walk straight from the long-stay car park to the Metro station. Next we bought a selection of papers from Smiths and then went into Cafe Ritazza to read them. Both the Mail and the Telegraph had front-page stories on Tim Harris, both of them praising his intervention and exhorting the Tory Party to clean up its act and get back to its Christian roots. The Guardian and Independent were far more cautious and very worried about bringing

Evangelical Christianity into British politics. It was the Times that had a leader commenting on the possible repercussions of Harris's actions on the stability of the Government. I hadn't thought of that, but apparently the more liberal, Remainer Tories were not happy about Tim Harris and American style religion, and were even less attracted to the extremist anti-Muslim groups in Europe.

We walked over to the Metro station, and only had to wait a few minutes for a train to Newcastle Central station. It was the first time I'd been on an underground outside London and I was most impressed as a gleaming yellow and black train pulled into the platform. The station was above ground and the train looked like a train rather than a tube, nevertheless we were soon underground speeding to Central Station where we arrived some twenty minutes later. This station was more like a tube and we had to use an escalator to get up to the rail station level.

We had fifty minutes waiting time before our Virgin East Coast train to Aberdeen arrived. I had thought we might stand out waiting on the platform, but Newcastle was far from being mono-ethnic or mono-cultural, it was as ethnically mixed as any big city and Jazz and I just blended in. Even so, I found myself examining the faces of those around and trying to memorise them in case we found them following us in Aberdeen. I have to admit that I was also searching for a glimpse of birdman just in case he had come up from London looking for us.

"Simon calm down. How can anyone know we are on Newcastle railway station?" Jazz reproached me as we sat at a Costa table on the station forecourt. "The only way they can check on us is my car which is at the airport. It will be ages before they think of checking the station rather than the airlines, and even then, what can they check us with? You paid cash for the tickets! Now let's get on this train that's pulling in and enjoy our rail trip north. I'm looking forward to going over the Forth and Tay bridges. I've never been over them and I've always wanted to."

I tried hard to forget why we were heading north and just tried to enjoy the ride. The ride was brilliant. I had no idea that the line hugged the coast almost all the way to Edinburgh, nor that Berwick was approached on a fantastic viaduct which led to an impressive barracks-like station. The Forth Bridge was awe-inspiring. I hadn't realised how long it was with the Forth below looking more like the sea than a river as we gazed down at islands. The Tay Bridge was even longer and a little scary as we could see the bases of the pillars left from the bridge that collapsed in the nineteenth century.

I was wondering what we were passing just north of Montrose (and of course Jazz knew and told me it was the largest saltwater basin in the UK) when my mobile rang, "Hi Si," without even recognising the voice, I knew it was Pete. He'd always loved to greet me with that phrase.

"Is it going according to plan?"

"Yes mate. We're not far from Aberdeen, just one more stop."

"I don't suppose you've heard the news then?"

"No Pete, we're just enjoying the train ride. Has something happened?"

"I think so, but you might not," Pete's answer was somewhat enigmatic.

"Try me Pete. I can't imagine that you've phoned me without a very good reason."

"They've just announced that the 1922 committee is going to vote on a motion, proposed by the chairman, to express support for the Rev Tim Harris and his campaign."

"Not altogether surprising Pete. I don't really think that's worth an emergency phone call."

"You might think differently when you know who the chairman of the 1922 Committee is Si."

"Go on then."

"It's George Blenkinsop."

I gasped at this news. George Blenkinsop had been at the meeting in Ripon with Tim Harris and the bishop.

"And get this Si," Pete continued. "George Blenkinsop was also the Chair of the North Yorkshire Police Authority until it was abolished to be replaced by a Police Commissioner."

"Thanks Pete. Now I understand why you had to phone. There's a lot of connections there. Give me a chance to bring Jazz up to date before we get to Aberdeen. I'll phone you when we're settled into a hotel."

Jazz had been leaning as close as she could to try to hear what Pete was saying, but had only managed to become more exasperated. As soon as I'd broken the connection to Pete, I filled her in on the gist of what had been said.

"My God Simon! We are in trouble. We're mixed up with powerful people. This George Blenkinsop brings them all together. He would know shady police like Byrom from being Chair of the Police Authority. We saw him with both Lord Jim and Tim Harris. This is becoming more and more frightening!"

I tried to re-assure her, "Don't worry my love, it'll be alright."

"Don't you patronise me Simon Keep. I'm not your little woman; and by the way I did notice that the 1922 Committee has a chairman whereas the police authority had a chair! No wonder the Tories have lost the female vote."

By this time the train was pulling into Aberdeen and everyone was getting ready to get off as the train terminated here. We sat still until the carriage was empty to make it easier to see if anyone was trailing us, and this time Jazz made no objections. Obviously Pete's news had worried her. The train and the platform were empty of all but railway staff by the time we walked along the platform and out to what appeared to be a new station concourse. I had heard that Aberdeen was the wealthiest city in Scotland and the new station seemed to confirm this.

Pete had pre-booked the Aberdeen Premier Inn at the same time as the Leeds airport one – he assured me that the anonymity and guaranteed quality whatever the location made this budget chain our best bet. As we came out of the station concourse we found ourselves slap bang in the middle of the harbour. It was incredible: two large North Link ferries for the Orkneys were almost beside us and they were surrounded by numerous orange coloured supply boats for the rigs. Clearly, despite the collapse in prices, oil was still big business up here.

Leaving the harbour, we climbed up to Union Street to walk along to the hotel. At 5.30 in the afternoon, it was rush hour and we were both amazed at how cosmopolitan the city was. Colours and ethnicities abounded. We heard several languages and also quite a few American accents, and not from tourists, these were clearly people who worked in Aberdeen. This was the unexpected, but the expected was just as good. I knew it was known as 'the granite city' and had been told the granite sparkled in sunlight. Well the sun was shining and the granite was sparkling. It was quite beautiful.

The hotel in North Street was not so beautiful, it was a Sixties concrete edifice. Nonetheless it suited us perfectly with its central location obviating the need for a car. We booked in, again as Mr and Mrs Turner, took our cases to our room and came back down to the lounge. The in-built lounge and restaurant was apparently a feature of the city-centre hotels in the chain, and it suited us perfectly. Being able to sit and drink whilst watching the only entrance is an obvious bonus when you're watching for people who might be following you, or even want to attack you!

There was a rack with tourist guides next to reception and I raided it before going into the lounge and ordering a pot of tea for two and some scones at the bar. We sat down and began to plot our strategy for the next day. We needed to find either Mark's office at the university or his flat/house. The big question was how to do that without arousing suspicion or revealing our motives!

We flicked through the brochures looking for inspiration. I had already discovered from the website that the Religious Studies Department was based in the King's College quadrangle in the heart of old Aberdeen next to the Visitors' Centre. Looking through the tourist literature, it seemed that one could easily approach the Religious Studies Department in the guise of a tourist. It was Jazz who spotted the guide to Aberdeen's St Machar's Cathedral which was situated on the edge of the University. She suggested that if we went there first and found out about some of its interesting history, we might find something which would give us an excuse to research it further in the King's Library which was just next to the Religious Studies Department. She also discovered a direct bus route to the old town from just across the road.

As ever, Jasmine was far more on the ball than I was and not only did she come up with the cathedral idea, she also suggested that Pete ought to be trying to find out something about Michael Brown, the London teacher who had allegedly confessed to murdering Mark, or more correctly Paul Williams whose name had been substituted for Mark's. She felt there ought to be some sort of clue there.

I thought I'd better phone Pete from our room and, surprisingly, Jazz made no protests when I said I didn't want to leave her in the lounge on her own. This was not treating her as 'the little woman', and she knew it. The news about George Blenkinsop had hit us both hard. Knowing what we did meant we were in a dangerous position, though, paradoxically, we didn't really know what we knew. Mark was at the heart of it, but why? What had Mark known and why had his murder been investigated as someone else's murder? Nevertheless, we were the only people who knew what had happened and as such we had to be a threat, and so we had to be in danger.

I phoned Pete, and Jazz made me put the phone onto speaker mode so that she could join in the conversation.

" Hi Si, how's it going?" Pete replied after the first ring.

Jazz chipped in, "Hi Pete, this is Jasmine. We're in our hotel room on the speaker phone. It's a long time since the two of us last spoke to each other."

"Bloody hell! Jasmine Baker. Good to hear your voice Jasmine. I hope you're looking after Si for me. He's not fit to be let loose on his own you know!"

"I know Pete. Innocent abroad isn't he"

At this point, I felt it was time for me to butt in, "Enough of the pleasantries you two. Listen Pete, have you found out anything about this Michael Brown, the chap who Byrom claimed was the murderer?"

"Not yet, but I bloody well hope to tomorrow. I've tracked down the school the bugger taught in – it's in Ealing – and one of my staff is having a meeting with some of his friends there tomorrow lunchtime."

I laughed, "What do you mean, 'One of my staff' you pompous twit. We went to D and K's, a Hornsey Comp, not Eton!"

"OK, Sue from the shop is doing it," he laughed. "I'm still keeping a low profile in case any of your bleedin friends are looking for me. And I've discovered that another MP you mentioned is a bit worrying. Henry Smythe is a bloody entrepreneur with some dodgy contacts through his press ownership. No bugger understands how he's avoided the Leveson Enquiry. It's probably just because he's not as big as Murdoch."

"I thought I knew the name," said Jazz. "He owns 'Where It's At' magazine doesn't he?"

"What's that?" I asked. "I've never heard of it."

"The soddin vicar strikes again," laughed Pete. "Have you heard of Hello and OK magazines?"

"Yes," I replied, "though I have to admit I seldom recognise the people on the front cover!"

"Well, 'Where It's At' is similar to them babe," Jazz put her arm round me and squeezed me in a very loving gesture, "but it rakes up more dirt. I'd no idea it was owned by an MP."

"You won't find his name anywhere on it," replied Pete. "He tries bloody hard to keep his ownership secret. It took quite a bit of trawling through sodding Companies House to find the connection. Word on the street is that not only is his bloody magazine connected with hacking, but also that it has contacts with some very tough cookies, who are not averse to using strong arm tactics to get the information they want. But, of course, that's all at several removes from Sir Henry bleeding Smythe Bt MP."

Jazz and I looked at each other. Our expressions were clearly asking why and how had we got ourselves mixed up in something like this.

"I was going to ring you two anyway," Pete continued. "I reckon you need a car up there. I know Aberdeen is the oil capital of Europe with the lowest unemployment etc etc, but it's not like London for public transport. If you need a quick getaway, you're going to be stuck. I've sent you an e-mail attachment of a driving licence for Simon Turner. It has your date of birth Si and a London address. You'll be able to get a printout at the hotel and I reckon any car hire firm will accept it since it matches everything on your credit card. Please do me a bloody favour and get yourselves some wheels. I'm worried about you two fuckers up there."

Jazz squeezed me again and said, "Thanks Pete. That's very sweet of you. We'll get a car first thing tomorrow and keep you updated on what's happening up here."

When we rang off, the room was pulsating with lust. Whether it was engendered by fear, or simply the result of our new found love, it consumed us; and consequently, Aberdeen proved just as satisfying as Newcastle!

CHAPTER FIFTEEN

I woke before Jazz and spent five minutes just looking at her sleeping beside me. She was beautiful. Brown skin seems to have a natural glow and it made Jazz look absolutely perfect without any need for the make-up which had always been a pre-requisite for Sarah to face the world. The peace and beauty of Jazz's sleeping form made the panic I had been feeling when I awoke melt away. I slipped out of the bed, put the kettle on, placed a tea bag in each of the white mugs provided and woke Jazz with tea and a kiss.

We were jolted back into reality when I switched on the TV to be greeted by the sickening face of Tim Harris. Why is it that 'born-again' people have a constant smile on their face yet it never reaches their eyes? Harris's grin was there even as he berated the Government, "I'm sorry, Lorraine, but it is quite clear from the Bible that God made marriage to be between a man and a woman as the way to bring up a family. Since this government decided to change the law so that men can marry men and women can marry women, then it has to accept that it has rejected God, and so is symptomatic of a godless society."

One Way was in the public eye again, this time under the harsh questioning of TV's most formidable questioner, not Jeremy Paxman, but Lorraine Kelly! However, the Reverend Tim might have miscalculated here, I thought, as Lorraine came back with, "But can we accept what the Bible says on marriage Mr Harris (he wouldn't like that, he was always Tim or the Reverend Harris), after all it permits polygamy doesn't it?"

Harris simply side-stepped the question and continued his moral attack on the government, "Be that as it may. The fact is that this government is doing nothing to improve the morals of this country. It not only allows, but seems to encourage the murder of unborn infants. Do you know how many abortions there were last year? Nearly 190,000. That's 190,000 children murdered in cold blood by a health service funded by this evil government. The One-Way Group is calling on the good people of the United Kingdom to help us force our government to accept that we are a Christian country and follow the Christian policies which will help us become great once more."

No doubt Paxman would have gone for the jugular here and asked whether Harris was as opposed to killing full grown people in war as he was opposed to killing foetuses, but although it looked as if Lorraine wanted to argue, time is restricted on a breakfast show and someone was telling her to wind it up. "Of course, Mr Harris, you might find that agnostics, atheists and other religions take a somewhat different view, but thank you for sharing your ideas with the viewers this morning." And with that she turned her attention to cookery matters.

We were a little dazed by what we had seen. The One Way Group was becoming far more political and we were mixed up in it somehow. Was this even more reason to be fearful, or simply more reason to get to the bottom of Mark's murder?

Jazz, however, had noticed something different in the interview. "Don't you think it's strange Simon?" she asked.

"At the moment just about everything seems strange babe. What exactly are you referring to?" I replied.
"Well Tim Harris is making all these statements about marriage, but he never mentions his own marriage. Don't you think a happily married man would refer to his own marriage to back up his points?"

I had to agree, but thought we had more important things to worry about at the moment, like getting up to the university. Another of

Harris's comments had given Jasmine the idea that I should wear the clerical collar I'd found tucked in my lap-top bag. She thought the country was still sufficiently Christian for car hire employees to assume that a vicar would be telling the truth.

After breakfast, we walked up the road to the nearest car-hire company I'd found on the internet. I had intended to book a car on-line, but that involved giving an e-mail address, and we only had them in our own names, so it might not a good idea to use them given what Pete had discovered.

It seemed that the car hire companies all had contracts with Vauxhall and I opted for another Corsa since I had driven one for a short time in Leeds. I was a little worried about having to explain why I only had a photocopy of my driving licence, but no questions were asked. They photocopied my photocopy, I typed in the pin for the credit card and we were back with wheels.

I drove back to the hotel. We'd booked in for two nights, but our current situation made me think like a boy scout. To be prepared for any eventuality, we needed our luggage with us at all times – thank goodness Pete had thought about us needing a car. The boy scout instinct also told us to familiarise ourselves with the road layout of the area before going to the university, and to this end I had viewed a variety of maps and street plans on my lap-top. However, to check these on the ground, I took the main road past the university and continued northwards till we hit the A90 which by-passes the city. I then drove back down the A90 with both of us noting all the side roads and landmarks we were passing. At the southerly end of the by-pass, I drove right round the roundabout and went back north to check everything again. We had decided that if we needed to make a quick getaway, the city centre would need to be avoided at all costs.

By this time, we were ready for a coffee, so I drove back up to the old town, assuming there would be coffee shops near the university. We were now following the detailed street plans on Jazz's i-phone. We passed a nice-looking coffee shop on the High Street, but couldn't find anywhere to park till we were on a road called 'The Chanonry' which Jazz told me was also about the nearest place we would find to park for the Cathedral. It seemed to be a dead end, so I did a three-point turn and parked facing the way we had come, to be ready for a quick exit. Then we walked back to the coffee shop and chatted over a delightful cup of coffee and an Aberdeen buttery.

Jazz began the conversation, "Do you think people really get converted by nutters like Tim Harris, Simon?"

"What do you mean babe?"

"Well he alleges he converts people to his view of Christianity, but I never hear him say anything to prove that he's correct other than 'the Bible says so' and if I weren't a believer, just saying the Bible says so wouldn't turn me into a believer. You'd have to prove to me that it's the word of God. But I suppose that's just the same with converts to Islam. Wouldn't you need to know everything about the religion and have its truth proved to you before you could convert? Yet seemingly intelligent people convert without appearing to know lots about the religion they're taking up!"

Jazz, perhaps because she was an RE teacher, patently took a far more academic view of religion than the majority of believers, and I tried to explain to her what my experiences as a vicar had shown me as I said, "Most people who are involved in religion don't take such an academic view babe. It's an emotional response either to the passion and apparent integrity of the religious leader they're in contact with, or it's part of the biggest insurance policy ever. People really do worry about death and about eternity and religion gives them the hope of survival. They pay their premiums by worshipping at, and giving money to the Church, in the hope that they'll have a big payout if religion is proved correct when they die."

This learned discourse was brought to a sudden halt by the ringing of my phone, "Hi Pete what's up?"

"Hi Si. I don't think you're going to believe this. Michael Brown was indeed gay, but he had nothing to do with Paul Williams. Just guess who his boyfriend was?"

"Come on Pete. This is no time for messing about. I don't have a clue, who was his boyfriend?"

"His boyfriend was Mark Greenwood and he was meeting Mark in Ripon for something Mark told his friend was 'deadly serious'"

Pete's surmise was indeed correct and I was so gobsmacked that Jazz had to take the phone off me to continue the conversation!

"Did I hear that correctly Pete?" she asked. "Michael Brown was Mark's boyfriend?!"

"You did indeed Jasmine. But listen further. We found this out from the only one of his colleagues who classed himself as his friend. Apparently, his parents disowned him as a degenerate when he came out, which is no doubt why they were prepared to accept the police story about him. It seems Michael was very much of a loner whose life was changed by meeting Mark. He was trying to get a job in Scotland, but was having difficulties finding all the paperwork on qualifications that the Scottish Teaching Council requires for registration."

I motioned Jazz to leave the coffee shop, then I paid and walked back to the car. This was not the sort of phone conversation to have in a public place. When we got into the car, Jazz activated the speaker phone and I said, "Hi Pete. Do you think this means that Paul was also murdered and Byrom and his mates made to look like suicide? But how on earth did they get him to write the notes and everything?"

Pete's voice boomed out of the phone, "I don't think they'd have been too bloody worried about the handwriting accuracy. Who the fuck would have checked? Michael's soddin parents would have just accepted what they were told by Byrom. Murdering his homeless lover and then killing himself would have fitted in with their picture of him.
Buggers like them would just have done a bleedin formal identification and blamed everything on his homosexuality."

"Poor man," chimed in Jazz. "That's why I can't stomach what Harris and his One Way Group are doing. They're trying to bring back really nasty prejudices that had almost died out. Prejudices that have caused so much pain and suffering."

I tried to steer the conversation back to our situation, "Did 'one of my staff' find out anything about the deadly serious business happening in Ripon?"

Pete chuckled down the phone, "Okay that was a very stupid way for me to describe Jan, but no she didn't. The colleague wasn't that close to Michael Brown. I think we're probably lucky he knew as much as he did."

"Not to worry Pete. Thanks for finding out this much," Jazz interposed. "It helps us to understand how it all happened. Now all we have to discover is why it happened and we're off to St Machar's Cathedral to do just that."

"Pardon?" Pete asked incredulously.

"You heard. St Machar, a follower of St Columba. He built the first church in Aberdeen in about 580 A.D.," I tried to say it as if it was coming from what I knew rather than quoting from the travel brochure I'd read in the hotel. "We're hoping to find something in the cathedral to give us an excuse to get into the Religious Studies Department which is in the King's College part of the University just near the cathedral."

"Spare me the details Si, but keep me informed on what's happening; and both of you, take care. These are bloody dangerous, bloody fuckin dangerous people."

With Pete's cheerful warning echoing in our ears, we locked the car and walked down The Chanory following the signs to St Machar's Cathedral. It was an imposing structure with twin towers at the west front. The style was very Scottish, according to the brochure I'd read, 'a fine example of a fortified kirk'. The setting was idyllic with no sign of the urban sprawl of Aberdeen, nor of the oil industry funding the city's growth. The notice board outside was the first sign that this was no ordinary cathedral as it informed the world that this was not a cathedral, but a cathedral church of the Church of Scotland with a minister not a bishop. The truth of this information was made obvious when we entered the church and found something more akin to a nonconformist chapel in its simplicity.

We had read about the Heraldic Ceiling and wondered how it had survived the Reformation, but seeing it in the flesh, so to speak, made us wonder even more. As we gazed a voice with a soft East Scottish burr said, "Wonderful isn't it? I'm Alastair Cameron, the minister here, and I still marvel every time I look at it. Are you a minister?"

His question made me remember that I was still wearing my dog collar. It had served me well at the car hire, I thought, so I might as well go along with it here. "I like to think of myself as a minister, but most of my colleagues call themselves priests!" I laughed, sharing an ecclesiastical joke with a fellow cleric. "I'm Simon Keep from the Church of England rather than Church of Scotland and this is my girlfriend Jasmine Baker, an RE teacher. Is that really the Pope's coat of arms I can see up there?"

It felt really good to introduce Jasmine as my girlfriend!

Rev Alastair Cameron M.Th., I remembered from the notice board, was a tall sandy-haired man of similar age to me, and he answered my question with, "It really is Simon. It was completed in 1530 and represents Scotland as part of Europe at that time. I'm sure Nicola Sturgeon would love it! There are three lines of shields up there headed by King James V of Scotland followed by the major Scottish nobility; one of Pope Leo X followed by the Scottish archbishops and bishops in order of importance; one of the Holy Roman Emperor, Charles V, followed by the monarchs of the Holy Roman Empire. Of course, Henry VIII is there but he is only given the arms of England."

"How on earth did it survive the Scottish Reformation when anything to do with papacy was torn down?" asked Jazz in true teacher mode.

"To be honest, no one knows," he replied, "but maybe it was too difficult to get up there to tear it down. Now, of course, it's a unique record of Scots history. I'm always surprised we don't have more expatiate Scots coming to see it. Well now what are you two doing so far from England?"

A tricky one. Did we tell the truth, or prevaricate? I looked at Jazz and her nod confirmed my decision to go for the truth. "We're trying to find out what's happened to Mark Greenwood, "I said." He's a lecturer at the University here. I don't suppose you knew him?"

The minister looked at us more closely, as if he were analysing us before answering. We must have passed the analysis as he replied, "Yes, I'm a friend of Mark's. Why did you use the past tense?" he continued, looking at us even more suspiciously. "Where are you from? What's happened?"

His reaction made me think that this man really was a friend of Mark's, so I went into vicar and bereavement mode and put my arm round him before replying, "I'm sorry Alastair, but we have bad news for you. We're here because we found Mark's murdered body in a hotel in Ripon."

"Murdered? Mark? What do you mean?" Alastair stammered out the questions as he tried to come to terms with the shock of our news.

Jazz took over from me and explained to an incredulous Alastair about our finding of Mark's body and the way the police had announced it as the murder of someone else. She concluded, "We've come up here to see if any friends of Mark know anything that might shed light on what's happened. There seems to be some sort of plot going on with extremely dangerous people involved. Basically, we want to find out what's happened so that we can sort it out and get on with our lives."

I could see Alastair struggling to come to terms with what he was hearing. But there was also a look on his face that said this was not altogether unexpected. He clearly knew something and was grappling with the problem of whether to trust us with whatever it was he knew. More visitors were wandering around the cathedral, gazing up at the magnificent ceiling and trying to match the shields to the descriptions in their guides.

"How do I know I can trust you?" he eventually asked.

He did know something. I tried to look as honest and trustworthy as a man in a dog collar can. "Because we wouldn't have told you what's happened to Mark if you couldn't."

"The ones you can't trust are the ones who are keeping his death a secret," added Jazz. "They haven't even told anyone he's dead, they're pretending his body is someone else's."

Alastair looked from Jazz to me and back again, clearly trying to decide whether he could trust us. The looks continued as he asked, "Can I just put a question to each of you to check you're what you say you are?"

"Of course," we both replied immediately, though I must admit I wondered what on earth he was going to ask me.

"Simon isn't it?" I nodded, "If you really are a vicar, you should be able to explain to me the difference between a vicar and a priest-in-charge."

I tried to ignore the total weirdness of the situation and replied, "A priest-in-charge is only responsible for the spiritualities and has no tenure whereas a vicar is responsible for both the spiritualities and the temporalities and owns the freehold." I knew because technically I had been a priest-in-charge, but it seemed weird, and inappropriate to be treating Mark's murder like an episode of 'Who Wants to be a Millionaire'. This surreal atmosphere only increased when he asked Jazz, "What is the Buddhist equivalent to the Ten Commandments?"

I had no idea there was such a thing, but Jazz answered, quick as a flash, "The Five Precepts."

A sense of relief settled over Alastair. Then he looked around at the other visitors and said, "Let's go outside. I don't want anyone overhearing this."

By this time, we were used to the feelings of paranoia he was obviously experiencing, but mine were clearly more finely attuned because as we exited the cathedral church, I heard a rumble from above us, looked up and saw a large roof stone dislodging and making its way towards us. Perhaps my feelings for Jazz gave me extra speed because I grabbed her and pushed her out of the way.

As we lay on the ground, somewhat stunned, I looked beside me and saw poor Alastair. The granite block was across his shoulders pinning him to the ground. It had clearly crushed his organs as blood was leaking out of his nose and mouth. I crawled across and heard him mutter, "Mark's mother."

"Don't worry Alastair," I said, stroking his head as I tried to work out how to remove the stone block, "I'll get help." As I spoke his head slumped. I felt for a pulse in his temple. There was none. Alastair was dead and presumably the people who killed him were still around. Then it struck me. Not only were they still around. The block might actually have been intended for Jazz and me. If so they were going to be after us as quickly as they could.

Jazz was looking a bit dazed from my knocking her to the ground. She got to her knees, looked over at Alastair and screamed.

"No time for that Jazz," I said helping her up. "He's dead. I'm sure that block was intended for us as well. We've got to run for it babe. We need to make it to the car before they see us."

I grabbed her hand, and we were off.

CHAPTER SIXTEEN

Luckily, we were both joggers and got back to the car pretty swiftly. Thank goodness I had parked it, not only facing back into the city, but also out of view from the cathedral entrance. We leapt in, I thanked God for keyless ignition (thinking incongruously of the saying 'there are no atheists on the battlefield'), and we were away.

Where to go? I was following the route I had prepared in my head in case of being spotted and headed north for the A90 to go back south by-passing the city when Jazz spoke, "Shit Simon, these folks really are evil," she paused, still slightly out of breath from the run, then demanded, "Where are you going?"

"I thought that if we went north to hit the A90, we'd have a clear run south to get back home and sort things out."

I could feel the pitying look she was giving me as she said, "Look babe, they don't know this car, but they do know that I'm black! The route you're talking about is a pretty quiet one. White man and black woman in a car driving back to England. We'd be too easy to pick out. We need to split up Simon."

Her words filled me with dread. "There is no way I'm leaving you on your own with these killers on the loose," I replied, my voice no doubt revealing my fears.

Of course, I could see the logic of her argument. Outside Aberdeen, the roads would be quiet and the cars would be populated by whites only. I was beginning to think we'd made a big mistake in coming up here. Aberdeen itself might be multi-ethnic, but it was out on a limb and surrounded by huge swathes of almost empty white-only areas. To give myself time, I turned right for the city centre instead of left for the A90, thinking that the greater density of traffic would make us less likely to stand out.

Jazz saw what I was doing and it met with her approval. "Good thinking babe," she said. "Drive through the city centre and they'll never spot us. You can drop me off at the station and I'll get a taxi to the airport. There's a flight to Durham Tees Valley at ten past one."

Clearly Jasmine had been sorting out even more alternatives than I had. However, there was one thing she had not thought of as I discovered when I mentioned, "There's only one problem babe. Your passport."

"It's only an internal flight, I won't need my passport, Simon," she replied.

"It might be an internal flight, but since the London bombings, you need a passport for all flights."

"Are you sure?"

"Certain," I replied knowing I was sure ground here. "Not only have I flown Leeds to London, but Sarah loved the TV series about EasyJet and I've seen the trouble people get into when they're on an internal flight to or from Scotland and don't have a passport!"

Needless to say, Jazz had prepared for all eventualities so she came back swiftly with, "Okay babe. When you drop me off at the station, I 'll go in and catch the nine minutes past one train to Edinburgh and then the five past four to Darlington. Plane or train makes no difference. You're right. We'll be much safer if we split up. Anyway, if I catch the train, I can get back home and be free to get into work! That'll please my power mad head."

I thought about this as we became stuck in heavy traffic in Union Street. Yes, I could understand Jazz's point that as a black and white couple we stood out like a vicar at a lap dancing club, but they were after both of us, not just me, and I was not prepared to put her life at risk. I loved her. I was in love with her, and I would rather sacrifice my life than put hers at risk. Then there was the problem of where she lived and where she worked, the opposition knew both of those so she would be too much at risk to go back home. It was a no brainer. So, I drove past the signs for the station and headed as quickly as I could for the A90.

"What are you doing Simon? The station's down there," Jazz's enraged exclamation meant I had to tell her the plan.

"I'm sorry babe, but these people are just too vicious for me to risk them catching you on your own. And don't forget they know where you work and have no doubt discovered where you live. It might seem selfish, it might even be selfish, but I love you too much to put you in any greater danger than we're already in." I don't know whether it was the reminder that they knew about her, or my profession of love and concern, but my words calmed her down enough for me to continue. "I'm going to drive like hell to Dundee and swap this car for a people carrier with tinted back windows. Then we can take turns driving whilst the other hides in the back."

I could tell Jazz was now well recovered from the shock, as she was no longer too happy about me making all the decisions about what to do – though, of course, I was, quite literally, in the driving seat. Not a good thought for a woman like Jazz who, I was discovering, was very much her own woman.

She tried to regain control by asking, "But what about finding Mark's mother? We don't know where she is. She might be living in Scotland."

By this time, we were out of Aberdeen and by-passing Stonehaven on the A90. I still felt that my plan was the right one, but knew I had to justify it to Jazz! "I'm sorry darling," I said in my most conciliatory tone and immediately realised I'd used the wrong term of endearment. She didn't like darling perhaps because it smacked too much of our parents' generation and the upper middle-classes. I tried an immediate rectification. "Sorry babe, but we can't do much about Mark's mother, or Mark's murderer, if we're dead; and that's what these people want you know. I think that what's just happened to that poor minister shows us these people aren't playing games."

I could feel Jazz tensing up beside me, it was only a small car and our thighs were touching. She relaxed a bit as she spoke, "Yes babe," as she said this endearment, I realised I was forgiven, "I know that. It's just that I can't believe it. They did just try to kill us, didn't they? If you hadn't knocked me out of the way, I'd be dead now as well!"

"We could both have been dead babe," I answered, trying to downgrade my part in her survival. "And the worry is that they'll try again. We have no idea of what they were trying to protect by killing Mark, but the very fact that we're the only ones who know it was Mark they killed means they're going to keep trying to silence both of us. So, our first priority has to be to keep ourselves safe. The dead can't solve murders, except in zombie films!"

Keeping our eyes peeled for police cars that might object to the speed we were doing - speed cameras didn't matter as the people whose names were on the driving licences we were using didn't exist, we were soon by-passing Forfar and then approaching Dundee. Instead of staying on the A90 by turning right, I carried straight on and went into the centre of Dundee. We soon found a branch of the car hire firm we'd used in Aberdeen. They made no bones about changing the Corsa for a people carrier, perhaps because I paid up front for a week's hire. Less than thirty minutes later we were back on the road with Jazz in the back hidden by the privacy glass.

I'd been to Dundee before so I drove us out from the car hire, along the riverside with its strange narrow airport and back onto the A90. We'd decided we would sort out our next steps at the Kinross Services, but when I indicated to pull off for the services, Jazz suddenly shouted, "No Simon, don't turn in here!"

"Why not babe? I thought we'd agreed we were going to stop here and sort things out?"

"True, but I've been thinking. If they're looking for us, and they must be, where will they expect to find two people driving from Scotland to Teesside? Answer, motorway services. We need to go off the motorway. Let's try Inverkeithing, that was the first railway station after the Forth Bridge. There'll be somewhere like a supermarket there where we can get a drink and discuss what to do."

It was such a refreshing change to be with a woman who was not only bright, but insisted on using her intelligence. I was sure Sarah would just have followed me into the services, her only contribution being to moan about the state of the toilets.

"Good thinking babe. God I could have walked us straight into a trap! It wouldn't take many of them to cover the southbound services. You're right, there's bound to be something in a place with a busy station, and there seemed to be plenty of people on the platforms when we came up. "

The actuality proved even better. As I turned off the motorway following the signs to Inverkeithing, there was a garden centre with a cafe. Another plus was that it had free wi-fi so there would be no need for guarded phone calls. Pulling into the car park revealed yet another plus. It was clearly a venue for mums and toddlers and the car park was full of people carriers. We would not stand out.

It had taken us less than an hour and half to do the hundred plus miles from Aberdeen, and we hadn't paused since poor Alastair had been killed beside us and, putting first things first, we started off at the loo. There was a huge cafe with a large selection of food, but neither of us felt hungry.

I was pretty sure no one would be looking for us in garden centres, nevertheless we sat together at a table facing the entrance with a pot of tea and a toasted teacake. We had positioned ourselves very carefully so that we could check everyone entering the café, not that I would have had a clue what to do if some gangster had walked in with a sawn-off shotgun pointed at us!

I opened my laptop and logged on to the garden centre's network. Jazz looked over my shoulder as I composed an email to Pete telling him everything that had happened since the morning, including Alastair's final words and a request for Pete to find out whatever he could about the whereabouts of Mark's mother. I thought it would take him a while to reply, so I went and got us a couple of papers to see if Tim Harris was causing any more political waves. I don't know who thought of persuading tea and coffee shops to have free newspapers, but they deserve a medal. Jazz struck gold almost immediately with the Guardian.

"Look here Simon," she said pointing me to a feature article by the political editor, "see what the chattering classes are saying about the right-wing Tories linking up with Tim Harris."

We looked at it together and read how the political editor felt there was nothing strange about the link up because the right-wing Tories had taken over the mantle of UKIP after the referendum and now had so much in common with the Tim Harris view of Britain as a Christian country. It was interesting to discover that Jazz and I had such similar religious and political views. She too felt that Tim Harris's attitude to Jesus being the only way was likely to be very detrimental to Britain's community cohesion, especially if backed by a political party. But Jazz's attention had focussed on a small paragraph revealing a rumour at Westminster that George Blenkinsop was about to reveal information about the Prime Minister which would make his position untenable. Seeing as we had first come across the man, together with Tim Harris and the right-wing Tories at Ripon, Jazz wondered if Blenkinsop was going to reveal something about the murder.

I had never quite worked out how to get automatic alerts to tell me an email had arrived, so I had to keep checking. Of course, Pete, being Pete, was bound to have such a facility and he replied just as we were finishing our teacakes. Pete wanted to know if we had heard the breaking news that the Archbishop of Canterbury had announced his resignation and could I guess who the bookies were quoting to succeed him – the Bishop of Ripon and Leeds. I wondered why Pete thought this was important. Did he think it was connected to the plot?

Jazz thought we'd been in the cafe long enough and led me outside. It was strange, but I kept forgetting how conspicuous we were because to me we were just a couple having a cup of tea, but then I hadn't spent a lifetime standing out from the crowd.

On Jazz's advice, when we returned to the car, I e-mailed Pete back to say we were on our way out of Scotland and would think about our next steps on the drive south.

Jazz insisted on taking the wheel for the next leg of the journey and as we drove over the Forth Road Bridge, I felt quite relieved. I don't have a great head for heights and that was one of the highest bridges I had been across; just looking out of the window made my legs turn to jelly. I reflected on how much more secure I'd felt going over the Forth on the train than by car!

Once over the bridge the drive was uncomplicated: onto the Edinburgh by-pass, then straight down the A1, so I asked Jazz to switch on the radio.

"The Chairman of the 1922 Committee, the Right Honourable George Blenkinsop, has just announced the result of the Committee's vote on support for the Rev Tim Harris and the One Way Movement. Mr Blenkinsop revealed that the influential committee of Conservative backbenchers has voted to urge the government to come out in support of the Rev Harris's proposals to reverse the legal changes to same sex marriage, ban abortion and base government policy on Christian principles. Mr Blenkinsop added that he is sure the Prime Minister will follow the advice of the 1922 Committee. Here to give his analysis of the repercussions of this vote is our political correspondent, Anthony Redding.."

"What the..." exclaimed Jazz and turned up the volume so we could hear more clearly the views of the political correspondent.

"Well, there is no doubt that this is a vote the Prime Minister could have done without. Quite clearly his more liberal MPs will be opposed to this. They have always supported same sex marriage and abortion as a human right. Furthermore, they are very committed to community cohesion and multi-culturalism, and so will not want to be tied to the moral principles of any one religion. They have always been committed to the human right of freedom of conscience and religion which this vote by the 1922 Committee appears to be rejecting. So Prime Minister, Stuart Fairhurst, faces a tough choice. If he acquiesces to the 1922 Committee, the party could well split; but if he rejects the 1922 Committee's vote, he will be alienating many of the most vociferous of his MP's and could split the party anyway."

Jazz was the first to recover from the shock of this news. "Do you think it's a part of the plot?" she asked.

"Well I suppose it might be," I replied, still in shock.

"Simon! George Blenkinsop was in Ripon for that meeting. There must be a connection. But why would the 1922 Committee be connected with murder and swapping dead bodies?"

"I have no idea babe, but it's making me shit-scared," I replied. I had no need to apologise for my coarse language with Jazz, I certainly would have with Sarah, but it was the only language which adequately summed up how I was feeling. "By a pure fluke, we've got ourselves involved in a very big piece of nasty work. If we hadn't decided to stay at that hotel, and you hadn't known Mark Greenwood, this would have had nothing to do with us."

"But we did, and so we are involved babe," Jazz retorted, "whether we like it or not."

"We are not only involved babe, we are in deep shit. If the Chair of the 1922 Committee, the Chair of the North Yorkshire Police Authority, the Bishop of Ripon and Leeds, the leader of the most powerful Christian Evangelical group in the UK and various Tory MPs are all involved in this, and we are the only ones who know that it was Mark Greenwood, not Paul Williams, who was murdered, then there is no doubt that we are not just in deep shit, we are in very serious danger."

Silence descended as we both thought about this and about what we should do.

"I think we should split up babe," Jazz suggested. "We're just too noticeable as a mixed-race couple. I know it's too dangerous for me to go back home, but what if I stay with my friend Emma in Darlington?"

The idea appealed to me. Jazz would be out of danger and if she kept out of the way until Pete and I had got things sorted out, she would be safe. And her safety was becoming my priority. My feelings for her were getting deeper all the time, and I didn't want anything to harm her. But there was something wrong with Jazz suggesting this. She was not Sarah. She was no 'little woman'. She would not sit around doing nothing. She must have an ulterior motive!

"Then I could explore this One Way Group a bit more," she continued revealing a bit of the ulterior motive I had suspected.

"And how would you do that?" I asked.

"Don't you worry yourself babe," she replied," I'll stay in Emma's flat and do research on the net. I'll see what I can find out about Tim Harris and why he formed this group. I can use Emma's PC so nothing can be traced to me. I can also send messages to my Head via Emma so that I keep my job secure, whilst you find Mark's mother and find out what sort of information Mark left with her."

Well that seemed pretty well sorted. I just hoped I could trust her to stay in Emma's flat and not go out to do her research. The plotters couldn't have vast numbers of people available to search for us, and they would have no reason to be looking in Darlington. No doubt they'd be watching the flat in Yarm, and her school in Stockton, but surely that would be all? As we came into England, I racked my brains for any occasion we might have mentioned Darlington as somewhere either of us frequented. Of course, on the A1 between Edinburgh and Newcastle, you have to pay a lot of attention to the road as the speed limit changes from 70 down to 60 every time you come out of a bit of dual-carriageway: and they have lots of unmarked police cars. So, it was a while before Jazz spoke again, and I too had been silent as I tried to think of any possible snags in her plan.

"Cat got your tongue Simon?" came a voice from the driver's seat.

"Oh, sorry babe," I said jerking back to reality. "I was just trying to think of us making any mention of Darlington that the plotters might have picked up on."

"And did you think of any?"

I really wanted to say yes so I could dissuade her from staying in Darlington. My heart wanted us to stay together, but my head knew we ought to separate, and as much as I struggled, I couldn't think of any time we had mentioned Darlington, so I answered, "No babe."

"Right then," she said emphatically, "We'll soon be at Emma's. I'll stay there and you can get on to London to find Mark's mother."

"How do you know Mark's mother's in London?" I queried.

"You're not the only one who's been thinking Simon!" she shot back at me with a note of asperity. I flinched as I realised I must have been sounding patronising again. "I've been thinking back to uni and to Mark. I'm sure he lived in West London, somewhere like Ealing, or Brentford, or Isleworth. So that's what you need to do Simon. Get down there. See Pete and the two of you must be able to find the Mrs Greenwood in West London who's Mark's mother. Find out what she knows and then sort this whole mess out so that we can get on with our lives."

What a woman, I thought. But could I really sort this mess out? It seemed to be becoming too big for someone like me to clear up. I also rejoiced that she had said 'getting on with our lives'. 'Our lives' meant she intended to share my life which was all I really wanted. My life had been totally transformed at the same time that all of this brouhaha developed. I had no idea what a normal life was going to be, but a life with Jazz was bound to be wonderful.

I was also relieved she had suggested that the first thing I should to do was to contact Pete. He seemed to be much more at home in this world of intrigue and politics into which we had so unexpectedly been thrust. I felt that searching for Mark's mother whilst avoiding the plotters who wanted me dead, would be much easier with his help. But I knew I was going to worry about Jazz all the time we were separated.

CHAPTER SEVENTEEN

Emma's house was a large Edwardian terraced property in the west end of Darlington. Jasmine had not been there before and she appraised the high ceilings and ornate plaster cornices as she followed Emma through the spacious hallway into the kitchen. It was, perhaps, the ideal home for Emma and her family. The megabucks her husband Andrew made from working on the rigs had clearly been invested in restoring the house to its former glory: retaining the original features (as the TV Home channels would say) whilst incorporating the last word in modernity. The kitchen was as sleek and gleaming as the one in Jasmine's flat, but much larger so that the Aga in the corner appeared no bigger than an ordinary cooker.

"Come on then Jasmine. Let's have the lowdown on what's happening," Emma began as she switched on the coffee machine and packed the coffee pod like a professional barista. "Why have you been off work? Why do you need to stay here? And where's your car?"

"I'll answer the easy question first. My car's in the car park at Newcastle airport. I'll answer your other questions when you've finished using that steamer to make your very upper middle-class latte. Not that you'll believe half of what I have to tell you!"

Jasmine sat with Emma at the island in the middle of the kitchen drinking their coffees and telling her everything starting from the finding of the body at the Old Deanery through the misidentification, the apparent plot to kill them, the escape to Scotland and ending with the near-death experience at St Machar's Cathedral. Only then did she start to answer Emma's questions.

"So, Emma, now to answer your questions: first one, I couldn't go to work because whoever these plotters are, they are trying to kill me and Simon, and they know where I live and where I work, therefore it's dangerous for me to go to work. I suppose that also answers question number two of why I need to stay here. It's because it's too risky for me to return home, but I'll be safe here. There's no way the 'plotters' will suspect I'm in Darlington. Simon and I have been over everything with a fine toothcomb and they have no reason whatsoever to think I might be here."

Emma looked suitably stunned at Jasmine's explanation and sat sipping her latte for a few moments before replying, "There's only one problem Jasmine. Howard is going bananas about you being off, you know he hates paying for supply cover. You'd think he had to pay it out of his own salary. In fact, I think you have to get yourself back to work and teach your revision classes if you're not to lose your job!"

"But will I be safe at school Emma?"

"Of course, you will Jasmine. Just think about the security we have. No one can get in without being checked by reception, and we'll warn the receptionists to be extra vigilant. We'll go there and back in my Audi which has darkened windows in the back. You'll be safe; Howard will be mollified; your kids will pass their exams and your job will be safe. Now stop worrying and we'll catch up with what's been happening in Albert Square."

*   *   *   *   *   *

I needed advice and that could only come from Pete, but before I got to London, I needed to check on Jazz. I would have preferred her to be with me; no, it was far stronger than that, I wanted her to be with me, I needed her. It was ridiculous, two hours apart and I was desperate to see her. It was totally irrational, but I couldn't help myself. Presumably this was what being in love meant. It was an emotion I'd never experienced with Sarah!

I pulled into the services at Watford Gap and phoned her mobile as soon as I'd put the handbrake on. "Hi babe," I said as soon as she answered. "Are you okay? No signs of any trouble?" I cursed myself for sounding so protective.

"Of course, I'm alright Simon," Jazz replied in a tone of voice such as you would use when patting a young child on the head. "I'm still at Emma's in the quiet town of Darlington, as safe as houses. Don't tell me you phoned just to see how I am?"

The tone of voice for the last sentence was much more reassuring. It sounded like she was pleased that I cared so much, but I had to make clear that I was not appearing to treat my independent woman in the same way I had treated my needing-to-be-looked-after wife. So, I had to think up an excuse for phoning.

"Of course, I'm not," I lied while trying to think up an excuse. "It goes without saying that I'm missing you babe. But at this moment I'm even more desperately missing your perspicacity," I continued hoping that flattery might get me through. "You see, I've been thinking about what George Blenkinsop is going to reveal to the 1922 Committee," I paused as I wondered what on earth I could say I'd been thinking about.

Luckily Jazz spoke before the silence could become too worrying. "I'm missing you as well babe." These words gave my morale a huge boost. "And I'm sure you don't need to worry about the deliberations of a group of Tory backwoodsmen."

I was feeling more confident now and answered, "Come on babe. You know we need to worry. There's got to be some connection. Have you had any more thoughts on it?"

There was a pause, such a long pause that I began to wonder if my mobile had lost its connection. Then she said, "Sorry babe. I was just thinking. You're right. There has to be a connection between what's happening to us and that meeting between Tory bigwigs, the bishop and Tim Harris. That was some sort of political plot. It all sounds more like American nutters than British stiff upper lip. But what on earth could it have to do with Mark's murder?" she paused again, but for a much shorter period this time." On the other hand, you did find a connection between the bishop and Samuel Watkinson who was definitely connected with the murder and the Tory Party. Didn't Pete say he was big in the Tory Party at Oxford?"

"Yes, he was, but Pete hasn't found any record of connections with the Tories after Oxford."

I could almost hear Jazz thinking over the phone before she said, "There's got to be some connection babe, especially when you actually saw your bishop with Samuel Watkinson at the One Way publishers. Somehow Mark's murder is connected with this. But how? And why?"

I needed to know what Jazz had been discussing with Emma in Darlington. The plotters had been meeting in Ripon. The MPs were from the North. There was clearly a northern connection, and Emma could have connections with those connections. Maybe I was being paranoid, but we were talking about the safety of the love of my life.

"Have you told Emma what's been happening?" I asked anxiously.

"Most of it babe. Why?"

"What do you mean by most of it?" I tried to sound calm, but I needed to know what Emma knew in case she had told someone who might be connected with the plotters. "And has she spoken to anyone since you told her?"

"Don't worry Simon," Jazz said, but the way she was now calling me Simon rather than babe made me even more worried." I told her about the body, and about it being Mark, and why we had to go to Aberdeen; and, of course, I told her about the cathedral and that poor man being killed and his last words. But Emma's my friend, she won't have told anyone. You've got no need to worry Simon."

Oh God, that 'Simon' again. That meant she was trying to cover up something. Was she worried that Emma might have spoken to someone.

"Who do you think she's spoken to?" I asked as calmly as I could.

"I'm not sure babe." That sounded better. "I know she's been on the phone since I told her, but I don't know who to or what she said. I'm pretty sure that it had nothing to do with us, she's my friend. Even so, I suppose I can't be certain."

"Okay babe. But keep an eye and ear on Emma's phone calls and look after yourself. I'll phone as soon as I reach London. Love you babe," I ended the call hoping I sounded more reassured than I felt.

What did I know about Emma? Answer not a lot. And Emma had phoned someone as soon as Jazz had told her what had happened. And Jazz didn't know who she had phoned or what she had said. I couldn't help being nervous. I felt the need to make contact with Pete immediately. Fortunately, there was free wi-fi at the services so I switched on my laptop and sent Pete an urgent e-mail. Then I bought yet another coffee and waited for his reply.

The reply was not long in coming and it brought little relief:
Hi Si. Have a look at the breaking news on Sky News. Things aren't looking good. You're obviously involved in something really big. We need to meet. Phone the shop from a callbox when you get to London.

Reading this sent me straight onto the Sky News website where I was able to read about the 1922 Committee which had released this press statement after its meeting:
'The Committee has asked Stuart Fairhurst to consider his position after The Daily Mail gave the Committee a preview of its investigation which revealed that whilst the Prime Minister was a student at Oxford, he had a homosexual affair with Franz Schmidt, the current President of the European Commission. The Committee will be meeting again on Thursday to discuss the Prime Minister's response'.

This was followed by a report on the response of GBnotEU whose leader, Charles Matthews, was, of course, having a field day. He was claiming that it was no wonder Britain was just giving in to the demands of Europe over Brexit when Britain's Prime Minister was the EU's President's lover! Needless to say, he also had a few, or rather many, words to say about the reasons for the Government pushing through the legislation on same sex marriage, after all Charles Matthews had been making oblique, if not snide, comments about Schmidt ever since the EU elected an openly gay man to be President of the Commission.

Sky's political correspondent seemed as dumbfounded as everyone else, but she was sure that Mr Fairhurst would be made to pay for such a double rejection of his Tory grassroots supporters who had always felt that his Eton background and home in the Chilterns made Stuart Fairhurst one of them.

I closed my laptop and walked back to the people carrier, my mind pounding from what I had just read. This had to be connected to the Ripon murder. Such a big story revealed by one of the participants meant the Ripon meeting had to be tied in. But despite these revelations, we were still no nearer to answering the pivotal questions of why and how. Mark Greenwood had to have been connected to some sort of big political plot involving rich and powerful people. The sort of people I was only ever likely to meet by chance in the sort of hotel that was normally out of my league. Feeling more and more nervous, I jumped back in the people carrier and drove to London as fast as the traffic allowed.

Pete had insisted I should phone the shop from a call box, not go there, so I decided to avoid North London. I came off the M1, onto the M25 and came into West London along the A40. I pulled into a hotel I knew in Greenford and went into the call box I knew was outside (such things were becoming much rarer than Pete realised). I phoned the shop and listened to a number of automated responses telling me that my call was being diverted. Then I heard Pete say, "Stay where you are mate. I'll find you." Then the phone went dead.

I decided to wait by going into the hotel and booking myself in for the night. I took my Sainsbury's case up to my room and came back downstairs. As I walked through reception back to the car park, I saw a car pull up and a large figure extricate himself from the driver's seat. It was Pete.

The nerves disappeared as I rushed out and gave him a hug, and had the breath squeezed out of me in return.

"Hi Si, how's it going yer bastard?"

I replied to Pete's usual offensive greeting with a question of my own, "How the hell did you know I was here?"

"Your technologically aware friend has a trace on the shop phone that can tell me the location of any phone box calling the shop. I then put the postcode into my satnav, follow the instructions, and here I am," Pete's face lit up with a huge grin of satisfaction as he finished his explanation.

"And why was my call diverted several times before I spoke to you?"

The grin disappeared as quickly as it had arrived, and his face took on a worried expression as he began, "Well Si, you've got yourself involved with some very fucking dangerous characters. Characters who seem to have a lot of bleeding influence. Characters who have been monitoring the fucking shop phone – and before you ask, yes I have a device that tells me if some bugger is listening in to my phone calls. Characters who tried to break into the bloody shop, but were not quite expert enough to get through my fucking anti-theft gizmos."

I began to worry. Not only at what Pete was telling me, but also that his language had become much bluer and that he was telling me it in the middle of a hotel car park totally open to prying eyes and ears!

"Don't you think we need somewhere a bit less public to discuss this Pete?" I asked.

"You're right Si me old china," Pete replied in his favourite mockney accent. "Let's go in the bath and see if we can find a fucking quiet table. There's a lot you need to know."

It only took me a second to translate china to mate but it took a bit longer to move from bath to pub (China plate – mate, bath tub – pub) and as we walked over to the pub, I suggested, "Let's drop the rhyming slang Pete, I know you're a London boy, but I also know you're no EastEnder."

The bar was fairly empty and we found a table in a corner well away from any listening ears. I bought a pint for Pete and a lime and soda for myself – I'd definitely had enough coffee for one day. "Right Pete," I began, "Tell me more about these characters you've found."

A troubled expression appeared on Pete's face, which, of course, did nothing to lessen my worries. If these characters were troubling Pete, they were likely to scare the pants off me!

Pete looked around carefully, checking the occupants of the bar. His gaze lingered on a muscular looking man sitting at the bar. He was dressed in a dark suit with his tie pulled down and the top button of his formal shirt unfastened. I could see Pete thinking that he was a bit suspicious, but too far away to hear our conversation. Then an attractive young woman came out of the loos and sat next to him. Clearly the man ceased to be a threat when he started gazing into her eyes with obvious infatuation.

"Right Si. Let's start with your old friend Samuel Watkinson, the Reverend Samuel Watkinson as he is sometimes, but not always, known," Pete spoke without a single swear word which had me even more worried about the seriousness of the situation. "My hacking friends have discovered some very unsavoury pieces of information about Mr Watkinson. First off, he's a major shareholder in, and non-executive director of, 'Where It's At' magazine which, of course, make him close to Sir Henry Smythe. It seems that Samuel is a very wealthy man – we've discovered investments totalling at least five million pounds – and has fingers in many financial pies. Apart from the fact that it seems odd for an apparently insignificant clergyman to have so much money and influence, we have to wonder how this fits with his being the CEO of the Fisherman's Group and what any of this has to do with his being a clergyman!

Then we discovered it's probably all to do with the fact that he's the younger son of the Earl of Dawlish – old money and friends in high places! Anyway, probably of even more interest is the fact that Samuel is a major financial backer of the One Way Group and a substantial donor to the Conservative Party with several friends among the more right-wing members of the 1922 Committee. Perhaps even more important is the fact that he owns a security company – it was very difficult to ascertain the ownership of this company – which seems to have several ex-cons on its payroll. Now me old fucker is that enough bloody information for you?"

The swearing came back right at the end of his speech, but it didn't make me feel any better as I sat back in my chair and gulped at my drink trying to assimilate all this data about Samuel. I suppose I'd just assumed he was a fairly genuine, and fairly ordinary, clergyman, concerned to help the homeless who had somehow got caught up in the murder plot – whose meaning remained as much of a mystery as ever. But this news totally demolished that picture.

"What do you think made him behave like this?" I asked Pete. "Why did he become a vicar? Where did he get the money? What do you think he's trying to do?" The questions poured out of me as I tried to come to terms with this very weird situation.

"Slow down Si. Give me bleeding chance to give you my take on what's happening. First of all, it seems that Samuel was pushed into the Church. His family is very rich and very old. Eldest son into the army youngest into the Church has been their tradition for generations. Samuel's elder brother went into the Guards. About ten years into his career as a clergyman being prepared for great things (two spells as chaplain to the Archbishop of Canterbury and one as the Church's media spokesperson are not given away lightly). Then his father died and his brother's armoured vehicle was destroyed by an improvised explosive device in Helmand Province. Samuel became the head of the family fortune and gave up all his clerical duties, but not his holy orders. What he's trying to do now, we can only guess at it. He's a powerful man, with powerful friends in very high places, yet he spends a lot of time running a charity for the homeless and a downmarket security firm, Safe and Sound, several of whose employees must be counted as security risks. He has organised the cover-up of a murder, and I have to admit Si, I've no idea why he did that. The man is a bleeding enigma, but a sodding rich and powerful and dangerous enigma. And I'm sure he wants you, me and Jasmine out of the fucking way, which probably means dead!"

I thought about what Pete was telling me, once more the important bits with no swearing. What he was telling me about Samuel Watkinson was making me even more worried about Jazz up in Darlington on her own. If a seemingly upright and inoffensive vicar like Samuel had such secrets and posed such a danger, what about the unknown teacher Emma?

"What else have you discovered Pete?" I asked with growing trepidation.

"Your bloody birdman, the guy you thought was fucking following you round central London."

"Yes," I replied anxiously.

"Well, we think he's an employee of Samuel's security firm. Indeed, as far as we can make out, he's classified as the firm's Head of Internal Security. His name is Wayne Jackson and he is one seriously dangerous man. He's served two prison terms: one for beating a man with a metal bar until he lost consciousness; one for driving a car at someone who he wanted to frighten into paying the gambling debt he owed (at that time, he was working for a casino). You were right to be worried about your bleeding birdman: who, by the way, is actually known as birdie by his friends."

The more Pete told me, the more I began to appreciate why even a man built like a tank, as Pete was, would go into hiding from these people.

"There is one piece of good fucking news Si," I relaxed ever so slightly at these words from Pete, "We've managed to hack into the One Way Group's data bank. By morning, my friends will be able to supply us with almost any fucking thing you want to know about the bleeding group."

This might have been good news to Pete, but it did not send me to bed rejoicing as I thought of my ex-wife and her One Way acquaintances up in the North East!

CHAPTER EIGHTEEN

Jasmine woke up the next morning raring to go. Life was good. She was, unbelievably, in love with a decent man, and she was going to get back into the job she loved. Then she looked round the bedroom with its high corniced ceiling, the unfamiliar white cotton duvet cover, the mahogany Edwardian style furniture, and wondered where she was. This wasn't home and it wasn't a hotel. Then she remembered. She was at Emma's house in Darlington. Her mood changed somewhat when she remembered why she was at Emma's house. Memories of yesterday's events came flooding back. Her mobile rang just as she had a flashback to the stone hitting that poor minister.

"Hi babe. Alright?" It was Simon. The Aberdeen image faded to be replaced by the more re-assuring image of her lover. The word 'lover' had just sprung to mind and she was intrigued to realise that she had never thought of Simon in those terms before. Then she thought of the nights of passion and smiled as she realised that he was indeed her lover, and what an unexpectedly good lover her vicar had proven to be!

"Jazz?"

The agitated tone in Simon's voice made her speak, "Sorry babe," she apologised," I was just thinking about you and our hotel nights together, and how great they were!"

"Wow! Now you've made me think of them, and I can't remember why I phoned," he paused for a moment and then continued, " I phoned to tell you I love you, and to give you some warnings."

Jasmine sat up in bed as Simon brought her up to date on all of Pete's findings about Samuel Watkinson. Somehow, despite everything she had learned from her studies of religion about how some very nasty people had often used religion as a cloak for their nefarious doings, the way in which a man of the cloth like Samuel Watkinson could be so rich and so unscrupulous shocked her rigid. When Simon went on to tell her of Pete's discoveries about the birdman, she shivered involuntarily as she thought back to how close Simon had come to being attacked by him. She had no trouble in agreeing that these were very unsavoury, frightening people and in promising solemnly not to go out on her own, not to go near either of their flats and, after a bit of arguing, not to go near her school. Then she got up, showered, dressed and went downstairs.

Emma was waiting for her in the kitchen which was filled with the appetising aroma of freshly brewed coffee and freshly warmed croissants. Emma greeted her warmly and sat her down to a latte, a plate of croissants and a choice of jams.

"Sleep well?" Emma asked as Jasmine buttered her croissant.

"So so," Jasmine replied.

The doorbell rang and Emma went out to say goodbye to her daughter, Lauren, who was off to the free school down the road (which until recently had been a girls' boarding school!) with some of her friends. Jasmine glanced round the kitchen as she ate her croissant. One of the shelves had a few books on it, one of which immediately drew Jasmine's attention. 'God's Dangerous Book'. Hadn't Simon mentioned that as one of Tim Harris's books when he was looking in the One Way Publications window? What was Emma doing with a book like that? Surely she didn't have anything to do with the One Way Group? Jasmine wondered whether she should mention it to Emma, but decided to wait till after breakfast when she would have the chance to tell Emma about the horrors of the people connected to the One Way Group, and why she was not going back to school yet.

The coffee was good, if slightly bitter, and Jasmine was soon finished her first cup. As she sipped at her second cup, she suddenly started to find it difficult to lift the cup. She felt so tired...

*   *   *   *   *

I felt so much better now I'd spoken to Jazz and she'd promised me she would keep away from all the places where the plotters might get to her. I was particularly pleased that she was not going into school. That Colin guy really worried me. A weirdo scientist into the One Way, he had to be a potential threat. Thank goodness Jazz was going nowhere near him. And thank goodness Jazz thought the sex had been good. I was so inexperienced, I didn't really know whether I'd been doing things right, but clearly I had!

Pete had suggested that I change cars as a sort of double-indemnity, so I used my laptop to find the nearest depot where I could drop off the people carrier, then look for another nearby depot to pick up a more anonymous vehicle. I drove to the first depot but found more difficulty in getting to the second car hire. What seems nearby on a google map is much further when you are walking. Nevertheless, I was soon in possession of a one-year old silver-grey Focus, as anonymous a vehicle as it is possible to get, but with a 2 litre eco-boost engine, as powerful as anything I could hire, I felt more confident in being able to deal with anything sent my way.

After all I'd discovered, on top of all that had happened, I thought it best to comply with Pete's arrangement and drove off to find a phone box. They were becoming as rare as hen's teeth and I ended up in West London's most magnificent Tesco – the old Hoover building on the A40 where I'd eventually found one. As I'd done the night before, I phoned the bookshop and listened to the usual diversions until Pete answered. "See you," was all he said, and twenty minutes later he appeared in Tesco's cafe.

"Well Si, this is certainly a bloody fine building for a cheapo full English breakfast," he said as we tucked into bacon, sausage, black pudding, fried eggs and fried bread. "How's things this beautiful fucking morning me old mate?"

I reported my conversation with Jazz (omitting, of course, the references to our sexual exploits) and we agreed that it was good she'd promised to stay away from any possibility of danger. Then Pete reported on the discoveries his hackers had made. Apparently the One Way Group had regional committees known as 'the elect' (presumably a reference to the 144,000 elect mentioned in Revelation), and Pete had print-out lists of their members. When we'd finished our breakfasts, we put our plates to one side and began to flick through the lists.

My heart sank when we came to the list of the North Region Elect. Three names sprang out at me – Trevor Thompson, Christine Thompson, Emma Davies. As I read the last name, I involuntarily shouted, "Oh shit! Oh shit! Oh shit!"

We had thought Jazz was so safe, but how could she be safe in the home of one of the inner circle of the One Way Group?

"What's the matter Si? That's not the language for a bloody vicar, ex or not! What have you seen?" Pete was quite unaware of the significance of the names, but clearly disturbed to hear me swearing.

"That last name Pete - Emma Davies. Sh..sh…sh she's," I stammered, "she's the friend Jazz's staying with in Darlington. That's the worst thing. But that couple, Trevor and Christine Thompson, they're Sarah's mother and father – my ex in-laws. I've got to go Pete. I've got to get back up there and save her."

Before I finished speaking, I was up from the table and moving fast out of Tesco's. Pete caught me up just outside the store and pulled me back. He tried to remonstrate with me,
"Wait a minute Si. We need to talk about this and work out a plan of campaign."

I shrugged him off and headed for the car. "Bugger a plan of campaign! Bugger you! Bugger everything! They might kill her. I've got to stop it."

My terror, my anguish must have been impressive because Pete suddenly stopped his objections; put his arm round me to comfort me rather than hold me back and said, "OK mate, let's go. But I'll drive, you're far too upset to be safe." With that he bundled me into the passenger seat of the Focus and we set off heading west down the A40.

By using the M40 towards Oxford, then the A43 to join the M1 west of Northampton, we avoided any hold-ups on the M25 and the speed limits round Luton. Pete drove at a steady 85 mph and we were approaching Woodall Services south of Sheffield just before 11.00 a.m. when his phone rang. He glanced at the caller then pulled over into the services. It was a message from his manager at the shop. The shop had had an e-mail which they thought we had to see immediately. Pete, of course, had an I-phone and was able to access the e-mail on his phone, His face blanched when he read it and then passed the phone over to me.

As I read the message, I was filled with a mixture of rage, despair and horror:

We know this message will get through to you.
We have Jasmine Baker and we want both of you. Mention anything to anyone and she dies.
Jenkins and Keep, your only way to ensure she stays alive is to be outside the Fishermen's Group hostel in Cleveland Street at 9.00 p.m. tonight – no one else, no police, no friends, just you two.

I felt sick. This was no longer some sort of game with me pretending to be a private investigator. This was real. I was now on the inside and my love, my rediscovered first love, had been kidnapped by a bunch of religious nutters. Suddenly the sick feeling transformed itself into a burning anger. Whatever weird politico-religious game these morons were playing, I was not going to let them play it with Jazz. I didn't know how, but before the end of the day my beloved would be back with me. In capturing Jazz, they had crossed the line; and they were going to pay. I would not be in Cleveland Street tonight. I would be with Jazz. The anger pulsated within me as I tried to decide what to do. 'Think Simon, think,' I remember saying to myself. 'What do you know that can help you find her?'

My attempts to think were interrupted by Pete thumping me on the back and saying, "Bugger me Si, we actually have advantages here. The bloody sods think we're in London when in fact we'll soon be in the area where Jasmine must be being held. Secondly, we have access to some of their bleeding secrets in the One Way files. All we need do, is find out where they're keeping her and then rescue her."

His words of comfort had a hollow ring to them. I knew he had intended them to comfort me, even to prevent me from descending into the pit of despair he had seen me in when Mum and Dad died, but they smacked of whistling in the wind. All we needed to do? How could we find out where they were keeping her? How on earth could we rescue her?

Then I had a moment like Paul's on the road to Damascus, a moment when I clearly saw the answer. I knew where she was, and how to rescue her. I leaned across and gave Pete a big kiss on the forehead.

Pete looked at me as if I had taken leave of my senses as I said, "You little beaut! Of course! I've got it! The list: Trevor and Christine Thompson. The North Region Elect members. They used one member, Emma, to kidnap her, and I bet they used another two to keep her in captivity, and I know just where she'll be!"

My outburst patently confirmed Pete's view that the shock of the news of the kidnap had left me several sandwiches short of a picnic until I explained further, "They used Jazz's friend Emma, who's a member of the One Way Northern Elect, to kidnap Jazz because she could do it without arousing suspicion. Right Pete?" he nodded and so I continued, "I happen to know that Trevor has a soundproofed office at the bottom of his garden that would make an ideal prison cell. He and his wife are bound to hate Jazz, apart from whatever they have to do with the One Way plot. They're on the Elect, so they're bound to have some sort of influence on what's happening. They think we're in London, so what better place to keep Jazz than Redcar?"

I could tell from his expression that Pete was not altogether convinced by my impeccable logic. However, in the absence of any more concrete evidence, he agreed that we should proceed to Redcar to keep watch on the Thompson home for signs of confirmation. After all, if worst came to worst, we could always speed back to London in time for the Cleveland Street meet. Pete was still thinking more clearly than I was and made a small notice which he spent a couple of moments putting onto the bookshop website. It simply said - *Jenkins and Keep have received the message and will comply.*

CHAPTER NINETEEN

When Jasmine came round, she found she could not move. Her wrists and ankles seemed to be tied together. She tried to work out what was happening, or more precisely what had happened. She had been eating breakfast in Emma's house. She had just finished her first cup of that fabulous coffee when... Everything had blanked out. There must have been something in the coffee. Some sort of drug that Emma had given her. Why would she do that?

Jasmine began to struggle to release her bonds, and immediately felt hands pushing her down. It felt like she was on a car seat, and it also felt like the car was moving. As she struggled harder, she heard a voice say, "She's coming round, pass me the needle." It was a voice she'd heard before, something to do with the police she thought before she felt a jab in her arm and drifted back into unconsciousness.

*   *   *   *   *

*

As we drove from Sheffield to Redcar, Pete and I tried to work out a plan of campaign for the rescue of Jazz. Under Pete's instruction, I wrote down everything I knew about the house, garden and garden office of the Thompsons. Then I drew a map showing the layout of the garden and its relationship to the neighbouring houses and their gardens. We both agreed that if we were to have any hope of releasing Jazz, a frontal attack was out of the question. We needed to find a place in one of the neighbouring gardens from which to launch our attack. But first we had to have some sort of confirmation that Jazz was being held there, and that was going to be every bit as tricky as attacking a soundproofed garden office!

Pete and I were both racking our brains for inspiration when we passed one of those ubiquitous white Northgate hire vans, and I remembered a conversation from a few weeks back when I had passed just such a van doing Water Board repairs. We had discussed how the public utilities used to have their own vans, but now often seemed to hire them. What struck me now was that if we hired a white van and pretended to be BT men repairing the phones, no one would pay us any attention and we could see whether the nature of the visitors to Uttoxeter Road could confirm Jazz's presence.

The idea of the van was mine, but I had no idea about how to get the type of equipment that would make our presence seem genuine. Luckily that was Pete's forte, and he soon came up with the name, 'Fast Hire'. He reckoned he had seen their name on equipment like generators and pneumatic drills being used by utility companies. I phoned directory enquiries and located a Fast Hire main depot and a Northgate van hire depot almost next to each other in Stockton.

Of course, Pete had satnav on his phone, so finding our way round the two industrial estates off the A19 was quite painless. We went to the van hire depot first, as we would need to load the equipment into it. Luckily we had decided that I would hire and drive it – two different vehicles might give us more flexibility – but Pete was sure that hiring a van required far more in the way of security than a car. We felt it was safe to use my own card and driving licence, because, if all went to plan and we rescued Jazz, they would know it was me anyway.

The first question we were asked was whether we wanted to hire a small, medium or large sized van. We quickly decided on a medium sized. However, when I presented my own credit card for the transaction, I was asked for two utility bills from the same address as well as my driver's licence. It took some time for me to explain that I had been kicked out by my wife and therefore had no utility bills, but I did have a passport and was prepared to pay more than the £250 deposit they wanted to take from my credit card if necessary.

The guy who was serving me was about my age and looked at me with sympathetic eyes as he said, "It's a bugger isn't it. My wife had the soddin locks changed while I was at work. Let me take a photocopy of your passport and it'll be okay."

After thirty minutes of form filling and arcane promises, I got into the driving seat of a white Ford Transit. As I looked at the massive space behind me in the medium sized van, I wondered how big a large one would have been. Far too big for our needs!

Ever the cautious one, Pete had waited outside in the car to check for any unwanted visitors. As soon as he saw me get into the Transit and familiarise myself with the controls, he drove off to find the Fast Hire depot his satnav directions with me following in the Transit: a Transit that we hoped would be thought of as a BT service vehicle ready to restore the communications network in Redcar.

The Fast Hire depot was massive, and we decided that the best way to get what we wanted was to give a modicum of the truth, the type of truth that had worked with the van hire firm. So, I went over to the information desk and explained that Pete and I were private investigators employed by the DSS (I knew that the more correct DWP would mean nothing to the man behind the counter). We were investigating a couple who had been reported as claiming disability allowance and other benefits when they were fit and well and running a business, and that we needed a cover story so that we could get some photographic evidence for a prosecution. It was just the right choice of lie for the guy we were dealing with. Most people who have to work for a living dislike scroungers, but this chap absolutely hated them and couldn't do enough to help us.

As he typed instructions into his computer terminal and equipment began to be brought out, we realised why the depot was so enormous. A compressor and generator, plastic barriers, road works warning signs, one of those red and white shelters that BT workers put over the holes they are working in soon appeared, accompanied by a running commentary from Geoff (the guy who was serving us) on exactly how to use each one and what we needed to do to make our appearance look genuine. We even got nice orange overalls and yellow hard hats and, most important of all, a large portable radio to switch on so that we could have the pop music at full blast as the necessary accompaniment for the modern British workman.

After more chat and signing away a fair bit of money on the credit card (none of these firms seemed to like cash), we loaded the van and I set off for Redcar with Pete following in the car. The A66 goes through what is still, despite media moans that we no longer make anything, an industrial heartland. A haze of pollution, fuelled by vast columns of smoke and steam from what is left of the steelworks, covered the horizon making the clear blue sky grey and forbidding as we headed eastwards to the coast. As grey as my spirits, and as forbidding as the task ahead of us.

*   *   *   *   *

This time Jasmine knew exactly what had happened and so, as consciousness slowly returned, she resisted the urge to move her limbs. Clearly, if her captors knew she was conscious they would give her another dose of whatever drugs they were using to keep her under. Jasmine was an intelligent, strong woman who understood the need for extra knowledge in whatever situation you found yourself.

She was in her worst situation ever, therefore anything that gave her one up on her captors was to be savoured and utilised.

Jasmine stayed absolutely still, using her senses of hearing, touch and smell, as she tried to work out what was happening. She could no longer feel movement and she no longer felt as if she were on a car seat. It didn't take an Einstein to work out that she had been kidnapped and transported from Emma's house to wherever the kidnappers intended to keep her.

Emma's house! She had thought she was safe there. Emma was her friend, her buddy, her confidante, and she had betrayed her. Why? There was something niggling in the recesses of Jasmine's brain; something she had seen just before drinking the coffee that sent her to sleep. A book? Of course, it was a book. It was a book on a shelf in Emma's kitchen. A book by Tim Harris. Presumably that meant that Emma was a member of the One Way Group; and they must have been involved in her kidnapping as well as the murder plot. She had been kidnapped because of what she and Simon had found out about Mark's murder. Maybe just because they'd found out it was actually Mark who'd been murdered. Jasmine had to use all her powers of concentration to stop herself from moving when she worked this out.

Jasmine's thoughts were interrupted by the sound of some sort of special knock on a wooden door. Two short knocks followed by two long knocks and then two short knocks again.

"The Lord be with you," a woman's voice said.

"And also with you," replied a man's voice.

As Jasmine reflected on the rather simplistic secret code they were using to gain entry to her prison. She suddenly realised that the man's voice was ringing bells; it was the voice of someone she knew. Someone she knew from real life not TV or films. Someone who would love speaking in the religious terms of that banal password. Of course! It was the voice of Colin Taylor, that insufferable right-wing born-againer. Through a huge mental effort,

Jasmine managed to stay absolutely still and silent, even though she wanted to scream and lash out at the stupid man.

'Stay still. Keep focussed. Listen to what they say. Knowledge is power,' Jasmine said to herself. She heard a door open and shut and listened carefully to the ensuing conversation.

"How is she?" asked Colin.

"She seems to be sleeping peacefully," the woman replied. "I haven't needed to give her any more injections. I've been praying for her. But I don't really know what to ask the Lord. Will you help me?"

Jasmine could almost feel Colin leap at the chance to be a prayer leader. She wondered what on earth they would find to say to the Lord about them having drugged and kidnapped an RE teacher!

"Oh Lord, you are full of power and might and deserving of our praise and thanksgiving," Colin prayed in the droning, respectful tone of voice which so many people used for addressing prayers to the deity. Jasmine thought it must be dreadful for God to have to listen to millions, if not billions, of such drones every day.

"Lord we thank you that you have delivered our enemies into our hands," he continued, "and we pray that this daughter of Satan may be used to bring your other enemies into our grasp so that we may fulfil your heavenly purposes. We pray that she, and all those who have sinned and gone astray, may be led into the light of your sacred love. May she see the error of her ways and through the redeeming power of your Son, our Lord Jesus Christ, let her sins be forgiven so that she can receive your gift of eternal life."

Colin paused in his prayer and Jasmine imagined God heaving a sigh of relief, but it was not for long. She heard an intake of breath as Colin readied himself to re-address the Almighty, "O Lord bless us your servants and fill us with the strength of your Holy Spirit as we strive to carry out your holy work. Give the Reverend Tim and the Reverend Samuel your heavenly strength and guidance as they prepare to lead this country back onto the narrow path that leads to salvation, so that all your people may rejoice in the loving salvation of your Son who lives and reigns with you and the Holy Spirit, one God for evermore. We ask this in and through the name of our Lord Jesus Christ. Amen."

The woman joined in with a loud, 'Amen' and Jasmine tried to work out what she had learned from the prayer. Well, of course, she had learned that Colin was not in school, but was one of her captors. He was clearly involved in the plot since he was involved in the kidnap and must have had no qualms about filling her with drugs. As yet she had no idea who the woman was, or why she was here. 'Hang on a mo,' she thought, 'I do have an idea why I'm here. I'm the daughter of Satan whose task is to bring the other enemies in. I guess the other enemies are Simon and Pete and they've kidnapped me to stop them from investigating Mark's murder. But how can intelligent people believe the Christian God will accept such unchristian behaviour?'

The woman spoke again, "Thank you Colin. I feel so much better for that. Don't you find that communing with the Lord is so uplifting for the soul?"

"I do indeed Christine. I think the Lord sort of transports us to another level of existence. A truly spiritual level where we are not constrained by the finite limitations of these mortal bodies."

Jasmine switched off from the spiritual claptrap and switched on to Colin's use of a name for the woman. He'd called her 'Christine' and Jasmine knew that Simon's mother-in-law was called Christine. Jasmine also knew that Christine and her husband, Trevor, were involved in the plot, she'd seen the police inspector at their house. She also thought that Simon had been pretty sure of their involvement in the One Way Group. Was this woman who had been giving her injections, Simon's mother-in-law? If she was, she had no doubt justified herself by her hatred of the woman who had destroyed her daughter's marriage. No doubt she had also created for herself a mental image of Jasmine as a wanton Jezebel. Jasmine could not help a silent chuckle at that image, she could not think of anyone less like an alluring seductress than herself.

She quickly plummeted back to reality as she thought about the careless use of their real names by her two captors. Had they just forgotten she was there? Did they think they didn't need to bother because she was unconscious? Or had they decided there was no need to bother because, given what Jasmine already knew, there was no way Jasmine was coming out of this alive?

*   *   *   *   *

The sun was shining and the seagulls were screeching as I turned into the road parallel to Trevor and Christine's. I took this as a good omen since it gave me ample excuse to wear the pair of sunglasses which previous hirers had left in the van. I reckoned that the glasses, together with the yellow hard hat and orange boiler suit would make me sufficiently unrecognisable to anyone driving past.

We had decided that we would park the Focus in the road of the house that backed onto Thompson's since, if my plan worked, we would be bringing Jasmine out of their front gate. Pete locked the Focus and got in beside me. I drove round the corner into Uttoxeter Road, relieved to see that the BT communications box was still on the corner, as I remembered. It was ideally situated to give us a clear view of the comings and goings at number fifty-five.

We parked beside the box, donned our overalls and hard hats, and put out the road signs for men at work and road narrows. We switched on the radio which seemed to be pre-tuned to the local independent radio station. Without a radio tuned into a local station, we would never appear to be authentic British workmen. As Pete unloaded things from the van, the radio station belted out the Spice Girls singing 'Wannabe' as part of their featured hits of 1997. I took some tools out of the van and went to look at the large green BT box in, what I hoped would appear to anyone watching, a professional manner. It took a bit of working out, but eventually I had the front off, exposing loads of wires, to make it look like we were doing a real job of work.

Pete banned me from touching anything else on the box, and sat himself down on a small portable seat unplugging and re-plugging wires and cables. I set up the red and white striped canvas hut, went inside and peered through a slit in the canvas down the road to number fifty-five. Nothing was happening, though there was a battered old Toyota Corolla parked outside the house. The wonderful sound of Aqua singing 'Barbie Girl' was interrupted by a newsflash:

"Independent Radio News has just heard that the Chairman of the 1922 Committee, George Blenkinsop, has announced that since he has received letters from more than 15% of the Conservative members of the House of Commons requesting a vote of no confidence in Stuart Fairhurst, the Prime Minister, as Leader of the Conservative Party, under the rules of the Party he is therefore organising such a vote to take place tonight. Such an event is totally unprecedented in British politics and is presumably connected to the Prime Minister's refusal to give public support to the Reverend Tim Harris's campaign to restore the UK to Christian values. In what some commentators are calling a connected event, Jemimah Percy-Gilbert Secretary of State for Culture and the Media has resigned her ministerial post. As usual, IRN will be keeping you up to date on what happens as it happens."

The radio went back to singing about the fantastic life in plastic of a Barbie girl who can be undressed everywhere, and I had some new thoughts to share with Pete. The MPs George and Jemimah had been at that meeting in Ripon and now they were launching a full-blown frontal attack on the Prime Minister. If Jemimah had resigned as Culture Minister to support the attack, she must have high hopes that it would be successful.

I went and knelt next to Pete and asked, "Did you hear that Pete?"

"Yeah. Bloody wankers."

Well I suppose it gave me an accurate description of what he felt about the two MPs, but it didn't tell me what he thought they were up to; so, I said, "OK Pete no arguments there, but what do you think it's about?"

"I don't have much of a bloody clue Si, except they want to get rid of that toffee-nosed dipstick as leader of the Tories. On the other hand, mate, if enough Tory MPs vote against him, he'll have to resign. If he resigns as leader of the Tories, he'll probably have to resign as Prime Minister. There's no official Deputy Prime Minister at the moment so I guess there'll have to be another bloody general election."

We went back to work. I mulled over what Pete had said whilst I continued my peering through the slit down to number fifty-five and the radio moved on in 1997 to Elton John and 'Candle in the Wind'. No one of a certain age can listen to that without thinking of Princess Di and conspiracy theories, and I was already thinking of conspiracies. Had we stumbled into a huge conspiracy aimed at bringing the One Way Group to power?

CHAPTER TWENTY

Jasmine had to move. Her legs were cramping and her back was itching. Though she wanted to continue listening to these two to discover more about what was happening, she really had little choice and began to wriggle.

"She's coming round," Colin said. "I'm off. She mustn't see me. And you'd better get your mask on."

Jasmine began to moan, but kept her eyes closed to give Christine, whoever she might be, plenty of time to get her mask on. Having heard that they didn't want her to recognise them, Jasmine was beginning to feel better. She would make sure she gave no sign of recognising any of her captors because whatever else happened, Jasmine quite fancied getting out of this nightmare alive. She slowly opened her eyes and groaned, "Where am I? What's happened?"

A hand softly stroked her forehead as a woman wearing a black velvet mask (Jasmine had to stop herself laughing as she imagined the embarrassment of Colin the physics teacher buying it from Ann Summers) bent over her and murmured, "Don't worry daughter. You're perfectly safe. The Lord has brought you here for safe keeping."

Jasmine now had to play along with the idea that she was only just regaining consciousness. "What do you mean? Where am I? Why am I here? I was having breakfast at Emma's. What's happened?"

"You are in the Lord's keeping my child. There is nothing for you to worry about. Just let me loosen your ankles and then you can sit up."

I am neither your child, nor your daughter, thought Jasmine and I'm sure the Lord has nothing at all to do with this, but she kept her thoughts to herself. She allowed the rope round her ankles to be loosened, sat up and looked around at her surroundings. She appeared to be in a small office. There were no windows and the walls seemed to be lined with some sort of insulated plasterboard which had not been painted. There was a high desk against one wall with a drawing board on it and an open Bible. Sitting on a high office chair with her back to the desk was a trim lady, probably in her mid-sixties, wearing a white blouse and black trousers. The top of her face was covered by the mask, the bottom half showed a lipsticked mouth fixed in that smile that Jasmine had come to associate with Evangelical Christians, a smile completely lacking in humour or feeling.

Christine, and Jasmine was now certain she was Simon's mother-in-law, said, "You have nothing to fear my child. I will not harm you in anyway. We are all the Lord's people here so you have nothing to fear. Our Lord said, 'Do not be afraid; just believe'. Do you believe?"

Jasmine struggled to prevent herself being freaked out by this weird woman. Had she no idea how bizarre she both looked and sounded? Nevertheless, Jasmine replied as if she were having a normal conversation with a normal person. She could not afford to anger someone who clearly had a lot of power over her, "Believe in what?" she asked.

"Believe in the Lord Jesus Christ as your Lord and Saviour of course," came the prompt reply. "Do you believe that? It's all there in the good book. As John 3 says, 'God so loved the world that he gave his one and only Son that whoever believes in him shall not perish but have eternal life'."

Jasmine was now feeling totally spooked. Was this woman actually trying to convert her at the same time as keeping her tied up and injecting her with anaesthetics? What sort of crazy logic was going in this supposedly good Christian woman's mind?

Then Jasmine suddenly realised what this was really about. The born-again Christianity was simply a cover for the woman to vent her spleen on the wicked Jezebel who had seduced her daughter's husband. Maybe this had been planned well in advance? Hadn't Simon said that Trevor and Christine had warned that he would be made to pay?

"We know you have been seduced by the Evil One my child. The Reverend Tim has told us that Satan has beguiled you into doing his work. You are working against God's plans to bring this nation back to the Lord's way. You are here so that we can prevent you from defeating God's plans. I am but the servant of the Lord. Why not confess your sin? Reject Satan and all his works and turn to the Lord, my dear."

Rather than being terrified, Jasmine was finding it hard not to burst out laughing when she used the patronising terms, 'my child' and 'my dear'. What this woman was saying was ludicrous enough, but sitting there saying it whilst wearing a black velvet Ann Summers mask made it totally outlandish. However, Jasmine knew she must not laugh; she had to keep this woman on something resembling an even keel if she was to learn more and work out how to escape. Jasmine thanked her lucky stars that she was an RE teacher who therefore knew how to talk the talk about religion, but she feared there was a long session ahead on evil and salvation.

*   *   *   *   *

I peered through the slit in the canvas looking at number fifty-five and stared at the old Toyota. I was getting dim memories of being told about someone driving an old Toyota as a sort of symbol of their eccentricity. Who was it? I racked my brains, but it was not till a man emerged from the house and drove off in the car that I remembered who it was. He was a grey-haired, slightly overweight man in his fifties wearing pale blue trousers and a bluish Harris Tweed jacket. That was exactly how Jasmine had described him. It was Colin Taylor, the born-again, right wing physics teacher from Jasmine's school.

After he'd driven off, I came out of the shelter to tell Pete. We agreed that this was a good sign that we were in the right location. This Colin chap was connected to the One Way Group, he was connected to Jasmine through the school, and therefore he was connected to Emma with whom Jasmine had been staying, and now here he was at Trevor and Christine's house.

I wanted to go straight in, break down the door and rescue my love, but Pete held me back.
He claimed we needed to be more certain and do a bit more in the way of reconnaissance before we leapt in. We needed to remember all the time that if things went wrong we could cost Jasmine her life. Of course, that calmed me down!

We made some tea using the equipment provided by the helpful guy at Fast Hire – tea making being an essential requisite for any group of outdoor British workmen – and sat down
to think things through. I was sure that the people whose garden backed onto the Thompsons had a feud going with Trevor. Their garden was more the cottage garden type than the municipal park variety favoured by Trevor. Consequently, Trevor had had many altercations with his neighbour about the neighbour's clematis and climbing roses daring to appear on his side of the fence. Given this situation, I felt fairly sure that the neighbour would give us his support and hopefully a means of unseen access to the Thompson's garden.

Pete was concocting a way of approaching the neighbours when final confirmation of Jasmine's location suddenly appeared as a black BMW pulled up outside number fifty-five. A tall fair-haired man in a dark grey Armani suit got out and went into the Thompson's house. It was Inspector Byrom looking more like a venture capitalist than a poorly paid police detective; the whiff of police corruption was definitely strong. I ducked into the shelter to prevent him from recognising me, but he never looked our way; we were just workmen and so beneath his attention.

I came out of the shelter and told Pete, "That was Inspector Byrom, Pete. That means she must be in there. Let's go!"

Without a word, Pete started putting stuff into the van. We replaced the cover on the green box and within five minutes we were in the van and driving out of Uttoxeter Road leaving no sign of our surveillance activities behind. We turned right, then right again and pulled up behind the Focus. Pete's plan was to tell the neighbour about the kidnap, but omit all mention of the murders and plots. We would simply blame everything on the nasty Thompsons, who I was sure the neighbour did not like anyway. Of course, if the neighbour wasn't in, we could simply go into his back garden and find a way through.

Leaving Pete in the van (we didn't want to frighten the neighbours), I walked up the path and rang the bell of the 1950s three-bedroomed semi. It was a well-kept house, but even the front garden had none of the manicured look of Trevor's. There were clumps of bluebells, just finishing flowering, aquilegias and poppies were starting to bloom and roses were coming into bud. To my eye it was everything a suburban garden should be, but I could see it being anathema to Trevor. The door was opened by a tall, thick-set man in his early fifties. He was wearing jeans and trainers and an open-neck button-down collar Oxford shirt with the sleeves rolled up. Trevor would have thought him far too casually dressed even for gardening!

I spoke first, "Hello there. I don't know if you've seen me around, but I'm Trevor and Christine Thompson's son-in-law."

"Poor you!" he replied, making me think we'd made the right choice. This was confirmed as he continued, "As they say, 'You can choose your friends, but you can't choose your relations. Oh! I'm sorry. I shouldn't have said that. Maybe you like the little shit?"

This was getting even better and I took the opportunity to build on it as I replied, "No I hate his guts, and that's why I'm standing here on your doorstep. The little shit, as you so rightly call him, has kidnapped my girlfriend."

The man's jaw dropped, "Your girlfriend? Aren't you married to the ice maiden?"

"Ah well, that's the problem. You see I've left my wife, who was, as you so truly describe her, an ice maiden, and to punish me the

Thompsons have kidnapped my girlfriend, and I'm pretty sure they're keeping her in his office shed at the bottom of the garden."

The neighbour's expression said almost as much as his next words, "I always knew that holy Joe act of his was just a bloody front. I don't believe in much, but I would never treat a neighbour in the way he's treated me, cutting off my plants, spreading weedkiller at the bottom of his fence, refusing to speak to me. Things like that make you think a person can't be a real Christian. Doesn't Christianity teach that you should love your neighbour? And now he's kidnapped your girlfriend? The bugger. Well come on in. Let's have a cuppa and you can tell me what you want me to do. Anything to cut that stupid prick down to size."

Pete and I were soon sitting in the neighbour's front room looking around whilst he made a cup of tea. The room was tastefully decorated and furnished, but yet felt like home. You got the impression that his wife didn't expect people to take their shoes off before they came in. The house was a home not a showcase, such as I had always felt the Thompson's to be. He introduced himself as Tony Harvey. As he gave us our tea in china mugs which celebrated the relighting of the Redcar blast furnaces, which had now shut down again, he informed us that he was a supervisor at one of the few remaining local steel processing works.

Of course, he had a few questions, the first of which was, "Excuse me, but I thought you were a vicar. They're always boasting about how Sarah married a vicar who will probably be a bishop before long."

"Well, I was a vicar, but the Church doesn't take too kindly to vicars who leave their wives for a girlfriend and even less to vicars who stop believing in God! So, I'm no longer a vicar and I don't think there was ever much chance of my becoming a bishop. And I have to admit that as far as the Thompsons were concerned, my stopping being a vicar was only marginally less popular than leaving their daughter for another woman," I replied with a sheepish grin and a shrug of the shoulders.

"And that was enough to make the stupid sod kidnap your girlfriend?"

How much to tell him? He seemed a nice bloke and I didn't want him to get involved in all the violence that was surrounding us. It would certainly be better for him and his family if we could make it look like he had known nothing about us using his garden, and therefore knew nothing about the murders. I answered carefully, "Of course there's more involved, and there are more people involved. The people involved are not only evil, they're violent. I don't want to get you mixed up in all of this. Where's your family?"

Tony began to look much less of an eager beaver as the import of my words sank in. "What's my family got to do with it?" he asked in a much less friendly tone of voice.

"The people we're dealing with use whatever they think will hurt you to get their way. That's why they've kidnapped Jasmine, my girlfriend. What we want Tony, is to find a way of getting into next door and releasing Jasmine without anyone being able to think that you might be involved. If your family are out at work, or something, that will make it easier to do."

"Well, well, well the sly git. Do you know, I'm not at all surprised? I've often said to the wife that there was something truly evil about that creeping Jesus next door. Anyway, family wise we're okay. Linda's at work at the M&S in Skippers Lane, she used to be in Redcar, but it shut soon after the blast furnaces. The kids don't live at home anymore: one's married, the other's at university in Leeds. You tell me what I can do to help your plan and then I'll bugger off so you can get on with things on your own. The hypocritical prat, I always knew..."

Tony spent a while talking to himself about the evil and the hypocrisy of his neighbour as Pete and I finished drinking our tea. Then Pete started asking the questions, "I suppose there are really only two things we need to know Tony. The first is whether there's any way of us spying on next door's garden from your garden without being seen. The second is whether there's any way of getting into next door's garden and carrying someone out without leaving much trace. Just two simple questions Tony, but I don't suppose the answers are that simple!"

Tony looked thoughtful for a couple of minutes, He was clearly visualising his back fence and its relationship to Trevor's garden. Perhaps he'd already done some thinking about just such a problem because his answer was just about as good as we could have hoped for.

"Spying wise, creeping Jesus has already sorted it for you. I've always thought he did it to spy on our daughter when she was sunbathing, but Linda said I had an evil twisted mind. From what you've told me though, I think I might have been right. Anyway, there are three knotholes in the fence where the wood has fallen, or been knocked, out. What made me suspicious is that they're only in places where they're not covered up by my climbing greenery that he hates so much. In any case, they presumably give a good view of next door's garden, though we probably need to check.

"As far as access is concerned, there's a couple of loose planks on the right-hand side that I've been meaning to nail back for ages. I'm pretty sure you'd be able to pull them off. Then if you screwed them back on after your escape it would be quick and noiseless and next door would have no idea anyone had been in from this side. Let's go and check it out."

Tony led us out of the backdoor and into his garden. As he had already told us about them, we found the knotholes standing out like beacons. As we looked at the fence and its holes, I got the definite feeling that Tony had been right about my prurient ex-father-in-law. There were plenty of knots in the planks that had not fallen out, but they were not at the right level for peeping through. Pete and I had a peep though the holes and agreed with Tony that they gave us a good view. In fact, they were perfect in that one gave us a good view of the door to the garden office, and the other gave us a good view of the French doors which I knew were the only access to the garden from the back of the house.

Next Tony took us to the corner where three fencing planks were held on by only a couple of nails each. Pete and Tony reckoned that a judicious bit of work with a knife would make it possible simply to lift the planks off thus making no noise. Then we could lift them back and two minutes to screw in a self-tapper and there would be no sign from the other side that they had ever been moved.

It seemed very important to me that we managed to get Jazz out without there being any chance of implicating Tony. He would be here after we left, and he had been so helpful to us. I looked at our footprints on the soil of the border and my heart sank. We were bound to leave a mass of footprints in Trevor's garden which would lead straight to the fence and make it obvious how we had engineered the escape. I was gutted. I just wanted to knock the fence down and drag Jasmine away from those bloody people.

Obviously, Tony worked out what I was thinking from my expression and what I was looking
at. "Don't worry mate," he said reassuringly. "That part of the fence backs onto a paved area where he has his compost bin. It's all neat and tidy but I think the damp from it is responsible for the state of the fence. You won't be leaving any footprints on the other side of there."

Tony showed us the side gate so we could get back into to the van after he left. Then he locked up the house got into his car and drove off to town to have a coffee. We went to the van, found a crow bar, a screwdriver and a few self-tappers and the balaclavas Pete, for some reason, had brought from London. Had he known we might need to conceal our identities?

CHAPTER TWENTY ONE

As far as Jasmine was concerned, although her situation was terrifying, it was also totally ludicrous. This woman clearly hated her with a venom verging on the obscene, and yet she had felt constrained by her evangelical beliefs to try to show Jasmine God's love in order to make her accept Jesus as her personal Lord and Saviour! Although, as far as she was concerned, this was an attempt doomed to failure, Jasmine felt she had to play along with the masked avenger (as she had christened the woman in an attempt to lessen the terror that was beginning to envelop her) since she was totally under her control - as evidenced by the fact that she had been made to lie down again on the sofa whilst the woman re-tied her ankles.

The sound of two short knocks followed by two long knocks and then two short knocks again came as a great relief to Jasmine. Although she had no idea who it was, what they were like, or what they were going to do to her, anything had to be better than the endless pseudo-religious claptrap she was being forced to listen to.

"The Lord be with you," the masked woman said.

"And also, with you," replied a man's voice.

The woman got up, walked over to Jasmine, blindfolded her with a scarf, then Jasmine heard the sound of the door opening before she heard the same man's voice ask the woman to go outside, then she heard the door shut. Although she had only heard a few words, there was something she recognised about the man's voice. The sound of the door closing made Jasmine try, as she had so many times before, to wriggle her hands out of the rope that was fastening them so that she could remove the scarf. Whether her previous attempts had stretched the rope, or whether it was because her hands were colder and therefore smaller, she didn't know, but as she managed to slip one hand free, she stopped caring about how or why it had happened and simply got on with freeing her hands and removing the blindfold.

*   *   *   *   *

Pete insisted that we start the rescue bid by surveillance, for which we did not need the balaclavas, just a preparedness to kneel on damp soil with one eye pressed against a small hole in a wooden fence! I took the hole facing the garden office door, Pete the one facing the French doors.

It was very uncomfortable and so it was a great relief to hear Pete whisper, "There's someone coming out of the house. It's a guy, tall, fair hair, posh suit."

It sounded like Byrom, and when a figure suddenly came into my view, I recognised him straight away. It was indeed the double-dealing police inspector. He knocked on the wooden door in some sort of special way, then the door was opened and a woman wearing a black velvet mask came out and closed the door behind her. As she took the mask off, I realised that far from being an escapee from 'Celebrity Big Brother', it was my bitch of an ex-mother-in-law who was now deep in conversation with Inspector Byrom.

I struggled to hear what they were saying as I watched Christine lock the door to the office and follow Byrom back into the house. As I puzzled over the few words I had made out, Pete dragged me over to the corner and started removing the loose planks.
"Quick as you can Si. Let's get her while they're in the house. I'll break open the door, you go straight in, pick Jasmine up, carry her straight to the van and drive back to the van hire. I'll sort everything out here."

Pete's words helped me to make sense of what Byrom and the bitch had been saying. They were planning to take Jazz away, and pretty soon. We only had a few minutes to rescue her, so speed was indeed of the essence. I went through the fence after Pete, pulling a balaclava over my head, and sprinted across the garden as Pete put the crowbar into the gap beside the lock and prised open the wooden office door. I was through as soon as it opened and was met by the best sight ever: Jazz sitting on a small sofa rubbing her wrists and trying to sit up even though her ankles were tied together.

"It's me babe! Keep quiet till we get into a white van. They mustn't hear us," I whispered. Then without further ado, I slung Jazz over my shoulder in a fireman's lift and raced back through the fence desperate to get her out of this religious hell-hole.

How good it was to feel that sensuous body touching mine again after the day I'd spent worrying that she might be dead. Was it really only this morning that she'd been kidnapped? It felt like weeks. Worry makes time pass so slowly. Pete followed me though the fence and I heard him replacing the planks, but I didn't stop to look.

I went straight through the side gate Tony had shown us and put Jazz into the back of the van.

"I love you Jazz, but we've no time to chat. You unfasten your ankles and hold on tight because I'm going to drive us out of Redcar as quick as I can. I'll stop and let you out of the back as soon as it's safe."

Without waiting for a reply, I removed the balaclava, kissed the top of her head, slammed the doors shut, leapt into the driving seat and drove off. I wanted to speed away, but with a police inspector looking for us, I couldn't risk breaking the speed limit and being stopped by the police. There was no way Byrom knew that I'd ridden to the rescue on a Transit charger, but a description of Jazz would be all the police would need to detain me if they stopped me for speeding.

I drove out of the estate a different way so there was no chance of us being seen from Uttoxeter Road. I needed to make sure I was not held up in traffic, so I avoided the centre of Redcar and took a circuitous route back onto the trunk road to Middlesbrough and then into a deserted factory yard I remembered on the Skippers Lane Industrial Estate. I pulled in about fifteen minutes after leaving the awfulness of the Thompson's garden shed, looked all round to check there was no one in sight, then I opened the back doors of the van and Jazz leapt into my arms.

We hugged and kissed and murmured endearments into each other's ears. It was wonderful, a transfiguration. We felt like two chrysalids metamorphosing into beautiful butterflies. The dereliction of the abandoned factory took on a strange beauty; helped, no doubt, by the brilliant sunshine and blue sky. But, of course, we had to come down to earth. The only thing that had changed was that Jazz was now free, everything else was the same. We were still in deadly danger and to remove that danger, we needed to meet up with Pete, who had hopefully got away from Redcar without leaving a trail.

Needless to say, as far as I was concerned that 'only thing that had changed' meant that actually everything had changed. It was as if an impenetrable fog had lifted from my head. Although I had been so frantically busy working on Jazz's release, I had been operating on a sort of auto-pilot. The dread that she would be harmed, even killed, had been an ever-present nightmare; and now it was gone.

As we got into the front of the van, I leaned over and gave her another kiss before saying, "Right, off to meet Pete and then we three musketeers can set off to slay the One Way dragon!"

Jazz laughed, "Oh Simon, it's so good to be free. You wouldn't believe how petrified I was when I woke up to find myself tied up and that mad woman spouting religious mantras at me. Then you arrived, and it's true you did seem like a knight in shining armour. But I still don't know what happened. Where was I? What day is it? What time is it? I was at Emma's house when I got up on Thursday. I drank a cup of coffee she made, and the next I knew, I was in that office shed where you found me. How did you find me?"

Poor Jazz, I gave her leg a squeeze as I tried to answer each of her questions, "As to where you were, you were at the Thompson's house in Redcar in the garden office my ex-father-in-law made for himself. The day is still Thursday and the time is four o'clock in the afternoon, so you were only kidnapped for about eight hours. I bet it seemed a lot longer. It certainly did to me babe."

"Is it really only four o'clock on Thursday? I thought it was probably Friday. There must have been a drug in the coffee. That must have been Emma. I can't believe it. She's my friend! Why did she do it? Anyway, after that they injected me with something when I was being driven here. I thought I'd been unconscious for hours. So how did you find me?"

My heart went out to her. I just wanted to run away somewhere with Jazz and forget all about these horrific people we were embroiled with, but I knew that was out of the question. We now knew even more about them (even though we still didn't know the whys and wherefores of their plan) so we must pose a bigger threat to them than ever, and they had proven to us just how ruthless they could be. There was no doubt they would hunt us down to destroy us unless we could put a halt to their plans. What we needed to do asap was to find somewhere safe where we could plot the downfall of this One Way Group.

"How did I find you? Well it was thanks to Pete and his computer geeks. They found a list of the northern leaders of the One Way Group and, as soon as I saw Emma's name on it, we knew what had happened and Pete and I started driving north. Then when I saw Trevor and Christine's names I knew where you were, because I knew about Trevor's office and how ideal it would be for keeping a prisoner," as I said this, I spotted Pete pulling into the Fast Hire car park. "Anyway, there's Pete. You stay in here whilst I return all stuff we hired from this place so we could pose as BT engineers."

Jazz's face was a picture as she queried, "BT engineers?"

"I'll tell you all about it soon, but first we need to return the stuff, then the van and then get out of the North East. We can't risk being seen!"
Pete jumped out of his car and brought a trolley for us to unload the stuff we had hired. Geoff, the benefits cheats hater, was still at his terminal and greeted us with the question, "Did you catch the thieving bastards?"

Quick as a flash Pete replied, "Red bloody handed mate. Thanks to you we've got video of the cheeky sods replacing the drive with block paving when they're not bloody well supposed to be able to bleeding walk!"

Geoff was delighted at this news and processed everything in double quick time so we were soon back outside. Next it was back with the van, which was a totally straightforward process. As we had used so little diesel, a tenner into the back pocket of the guy behind the counter had us out of there in less than five minutes. Jazz and I cuddled up in the back seat of the Focus as Pete drove off.

"Si mate, where the hell am I going?" he asked.

"To my flat for a quick shower and change of clothes, and then somewhere for a coffee and something to eat. I'm desperate," Jazz piped in. "I really do need to go back there just for fifteen minutes or so, and it's bound to be the last place they'll expect to find me now."

"No way," replied Pete. "I want us out of this area pdq."

I could see where he was coming from, and the lack of swearing convinced me that he thought we were in deep shit, but I felt so sorry for Jazz plus, as I looked at her I realised that rather than lessening her independent spirit, her capture and imprisonment actually seemed to have increased it. An impression confirmed as Jazz interjected, "Look Pete, you might be used to women who enjoy doing what their man tells them, but this woman here is no Barbara Cartland heroine. I need a shower and a change of clothes, no ifs, no buts, that's it, end of story. There's no way they'll be looking for me back at my flat, but, if you're too scared, fair enough, just stop the car and I'll get a cab out of here, after my shower!"

Jazz's outburst reminded me of just what she'd been though and how much she'd suffered. I understood immediately why she was so desperate to wash it all away with a shower and change of clothes, but I also knew that I had to jump in quickly to lower the temperature since I was sure Pete would not have enjoyed being talked to like that. I decided to butter him up.

"Did you get out without being seen Pete?" I asked

"Yeah. No bloody problem, screwed the planks back and everything. Even dug the border over so there's no sign of footprints on the neighbour's side. They won't have a clue how we got her out."

That use of 'her' rather than Jasmine made me think that maybe Pete was even less used to charming women than I was, so I jumped in again, "So there's no way they've followed us. There's no way they've seen the car. They'll have people looking for us on the A19 and A1, but not at Jazz's flat. Emma's no doubt told them about Mark's mother having a secret and they'll be expecting us to go back to London to look for her. I reckon they'll be concentrating on finding where Mark's mother lives and setting a trap for us there." I could see Pete giving my suggestion consideration. His reply showed he'd been giving other things consideration as well. "Sorry Jasmine. I know I'm a bit of an insensitive prat, and it must have been absolute bloody hell for you. You must want to wash every bit of the buggers off you. Tell me the way and we'll soon have you at your flat, but fifteen minutes max. Can you manage that? It's not that I'm scared, it's just that these people bloody well worry me. These folks are not just bad, they're fucking resident evil!"

"Apology accepted," my heart went out to my babe as she used just the right words to calm Pete down, and also get exactly what she wanted! "But we'd better do a recce first," she continued, "just to check the coast is clear. If you're worried Pete, so am I. Perhaps it would be best if you two kept watch while I'm inside just in case they do decide to check my flat – though I'm sure they won't."

I was not as sure about the wisdom of going to the flat as I had indicated to Pete, and so was glad to agree to Jazz's plan. We parked in the High Street, after the usual queuing in traffic to get over the bridge into Yarm. We could see no sign of either Byrom's BMW (though there were plenty of those about) nor of Colin's Toyota (though that would have stood out like a sore thumb in this up-market environment) on the High Street. Jazz and I walked down to the bridge so we could approach her flat along the riverbank while we directed Pete to an alleyway leading to the flats. None of us saw anything that looked remotely untoward.

We sent Pete back to get the car and drive into the parking places at the front of the flats. Jazz gave him the remote for the security gate in case we needed to make a quick getaway, and we waited until he was in place, watching our backs as we went up to the flat. I went in the building with Jazz. We used the stairs rather than the lift with me checking everywhere like I was the inspector from the 'Pink Panther'. The stairs and the corridor were empty. As soon as Jazz unlocked the door to the flat, I slammed it open so that anyone standing behind it would be smashed against the wall – at least I'd always assumed that was the idea when I saw it being done in films.

Thankfully the flat was empty. I gave Jazz a brief hug and kiss and told her to hurry, then I went out into the corridor to find somewhere from which I could keep an eye on the door to her flat within being visible to anyone approaching her door. There was nowhere. This was not a hotel, so there was no convenient cleaner's cupboard to hide in. However, the floor was tiled rather than carpeted so I reckoned if I hid up the first flight of stairs and listened carefully, I would hear anyone approaching Jazz's door. I was pressed against the wall of the stairwell when my phone began to vibrate. It took me a moment to realise what it was, as I seldom had my phone in silent mode.

"Si there's a bloke just come in who looks exactly like your description of the birdman. Watch out!" Pete was whispering, but there was no mistaking the bad news he was imparting.

What to do? I could hear that he was coming up in the lift! The stairs were straight opposite the lift. Should I retreat up the stairs and see what he was intending to do, or should I confront him? My last confrontation with him had worked well, so I stood opposite the lift waiting for the doors to open. I was going to keep this man right away from the woman I loved.

The lift doors opened, Birdman saw me and instantly pulled something out of his pocket. When I saw what it was my mind went into overdrive. It was a gun. I didn't have time to register anything else about it. The fact that it was a gun was enough, and the fact that it was pointing at me, and that birdman had recognised me.

My mind might have been in overdrive, but I think it was instinct that saved me. I put my head down and leapt off the bottom stair in a sort of rugby tackle except that I was leading with my head, not my arms. I remember zooming across the corridor before my head hit birdman in the stomach and he collapsed in a heap on the floor of the lift. I shook myself, grabbed the gun and lashed him across the head with it, just to make sure he was unconscious. Then I dragged him out of the lift, the lift doors closed and I knocked on Jazz's door shouting, "It's me babe! Come quick we have to get out of here!"

I almost forgot my panic as Jasmine opened the door revealing a beautiful naked body that had clearly just stepped out of the shower. I dragged birdman through the door after me and said, "Quick get dressed babe. I'll just find something to tie this spawn of Satan up."

Jazz began to giggle. It was totally inappropriate, I thought, for her to stand there in all her glorious nakedness with an unconscious villain at her feet giggling at my use of the phrase 'spawn of Satan'. But of course, giggling is what we all do in moments of stress, and this was stress with a capital 'S'. A kiss, a hug of that beautiful naked body – which threatened to turn into much more than a hug – then Jazz was getting dressed and I was securing birdman's legs and ankles with a couple of luggage straps.

We decided to put birdman in the lift and send it to the top floor. He would be found eventually, but we would have time to get away. Then we ran down the stairs to the car with me carrying a holdall Jazz had filled with spare clothes, and with birdman's gun in my pocket.

CHAPTER TWENTY TWO

"That was too bloody close mate!" Pete shouted as we leapt into the car, his worry clearly expressed on his face. "What the fuck happened?"

"I'll tell you in a minute. Just drive, and drive fast Pete. We need to get the hell out of here!"

Whether it was my totally unexpected ability to deal with violence, or the fact that I was handling a gun for the first time in my life, but suddenly I felt in charge. I directed Pete out of Yarm and onto the A67 to Darlington. I hoped that by heading west rather than south, we would be travelling in a direction our pursuers would not think of us taking. Then I filled Pete in on what had happened at the flat, omitting, obviously, all reference to Jazz standing there stark-naked giggling at me.

"You fucking beauty! The nerdy vicar knocked out and tied up one of the most dangerous thugs in London! And you put him in the lift and sent it to the top floor! Give me five man!" and with that he raised his left arm off the steering wheel and presented his open palm for me to slap with mine. As I did so, I felt as if my chest would burst, I was so proud.

Proud or not, however, this was not a time for prolonging confrontations. Our immediate task was to avoid the people who, as well as strangling their enemies, were, I now knew, quite prepared to shoot them. Worries began to assail me. I was worried that birdman might have seen Pete in the car on his way into the flat. I was also worried that two white men, one of whom was extremely large, and a beautiful black woman would present a very obvious target for people watching the motorways leading to London.

My mind went into overdrive and I came up with a plan as we drove past Teesside Airport (the name everyone used despite its name change to Durham Tees Valley). I suggested we should return the car in Darlington, then hire two different cars: one which Pete could drive directly to London on his own using the A1 and M1, the other which Jazz and I could use to drive a very circuitous route to West London. Surely going over to the West Coast and approaching London from the West was a route which they would never think of watching. After a bit of arguing, he thought we would be much safer with his strong-arm presence, Pete agreed. We soon found a branch of the same hire company in Darlington and I returned the Focus. Pete hired a car from the same branch whilst I completed the formalities of returning my car and Jazz sat in reception guarding our bags, about which I was now becoming paranoid. Having a Walther P99 (I had looked to see what type of gun it was!) in your holdall might be OK in the good old US of A, but would not go down too well if we were stopped by the police in the UK!

Pete then took us in the blue Corsa (we'd decided to hire something very different from the Focus) to another car hire firm where I rented a maroon Meriva, just two years old, but already with more than forty thousand miles on the clock. Pete was going to drive straight down to London in the expectation that no one would be looking for one man in a car. He would then go to the computer nerd hideaway and consult with his hackers to see what they had found out about the One Way Group and the whereabouts of Mrs Greenwood. We needed the information from her if we were to have any chance of getting anyone in authority to remove the threat facing us.

I knew Jazz must need to eat so we drove to a McDonald's drive-through and sat in a nearby supermarket car park to eat them. I positioned the car so we had a clear view of anyone coming in and left the engine running so that we could drive off immediately. Poor Jazz was both famished and thirsty, and when I was at the counter, I'd suddenly realised that I also hadn't eaten since breakfast. A quarter-pounder with cheese and a Big Mac had never tasted so good. As soon as we finished our coffees, we set off for Scotch Corner. My idea was to take the A66 over Bowes Moor, then drive through Kirkby Stephen to meet the M6 at Tebay, follow the M6 to the M42, then the M40 into West London. A circuitous route, but the timing should mean we would miss the rush hour round Birmingham and get into London between ten and eleven o'clock; and even more importantly we should avoid our pursuers.

As we climbed over the Pennines across the bleak Bowes Moor, Jazz switched on the radio and began to search for a news programme. It was strange to be driving on a dual-carriageway in such a desolate spot. It felt so high that we were on top of the world with the snow poles at the edge of the road reminding us that this was one of the most frequently closed major roads in England. We were passing the Bowes Moor Hotel, which picks up much of its winter trade from travellers abandoning their cars in the snow, when Jazz eventually homed in on Radio Five Live which was broadcasting news rather than sport.

The first report was from the religious affairs correspondent talking about an interview given by the Bishop of Ripon and Leeds to The Evening Standard today in which he spoke about the need for Britain to 'wake up to the dangers of moral relativism and re-engage with the spiritual and moral certainties which had made Britain great'. Apparently, he then went on to criticise abortion as 'an affront to the sanctity of life: life which is given by God and is not to be taken lightly by man'. He had also criticised the recent legalisation of gay marriage as 'another nail in the coffin of marriage which is the foundation of family life and therefore of society'. The correspondent mentioned that the Bishop is a strong supporter of the One Way Group and expressed the opinion that his interview was likely to be connected with the campaign the Group is waging to influence government policy in these areas.

"What a conniving, devious hypocrite," I exploded.

"I'm not likely to argue with that view, babe," replied Jazz. "Isn't he your bishop?"

"Well he was, babe, when I was a vicar in his diocese. Now he's just another bigoted religious hypocrite," I couldn't hold back and I didn't need to with Jazz, unlike sanctimonious Sarah. "Sanctity of life my arse! You know he supported the war in Iraq? There's the bloody, blatant hypocrisy. How can it be wrong to take the life of an unborn foetus, which isn't really a life because it can't survive outside the womb, but it isn't wrong to take the lives of people in wars? And if marriage is the foundation of society, isn't it better for gays to be married?"

"OK babe. Calm down. You're talking to the converted here. I agree with you. Is he really as much of a plonker as he sounds?"

"Oh babe! He's a total pillock. I can just about put up with the Eton and Oxford arrogance. I mean they can't help that can they? But to go on about Christian principles when you're living a totally privileged life with a family trust fund giving you complete financial security, that gets right up my nose."

"Shut up a minute," said Jazz. "What's this?"

Another news item had come onto the radio. Apparently, Sir Henry Smythe and Jemimah Percy-Gilbert were leading a group of Tory MPs in a campaign among Tory MPs for there to be a vote of no confidence in the Prime Minister for concealing his gay past and his relationship with the President of the European Commission.

"Didn't we see those two at the Old Deanery?" Jazz enquired.

"Indeed, we did. They were at that meeting with the Bishop, Tim Harris and George Blenkinsop."

"And isn't George Blenkinsop the Chair of the 1922 Committee who's going to be organising this vote of no confidence?" she continued.

"He is my darling, and not just that, he's also the ex-Chair of the North Yorkshire Police Authority. The man who could be responsible for Inspector Byrom's activities," I concluded.

"You're joking! This has to mean there's a connection between Mark's murder and these renegade Tories, doesn't it?"

"It does indeed babe, and lurking behind it all is the Reverend Samuel Watkinson and his nefarious friends like the birdman who go around pointing guns at people. People like you and me!"

We both descended into a stunned silence as I drove through Kirkby Stephen, under the Settle-Carlisle railway line and up onto the bleak, desolate moorland separating Kirkby Stephen from Tebay. We were roused from our daze by another news story coming out of the radio: "It has just been announced that the Reverend Tim Harris and other leaders from the One Way Group will be addressing a rally at the O2 Arena. Up to 20,000 One Way supporters are expected to be there, and the Group issued a statement this afternoon stating that Tim Harris will be outlining his vision of how to make Britain great once again. This statement was immediately denounced by several groups dedicated to community cohesion claiming that the Group is promoting religious divisions in the UK."

We turned onto the M6 and I saw that it was only fifteen miles to the services at Killington Lake. I thought we needed to stop and discuss what we'd heard on the radio without me concentrating on driving safely in the M6 traffic. Jazz agreed and ten minutes later we were sitting drinking a cup of Costa looking across at the beautiful lake which makes this one of the most attractive motorway services in the country.

"I'll tell you what babe," Jazz said with a rather puzzled expression on her face. "If they're having a rally at the O2 Arena, it must have been planned a long time ago."

"Yes," I agreed hesitantly, wondering where she was going with this.

"So, it must all have been on the cards well before that meeting in Ripon and therefore well before Mark's murder."

"Yeah.." I replied even more hesitantly still not knowing where she was going with this.

"And it must surely be connected with this scheme to get the Government supporting One Way."

"Yes..." I still had no idea what Jazz was getting at.

"Well babe, I reckon the rally and the scheme are all connected and all part of a long-term plan for the One Way Group to become political and join with GBnot EU and these right-wing Tories to try to run the country or something. And I think Mark found something out which posed some sort of threat to all their plans."

Light began to dawn. "So, you think Mark was murdered because he found something out that might have ruined the One Way Group's big plans?" I asked, wondering yet again what had made someone as bright, as well as attractive, as Jazz give someone like me a second chance.

"That's right babe; and I'm sure Mark discovered something that was so big, it threatened the whole scheme."

"What do you think this scheme actually is?" I queried, feeling totally dense for not having been able to work any of this out for myself.

"We already know that they're planning to get rid of the Prime Minister, otherwise there wouldn't be so many Tory MPs involved. I would reckon that the rally tonight is going to be about restoring traditional values in the UK and no doubt there'll be Charles Matthews and a lot of his anti-EU supporters their waving their Union Jacks. Don't forget that the GBnot EU supporters come from white backward-looking areas who are likely to see British values and Christian values as the same thing. I reckon either Samuel Watkinson or Charles Matthews knew all about the Prime Minister's affair with Schmidt and they timed releasing it to the press so that the Reverend Tim could use this O2 shindig to make some sort of case for Christians supporting the right-wing Tories and Matthews' anti-EU group to get rid of the Prime Minster and form some sort of Values Party in time for the general election."

"I don't suppose they'd want anyone to get in the way of that, babe," I surmised and then expressed the feelings that had taken me into holy orders all those years ago. "But I can't see how Christians can behave like this. Jesus taught about love and kindness and honesty. These are supposed to be Christian people, but there's so much hate in them, and a total lack of both kindness and honesty. No doubt it was dealing with people like them that's made it feel so good to have left the Church, even though we've been in nothing but trouble since I told the bishop what to do with the job!"

We then discussed how to get out of the deep shit-hole we were in. It was becoming more and more obvious that these people were far too powerful for us just to pop into the nearest police station and accuse them of murder. After all, who could we accuse? We knew 'they' had organised it. We knew Inspector Byrom had to have done some illegal things to swap the bodies, but there were now no bodies to prove that!

However, we both reckoned that if once we knew what the threat was that Mark Greenwood had posed, we would have some evidence we could use to get ourselves out of the insufferable mess we were in.
Jazz finished her coffee and announced, "Right babe. I'll drive from here. You can sit back and relax. Or better still sit back and think of how we can use whatever information we get from Mark's mother to get rid of these people who are ruining out lives!"

I knew better than to argue with this wonderful woman who was not just the equal of any man, she was far better than any man! So, when we left the services I went to the passenger door and settled myself in the passenger seat to think. My first thought was that whatever evidence we came up with was unlikely to be sufficient to convince the CPS, and without that level of proof any approach to the police would simply get us into more trouble. The reason being that to approach the police, we would have to come out of hiding and as soon as the plotters knew where we were, they would try to get rid of us.

The next thing I knew we were pulling into a Road Chef services, where it was, I had no idea as I did not often travel down the M6.

"Hi babe. Feel better for that snooze?" asked Jazz with a grin. That beautiful, slightly husky voice was definitely what I wanted to wake up to every day for the rest of my life.

"Wow! I must have nodded off," I yawned. "Where are we? How long have I been asleep?"

"Quite a while, babe. All that hard work digging holes for BT must have taken it out of you," she joked. "Or more likely it was carrying me across the gardens. I know I need to lose some weight!"

That made me fully awake. I quickly answered, "It must have been the BT work because you certainly don't need to lose any weight babe. You are perfect. I love you just the way you are."

"What a sleaze bag," exclaimed Jazz, "and it's not even an original piece of flattery! I think it's from a song was written by Billy Joel a long time ago, like 1977. 'Just the Way You Are' it was called and reached number 3."

"How on earth did you know all that? Don't tell me you're a pub quiz groupie! If you are we'll have to end our relationship. I hate pub quizzes," I joked. It felt good to laugh again after all that tension.

"No. My Mum loved Billy Joel and she bought me the single for my birthday in 1977. You always remember your first single."

I didn't argue, but I had no idea what my first single was. Indeed, I wasn't at all sure that I had ever bought singles. Maybe I was always a geek and just bought classical. I could certainly remember buying my first LP, Rachmaninov's second piano concerto with Vladimir Ashkenazy. Maybe I needed to keep that quiet!

Of course, this conversation was just an attempt to lighten the atmosphere of tension and threat which had enveloped us ever since the death of Alastair at St. Machar's Cathedral. Jazz had stopped at Stafford Services (the Road Chef I woke up in!) so we could decide whether to go on the M6 toll or straight down the old motorway.

Although it was after seven thirty, I thought we'd be better off on the toll than going virtually through the centre of Birmingham. We swapped seats and Jazz used her i-phone to check what and how you had to pay before we reached the toll. I tossed six pounds in and we were away.

CHAPTER TWENTY THREE

Pete's straightforward route and the smart motorway round the edge of Luton meant he arrived in London by seven o'clock. He drove to his favourite McDonalds for a Big Mac with large fries, checked in at the shop and identified the watchers he'd been told were there. Then he drove over to the secret hideaway, an under the arches lock-up in Wembley, part of the viaduct carrying the main line from Euston to Watford Junction. Pete knew from the even more sophisticated surveillance equipment they had there, that there were no watchers. He put the car in the next-door lock-up which they had hired so that no one would notice what activities were going on. He then knocked on the small door fitted into the large doors of the lock-up and was let in by a small man in his early forties. Although no more than five feet tall, he was squat, well-made and extremely muscley, not a small man to be pushed around.

"Hello, you pile of lazy tossers!" Pete shouted into the cavernous room.

"Hello you wanker!" came the reply from half a dozen men and women in their late thirties, early forties.

The room was filled with monitors, terminals, servers and other computer paraphernalia. It was a hacker's paradise with all the equipment needed for some serious hacking work. It was in fact the headquarters of a group (which was very difficult to track down, and even more difficult to join) which called itself North London IT Research Group, known to its members as Hackers United.

"And welcome back to all of you," Pete commented." That was such a charming way to welcome me back from my trip to the frozen North!"

This comment received even more raucous replies as many of the hackers were ex-pats from the North forced to come to the South East to earn a decent living. They were, of course, well aware that the North was not frozen, and was, in fact, often much warmer than the South East. Pete was also well aware of this, but knew he needed to start off with some harmless banter to put all these geeks at ease. They all knew they were geeks in the eyes of the world, but, although the geekiness was genetic, part of being a super-brain for most of them, they liked to be treated as normal members of society, especially as people with a sense of humour and a non-serious take on life.

Pete then got down to business. He wanted to know: what they had found out about the One Way Group; what they had found out about the Reverend Samuel Watkinson; and what they had found out about Mrs Greenwood.

He went over to a group of three sitting at a set of connected monitors. One was an earnest looking woman in her early forties whose mousey hair was pulled back into a bun which only served to highlight her very plain looks; looks whose plainness was slightly alleviated by the large thick black glasses she was wearing. The other two were men in their forties with hair far longer than suited men whose hair was thinning fast. They had discarded their anoraks and were sitting in jeans and message T-shirts one of which read, 'Thank God I'm an atheist', the other, 'I'm with this idiot' with an arrow pointing to his friend.

The woman acted as spokesperson for the group, and she began, "Well Pete we've discovered a couple of things about the One Way Group that you might be interested in. Firstly, this Tim Harris just suddenly appears in 1985, we can find no record of him before then, not even a birth record. Secondly, the Group's financial base is strong, but the original finance, that paid for the advertising campaign that made it so strong, came from a front company which, after a lot of searching, we discovered was set up by Watbros, the family bank of Samuel Watkinson."

Pete now went over to a similar size group, but rather younger, early thirties rather than early forties. They looked much less geeky perhaps because they were three women and only one man. They also had a woman spokesperson who looked as if she had walked out of a Next catalogue, very svelte, and very attractive.

"Well Pete," she began. "This Samuel Watkinson comes from a very rich and very old family, his father was the eleventh Earl of Dawlish. After Eton and Oxford, where he was active and prominent in the Conservative Association, Samuel was pushed into the Church. Apparently, eldest son into the army, youngest into the Church had been the Dawlish tradition for generations. Samuel's elder brother went into the Guards."

"Yeah, yeah. We know all this," Pete moaned at her.

The woman frowned at this, but continued, "About ten years into his career as a clergyman being prepared for great things, his father died, and his brother's armoured vehicle was destroyed by an improvised explosive device in Iraq. Samuel became the head of the family fortune and gave up all his clerical duties, but not his holy orders. It seems that Samuel is a very wealthy man, we've discovered investments totalling at least ten million pounds and he has fingers in many financial pies apart from his stake in the family bank. Samuel is a major financial backer of the One Way Group and a substantial donor to the Conservative Party with several friends among the more right-wing members of the 1922 Committee. Perhaps even more interesting is that he owns a security company. It was very difficult to ascertain its ownership but it seems to have several ex-cons on its payroll."

"Bloody hell Pam, we know all this shit," Pete expostulated. "Haven't you found out anything new?"

Pam's response to this criticism was a triumphant look as she announced," Samuel is also a non-executive director of 'Where It's At' magazine and his family bank provided the initial funding for the magazine. We've also discovered that Samuel is the executor of the blind trust set up to look after Jemimah Percy-Gilbert's assets when she became a government minister. His most recent recorded activity was to renounce his holy orders and take up his late father's peerage. Samuel has very recently been elected to a vacant hereditary peerage place in the House of Lords (of course nothing to do with his contributions to the Conservative Party!) and rumours are circulating that he may be offered a cabinet post."

Wow, thought Pete as he assimilated this information. Despite his cajoling of them, his friends had discovered quite a bit of new, and intriguing, information. Pete rapidly worked out that they now knew that: Tim Harris had no history before 1985; without Samuel Watkinson's money there would have been no One Way Group and no 'Where It's At' magazine; Samuel was also closely connected with Jemimah Percy-Gilbert, and, most intriguingly of all, was a voting member of the House of Lords.

"Fucking hell," said Pete. "And yes, I know, I hope they do. But what you've found out fills in a lot of bleeding gaps. Well bloody done Pam!"

The final group was a larger group, six members, and much more diverse in terms of age, ethnicity and geekiness. Their spokesperson was a handsome black man in his late twenties. He was dressed in a Nike sweatshirt and jeans with a pattern running down the outside seam of one leg. He did not look at all like a computer nerd, but his group had discovered some very worrying information about Mrs Greenwood. "We've discovered her address in Isleworth, but our equipment is so top of the range, it tells us if anyone else is trying to hack into the same info, and it's picked up some other hackers searching for a Mrs Greenwood in West London. Some of us have been working at trying to trace them and we've just linked them to a security firm called Safe and Sound."

"Bugger, bugger and buggeration," shouted Pete. "That's one of Watkinson's companies. Do you think they found her address yet?"

The man in the Nike sweatshirt looked round his group. A plump young woman with frizzy ginger hair shouted, "Here Pete. I've been tracking them and they've just made the same hit we did. They found her address just this minute!"

*   *   *   *   *

As we passed under the M25 and onto the A40, Jazz rang Pete for an update. It was a brief update which only consisted of Pete giving us an address in Isleworth and telling us to get to it as quickly as we could. He was on his way, but if we got there first, we had to put Mrs Greenwood in our car and get her out of the area because 'they' – that was how he defined the plotters – were onto her.

Jazz was a West London girl and when Pete mentioned Linkfield Road, Isleworth she immediately said, "O.K. Simon take the next slip road, it's the Greenford Roundabout. Now turn right onto Greenford Road. This time of night we'll be in Linkfield Road in twenty minutes."

Sure, enough the road was pretty empty as we took a lonely drive past Osterley Park, onto Syon Lane and suddenly we were in Isleworth going past the huge West Middlesex Hospital. "Slowly now babe, it's on the right. There it is, Linkfield Road."

I turned right and drove slowly down the road looking for the number Pete had given us.

"Oh shit! Oh shit!" we both yelled together as we saw a lady being bundled out of our target house into a waiting black Audi A4 estate. She didn't look as old as I'd expected, but then my own mother would only have been seventy if she'd still been alive.

I wasn't sure what to do, but I instinctively slowed down. Jazz was far quicker on the uptake and was immediately on the phone to Pete. "Where are you Pete?" she shouted. "They've just bundled Mrs

Greenwood into a black Audi estate. They're driving down Linkfield Road towards Isleworth station. Where are you?"

I assumed I needed to follow the Audi and accelerated as it sped off with a squeal of tyres and the smell of burning rubber. It was a lot faster than our beaten up Meriva and I knew we were going to be left behind as soon as they got onto an open road.

"They're turning right Pete, heading into London," Jazz shouted. She was impressive, anyone would think she'd been organising car chases all her life. And how did she have this encyclopaedic knowledge of West London roads? "If you're on the Great West Road come off it. I think they're going to drive through Brentford and onto the North Circular. If you come down Kew Bridge Road, you should meet them somewhere around Brentford High Street."

I was trying my best but the Audi was pulling away all the time and was soon out of sight, but Jasmine was still on the case. "There should be some parked cars on the High Street," she continued to Pete, "if you crash into the Audi, it will bang into a parked car and be unable to drive. We'll be there in a couple of secs and get Mrs Greenwood out and away. You just pretend to be a shocked and horrified motorist."

I was coming through some traffic lights beside a Holiday Inn when I heard an almighty bang and then the sound of rending metal. I kept going and just round a corner saw the Audi slewed across the road. Its front end was crumpled, the huge bumper was hanging off, connected to the car only by its remote parking electrics, its nearside was dented and scraped where it appeared to have banged into the side of a parked white van. The Focus didn't seem too badly damaged, but Pete was out of the car shouting and gesticulating as if it had all been the other driver's fault.

I'd seen Jazz out of the corner of my eye, fumbling in the holdall as I drove along. As soon as I stopped alongside the Audi, she handed me the gun and shouted, "Quick you use this to threaten them to let her out. Then jump in the back with her and I'll drive off!"

I took the gun and jumped out like someone in a James Bond movie, pulled open the rear passenger door of the Audi and brandished the gun at the guy facing me. I didn't know whether it was loaded and anyway the safety catch was probably on, but of course the guy in front of me had just been crashed into and was now facing a Walther P99: he was in no condition to discern the finer points of the gun I was waving at him. I gestured to him to get out and he staggered into the road making it easy for me to pull a frightened Mrs Greenwood out of the Audi and across the road into our Meriva.

I'd hardly got the door closed before Jazz hit the gas and we were off onto the North Circular just as blue lights and sirens were starting to appear.

"It's OK," I said re-assuringly to the frightened lady sitting next to me. "I'm Simon Keep, I'm an ex-vicar and I was at King's with your son Mark."

"And I'm Jasmine Baker," piped up a voice from the front seat. "I was a friend of Mark's at King's. We were doing the same degree."

"Wh...wh...what's happening," stammered Mrs Greenwood in a tremulous voice which, combined with the quivering I could feel from her body, revealed how terrified she was. "Those men came to the door. They asked me if I was Mark's mother and when I said I was, they grabbed me, bundled me into that big car and set off at great speed. I kept asking what they wanted and why they were taking me, but they just told me to shut up. Then we crashed into another car, then you came and grabbed me. Are you going to tell me what it's all about?" and with these words she began to sob.

I put my arm round her and, using my practised, comforting vicar voice, tried to explain and console at the same time. That would have been a difficult enough job if it was just the kidnapping and crash to explain, but I also had to break the news that her son was dead.

"I'm sorry we had to grab you like that," I began. "Those people who tried to kidnap you are extremely violent and evil men. They were not going to treat you very nicely. They think you have some information that could threaten their evil scheme."

I turned to her so that I could look into her eyes as I broke the tragic news about her son. "Did Mark tell you what he was investigating?"

Experience of breaking bad news told me that the expression on her face meant that Mrs Greenwood had guessed from the way I was speaking that I had bad news about Mark, and that she did indeed know something of his investigation.

"What's happened to him? It's bad isn't it?" A few tears began to trickle down her cheeks as she asked.

"I'm sorry Mrs Greenwood. As you've probably guessed, Mark's dead."

The sobs became convulsive, but she managed to ask, "How? How did he die?"

I gave her another hug as I broke the news, "He was murdered Mrs Greenwood, most probably by those very same men who just tried to kidnap you."

"Murdered! Oh God. I warned him when he told me what he was researching. I told him that religious people are much more dangerous than they appear. What about his friend. No don't be silly Pat, he wasn't just his friend, he was the love of his life. They were going to get married you know. What about Michael?"

"I'm sorry Mrs Greenwood. Pat did you say your name is? I think we're beyond formalities. I'm sorry to have to tell you, but Michael was also murdered. Whatever they'd found out, these people wanted to make sure it died with them. We think that's why they wanted you. They think Mark told you something and they wanted to make sure you didn't pass it on."
By this time, we were so far along the North Circular that we were almost passing the Wembley Arch and Jazz asked, "Where should I be going Pat? I think we need to take you somewhere where you'll

be safe from these people. Have you got any friends who wouldn't be known in West London?"

"Well there's my sister in Enfield."

"No!" Jazz and I said in unison. I let Jazz explain, "They'd trace her straight away. In fact, it's probably a good idea for you to phone her and advise her to go away to friends. You need to go somewhere that wouldn't be obvious to anyone trying to trace you, so no relatives."

Eventually Pat came up with the name of an old school friend living in North Finchley. Luckily Pat had had her mobile in her trouser pocket and so was able to phone her friend. Even more fortuitously, her friend was still up and ten minutes later we were depositing Pat at her friend's and explaining the whole saga over a cup of tea and some very welcome HobNobs. Of course, it was not the whole saga that we explained. We wanted to keep Pat's friend out of the political implications. Nevertheless, recounting things certainly brought us up sharp with the magnitude of what we were facing.

Before we left to find somewhere to stay, we managed to get Pat on her own and ask her what her son had said to her before he left for Ripon and she replied, "He said that if anything happened to him I was to tell anyone investigating that it was not Tim Harris but Paul Connor."

CHAPTER TWENTY FOUR

After some furious searching on our laptops for a hotel with a room that would take us at this time of night, we eventually booked in to the Premier Inn, Bricket Wood. Classified as St Albans it was down a narrow country lane south of the M25 by less than 50 metres. It was very difficult to find in the dark, and, even at nearly midsummer, it is still dark in the South of the UK at midnight. Once more we signed in as Mr and Mrs Turner using the card provided by Pete hoping it was still keeping us off the radar of the plotters.

Whilst Jazz went for a bath, I switched on the TV and found one of the 24-hour news channel provided by Freeview. I was relieved to find nothing about a car crash in Brentford. That must mean that Pete had not become involved in a fight with the people in the black

Audi. However, just as I had expected, there was considerable coverage of the One Way Group event at the O2. At first the event went just as I'd expected: lots of born again stuff from Tim Harris; an horrific condemnation of any form of abortion with photos of foetuses appearing on the huge screens; a sickening condemnation of same sex marriage which revealed a disturbingly anti-gay prejudice; and then came something totally unexpected.

I shouted to Jazz to come out quickly to see what was on. She came out wrapping a towel round herself in such a provocative way that I almost forgot about One Way and the O2. There on stage next to Tim Harris was Samuel Watkinson and Jazz was just in time for the announcement, "Brothers and sisters in Christ. I want to introduce to you one of the finest Christians I know. The man whose vision and philanthropy made it possible for the One Way Group to get started – the Reverend Samuel Watkinson."

Samuel stepped forward and the backing band began to play 'Amazing Grace'. All twenty thousand in the audience (though no doubt they thought of themselves as the congregation) joined in the hymn, after all every one of them believed that amazing grace had found them and brought them out of their sin. The news bulletin then cut to Watkinson speaking, "Dear friends, what a heart-warming experience we have had here tonight, and I can promise you even better things to come for this green and pleasant land of ours. Tomorrow I shall take up the seat in the House of Lords to which I have been elected and lead our One Way campaign to turn our British Parliament back into a Christian Parliament which will reject the killing of unborn infants (there were choruses of 'Alleluia' and 'Praise the Lord' when he said this), which will reject the abomination of euthanasia, which will reject the legalising of same sex marriage in contravention of God's laws (there was a crescendo of 'Alleluias' at this)"
The news broadcast cut from the O2 back to the studio where a variety of political analysts and religious affairs journalists began to discuss the political and religious implications of the event. Jazz looked at me, I looked at her and we both said, "What the hell is that all about?" Then the bath towel fell off and more important matters interrupted our religio-political discussion.

We were woken early the next morning by my mobile ringing. "Hello," I mumbled groggily, trying to concentrate whilst Jazz giggled beside me as she caressed me rather intimately. Despite Jazz's attentions, I managed to sit up and give the phone my full attention. "Pete? Where are you? What happened?"

"Hi Si! How did it go with you two last night?" Pete asked with no attempt to answer my questions.

As soon as she realised it was Pete on the phone, Jazz sat up and leant her head on my shoulder so she could hear the conversation. "Hi Pete," she shouted in the direction of my phone. "Where are you? What happened to you last night?"

Obviously, Jazz had more influence than I had because Pete answered her questions immediately. "It was no problem. As soon as they heard the police sirens, the three of them scarpered, one of them limping very badly. Then it was just me and the police. Turns out the Audi was stolen, so the police believed me when I said they had hit the van and then bounced across the road and hit me. I was exonerated. I phoned the car hire firm, they spoke to the police and all is hunky dory. What happened with you?"

"We're OK, but we need to meet," I replied. "How about breakfast in St Albans?"

"Pardon?"

"You heard me Pete. We're in a hotel in the middle of nowhere that calls itself St Albans, but is about 5 miles nearer London. It's not far from North London and by the time you get here we'll be showered and dressed and ready for a breakfast meeting."

I gave Pete directions to reach the hotel and switched on the TV whilst Jazz showered. The news was full of the O2 rally and Lord Dawlish's announcement (he was no longer being referred to as the Rev Samuel Watkinson). There was also a small item which claimed that Jemimah Percy-Gilbert was being named by senior Tory MPs as the most likely successor to the PM should the vote show that he had lost the confidence of Tory MPs. Thinking of Watkinson made me think of the Birdman and I shuddered as his hate-filled face when he saw me on the stairs came into my mind. I wondered who had found him in the lift and how he had explained his being there tied up with luggage straps. More worryingly I thought about him finding out we were in the London area and coming to find us.

These macabre thoughts were banished, however, when we walked out of the hotel. The exterior of the hotel in the daylight was a revelation. We really were in the country, yet right next to the M25. In fact, as we walked across to the restaurant, we had to dodge the ducks waddling over from the small river. There was also a pond with a bridge and viewing area to watch the variety of waterfowl swimming on the water and patrolling the banks. The restaurant itself was in an old watermill and opening the door, we were greeted by a few strange sounds: the creaking of a wheel, the slap of paddles as they were hit by the running water, and above all the turning cogs giving a sort of hum that filled the building. We walked past the glass screens protecting guests from the splashing water and walked up the stairs following the heady aroma of grilling bacon to the dining area set out with the breakfast buffet.

As food was on offer, Pete had beaten us to the dining area and was already sitting at a table digging into a massive plate of bacon, sausages, beans, hash browns and three poached eggs. He signalled us to sit beside him and spluttered a greeting through his latest mouthful. We greeted him back and organised a more modest repast, though the night's amorous exertions had made us both very hungry.

When we got to the toast and marmalade part of breakfast, Pete went and got each of us a fresh mug of coffee, put them in front of us and then pulled a sheaf of newspapers from the capacious inside pocket of the waxed Barbour jacket he wore for every season apart from heatwaves. He opened them out on the table one by one and the headlines told the story. The One Way Group was front page news and its campaign to bring honesty, integrity and old-fashioned Christian values back to British life was receiving the full support of every paper except 'The Guardian', 'The Independent' and 'The Mirror', but how many voters did these papers represent?

Well they certainly represented Jazz who immediately said, "Bloody Tory chauvinist press," I was beginning to realise that male chauvinism was the blue touchpaper for Jazz's anger. "Did you notice they were all men leading that O2 event last night. At least American evangelists always have their botoxed wives with them!"

"I think their male chauvinism is the least of our worries," said Pete. "Just take a butchers at this," and he produced a glossy magazine from his outside pocket. "The bloody buggers are attacking on all bloody fronts."

The magazine was the latest edition of 'Where It's At' and it was hot off the press. I'd expected it to have a photo of Tim Harris, or Samuel Watkinson on the front cover, but no it was the Deputy Prime Minister, Chris Foster, and two of the Remainer members of the cabinet sitting with half a dozen Arab Muslims dressed in what is generally seen as Saudi-Arabian princes' uniform – white thawb with white keffiyah held on the head by two black headbands. The headline read 'Where's the Money Chris?'

"Oh God! What have they allowed themselves to be tricked into this time?" asked Jazz.
"I don 't know why they can't tell the bloody difference between sodding actors and real bloody Arabs, or why they don't just say, 'bugger off' when people try to get them to talk about things they shouldn't bloody well be talking about in the first place," Pete replied.

"Anyway, it seems the Remainers don't have the financial backing the Brexiteers have since they're not really a group and have no special policies except to keep leaving the EU as painless as possible for the economy. Anyway, they agreed to meet the Saudi princes who are the owners of a British High Street Bank to get funding by the Bank, which would be perfectly legal because the bank is based in Britain and pays British taxes. But of course, they weren't Saudi princes, they'd been hired by sodding Henry Smythe's bloody journalists and the whole interview was videoed and now it's in this bloody excuse for a news magazine."

Jazz realised the ramifications of all of this long before I did. "S'truth Pete. This is going to be curtains for the PM isn't it? Stuart Fairhurst is bound to lose the confidence vote now which means the Tories will start supporting One Way. So however you look at it, this means the PM is doomed, and that the forthcoming election is going to be fought on One Way's terms."

"Right in bloody one, Jasmine," answered Pete.

I struggled to comprehend all of this and sipped my coffee to let it all sink in. Then, when I'd grasped the enormity of it all, I spoke up, "Hell's teeth! It's one huge, ginormous conspiracy isn't it? And one they'd started planning a long time ago. Booking the O2 and planning the entrapment of the liberal Tories must have taken ages. But OK, they want rid of the PM and they want an election fought on One Way policies to get a 'Christian' – with massive inverted commas round the Christian – government, fair enough but where on earth does Mark's murder fit into it all?"

Jazz is a woman with a mind, a very good mind, and she was onto it before either Pete or me.

"Mark must have found something out," she exclaimed. "Something which put their complex scheme in jeopardy. Perhaps he'd found out about the meeting in Ripon – all the leading lights were there – and gate-crashed it to announce what he'd found out. And what he'd found out was such a threat that he had to be removed so that the plot could still go ahead."

Jazz's ideas sparked off my own thoughts, so I chimed in with, "Of course, his message to his mother; that's what he'd found out. What was it he told her? 'Not Tim Harris but Paul Connor.' What do you think that means?"

Pete was first to reply, "I don't know what it means except that I've got to get every bleeding hacker I know trying to find out anything they bloody well can about this Paul Connor prick."

Jazz suddenly burst out laughing and it was some time before she calmed down sufficiently to be able to explain to us. It was all down to Pete's over colourful use of language. Apparently, she had misheard Pete and thought the hackers would have to search for Paul Connor's prick! Of course, this sent me into fits of laughter as well, but Pete remained totally sober-sided, clearly somewhat embarrassed by the effects of his swearing.

Jazz's mishearing not only lightened the mood, it also had a cathartic effect on Jazz's thought processes as she suddenly shouted, "Got it! Didn't you say you and your friends were finding it difficult to discover anything about the early life of Tim Harris, Pete?"

"Yeah," Pete replied. "They came to a bloody dead end. Nothing at all about the bugger before 1985! Why?"

"Well what if he didn't exist before 1985? What if before 1985 Tim Harris was actually Paul Connor?" Jazz asked, with a look on her face like a vicar who finds fifty youngsters turned up for his confirmation class.

I was still a bit slow on the uptake and asked, "What do you mean babe?"

"What I mean is this. What if Paul Connor changed his name to Tim Harris in 1985? If he did it by deed poll, there'd be no trace of Tim Harris before 1985."

"But why would he do that?" I asked.

"That my darling is what we have to find out, because it was probably finding that out that cost Mark his life!"

CHAPTER TWENTY FIVE

Pete suggested that we start by going to the North London IT Research Group where we'd have access to a computer each and a range of search engines. He reckoned it would most likely be empty as the hackers had jobs and so did their research in the evenings and at weekends.

As we followed Pete through Radlett and Elstree, then onto the A409 to Wembley, we listened to news and interviews on Radio 5.

Two other stories were given prominence and linked to the headline news. The lead story was of course about the article in "Where It's At" magazine and its amazing effect. Apparently, Chris Foster, the Remain supporting Minister of Transport had resigned stating in his resignation letter to the Prime Minister that the allegation in magazine was completely untrue and that although he would be suing the magazine's owners for libel and defamation of character, the process would far be too damaging for if he tried to carry on in government whilst trying to clear his name.

This was followed by much comment from political editors and pundits on the possible effects of the Remainers losing confidence just as the Conservative MPs were about to vote on the PM's leadership.

Then there was an account of an interview given earlier by the Tory Minister of Education who had apparently had a change of mind about the core curriculum and decided that GCSE Religious Studies would definitely count as part of the EBacc. He was claiming to have been misinformed by his civil servants about the nature of the current GCSE, but the people phoning in were not taken in by this and believed he was re-positioning himself to curry favour with the

One Way Group in preparation for the Prime Minister losing the confidence vote.

The last news we heard was an interview with, as they announced him, the Right Reverend James Scott-Philips, Bishop of Ripon and Leeds. Dear old Lord Jim kept it simple – what else could he do – and related the fact of 'broken Britain' to the loss of Christian values in our society. Jim claimed that what Britain needed was not more politics, or a change of government, but a return to old-fashioned values, the love of neighbour which had been at the heart of our society in the middle of the last century (I was quite surprised to hear that Jim actually realised we had moved into a new century!). A time when ordinary people could rely on each other rather than relying on the state as they do now. I was quite surprised that Jim managed to cope quite well with the interviewer who did ask him some more searching questions, but then if you set out to be simple, you reduce the amount of challenges.

Jazz and I were both somewhat taken aback as we followed Pete into some tatty lock-ups under the railway viaduct at Wembley. I supposed we'd expected something a bit more grandiose. The nerve centre of 'Hackers United' was empty and Pete soon had the three of us sitting at terminals to see what we could find out about Tim Harris and Paul Connor.

Jazz got us off to an inauspicious start when she shouted, "Great everyone, listen to this. I'm on the website of the UK Deed Poll Service and this is what they say about searching for someone's original name: 'Searching for someone's Deed Poll is like looking for the proverbial needle in a haystack. This is because there is no central register of all name changes by Deed Poll. Furthermore, in addition to ourselves, a Deed Poll can be prepared by any of the many thousands of solicitors throughout England and Wales. Even if you discovered who prepared your relative's Deed Poll, client confidentiality prevents the disclosing of any information about the Deed Poll'."

"Bloody typical!" I exclaimed, my heart sinking at this information." One step forward two steps back. How the hell are we going to get the evidence we need if you can't find out about deed polls? Where do we go now?"

"Oi mate!" Pete interjected." No slipping back into that bloody slough of despond you used to love being stuck in. That might be a website, but it doesn't mean they bleeding well know about the bloody web. We don't bloody well start with the sodding deed poll, we start with this tosser Paul Connor and see what we can find about him."

Jazz was silent. I looked over and saw that she was deep in thought. Then she spoke, "Mark gave us a clue from the grave. We don't need to go searching the internet. If Mark knew this Paul Connor from before 1985, then Paul Connor is probably connected with Mark's student days in London, and if we find someone from that same scene, they might be able to help us find the link. And actually, we already know someone don't we Simon?"

"Andy Rogers!" I blurted out. "Of course! If he remembers this Paul Connor guy, it might lead us to what Mark had discovered."

Pete was looking puzzled, so I explained to him about Andy and how he'd found the photo for Jazz which had enabled us to identify Mark as the murder victim. We were just deciding what Pete should do whilst we went to Brockley to find Andy when we heard a key in the lock and the door opened. In came two guys in their forties with hair far longer than suited men whose hair was thinning fast. They were both wearing the same message T-shirt with a large number 11 underneath which was written, 'Thou shalt not annoy'.

"Hi you buggers," shouted Pete. "Just the two tossers we need. We've got to find a link between Tim Harris and someone called Paul Connor. Are you up for it, after all you've been researching Harris's One Way Group?"

Of course, they were up for it, so Jazz and I set off for Brockley. Not an easy drive from Wembley, but Jazz took the wheel and made light work of driving through Willesden, Paddington and Euston. We took the Waterloo Bridge over the Thames, then the Old Kent Road to

New Cross and on to Brockley. They say North Londoners are never happy south of the river and I always feel a bit disoriented when I go south of the Thames, but Jazz had no problems, and so we were soon knocking on the door of one of the large Victorian houses in Arica Road.

The door was opened by a man of about my age who had clearly modelled his persona on Mr Humphreys from 'Are You Being Served'. His dark pink trousers were figure hugging; his bright pink shirt was double cuffed, but the cuff had a rather bold paisley pattern to contrast with the plain pink of the shirt; his hair was too blond not to be out of a bottle and was coiffed into a bouffant style. My Dad would have called him 'as camp as Christmas', a term I'd never really understood as Christmas had never struck me as a particularly effeminate festival.

"We're looking for Andy Rogers," I said. "Does he live here?"

"He does indeed sweetie," he replied and then shouted, "Andy there's a man and a divinely beautiful woman here for you. Shall I bring them in?" He swung round to face back down the hall, his lower arm swinging out with his hand drooping limply from the wrist and a familiar face came into view. It was Andy, still incredibly handsome, still looking as straight as they come in his jeans, pale blue Ralph Lauren Oxford shirt and a pair of white Reebok trainers.

"My God! Is that you Si? And Jasmine? Wow! What a surprise! Where are your manners Jonathan? Bring them in!"

Jonathan minced ahead of us into a light and airy sitting room. It was full of what an estate agent would call original features: a high vaulted ceiling, lots of decorative plasterwork, a fine Victorian fireplace, wooden shutters on the sash windows in the large bay. However, the decoration and furnishings were modern but simple: pale almond paint on the re-plastered walls, three pale brown sofas in a retro design, solid oak coffee tables, concealed lights in the ceiling, a few tasteful abstract paintings on the walls. It shouted interior design and was probably just the sort of sitting room one would expect a gay couple to have chosen.

"Please excuse Jonathan's camp act," Andy said after our hugs of greeting. "He's not really like that. It's an act he feels obliged to put on for all newcomers so that there's no doubting his orientation."

Jonathan shrugged his shoulders and said, "Sorry about that, but I've found it's the best way to avoid any type of embarrassing questions and conversations about our relationship. If I act like John Inman, people know where we stand. Well Andy, aren't you going to introduce me? You need complain about my manners."

It was good to see Andy in such a genuine and comfortable relationship. These two were the complete antidote to the evil slanders of the One Way Group. They were so clearly a happily married couple, why say they couldn't marry? As these thoughts coursed through my mind, Andy was busy introducing us.

He brought Jazz and Jonathan together with the words, "This is Jonathan Morris, my life partner, and Jonathan this is Jasmine Baker who was at King's with me in the gay days of my youth."

"Ah, Jasmine. Lovely to meet you in the flesh, so to speak," he laughed in such a charming way that not even a nun could have taken offence at his words. "We spoke on the phone the other day when Andy was away, didn't we? So, you must be Simon," he paused and turned to Andy. "He doesn't look like a vicar Andy, but he does look like he might be having an extra-marital!"

Jazz and I grinned and moved closer together, I put my arm round her as she said, "Let me explain…."

"Hang on a minute," interjected Andy. "We don't often get guests from the past. Please let us treat you properly and make you a drink."

Andy went into the kitchen to make coffee. Jazz and Jonathan discussed the furnishings in the sitting room. From the conversation about where to buy the curtains, table lamps and minimalist ornaments, it appeared that Jonathan had had the main input into the decor. Apparently, Jonathan was an art teacher and by the time Andy came in carrying a tray loaded with a huge cafetiere, four Cath Kidston china mugs and a cream jug, Jasmine and Jonathan were engaged in a deep discussion about the weaknesses of the government's education reforms.

Andy poured out the coffees and we began to explain why we were there. Of course, I had to start by explaining about my renouncing holy orders, Sarah leaving me, our love affair and the finding of Mark's body. On the way down from Wembley, we'd decided we needed to tell Andy everything. We had decided not to keep everything secret as we now felt it likely that the more people who knew, the less danger there could be, as the plotters would not be able to find and harm lots of people. However, it had been my job to make sure that we were not followed on our way down from North London, even though we were pretty sure we could not be followed since the plotters didn't know where we were or what we were driving. So, we told Andy and Jonathan everything.

Needless to say, they wanted extra details, especially when it came to Inspector Byrom's role in the swapping of the bodies and his attempt to inveigle his way into our investigation of One Way. They were also intrigued by the complexity and deviousness of the plot: the involvement of politicians, religious leaders and the press shocked Jonathan, but not Andy whose studies of religion at King's and involvement with politicians in the financial world had made him well aware of the lengths to which religious and political figures will go in their search for power and influence. As we recounted our changes of cars, dicing with death in Aberdeen, Jazz's kidnapping and rescue, and our release of Mrs Greenwood in Isleworth, their mouths began to drop open, and I have to say that as I listened to Jazz's exciting descriptions of some of those scenes, I could not believe that she was talking about me – the archetypal mild-mannered vicar!

As we were finishing our account of the car chase in West London, Andy asked, "So then, what do you want from me? Given the staggering things that have been happening to you two, and the danger you are still in, I can't believe that this is a purely social call to catch up on old friends – nice as that is!"

Never the quiet little woman, Jazz took it upon herself to reveal the raison d'etre for our visit, and of course she made a far better job of it than I ever could, "True Andy, though it has been great to meet up with you again, and to become acquainted with your delightful partner," she smiled at Jonathan and touched his knee as she spoke. "Mrs Greenwood told us that Mark's last words to her were, 'If anything happens to me tell anyone investigating that it was not Tim Harris but Paul Connor'. Does the name, Paul Connor, mean anything to you Andy? Think back to pre-1985."

"Paul Connor?" Andy paused as he spoke the name, clearly using the repetition of the name to take him back to his youth. "Paul Connor? Yes, got him!"

I looked at Jazz and she looked at me, there was an expression of great relief on her face and I'm sure there must have been on mine. "Great Andy! What can you remember about him?" she asked.

"Well he was a major player in the gay groups at Kings," Andy began.

"No surprise there then," cut in Jonathan ironically.

"OK darling," Andy said with his own twist of sarcasm on the darling, "but Paul really was a leading light. He was a leftover hippy. I remember him with very long bleached hair controlled with a hairband, John Lennon style glasses, flared jeans embroidered with flowers, flowery shirt. When he went somewhere the non-gays would always start singing the Mamas and Papas song about San Francisco and wearing flowers in your hair."

"Do you remember anything else about him? His friends? His job?" Jasmine asked trying to prompt his memories with her questions.

"I remember he was very promiscuous, really into cottaging." I felt Jonathan about to make some comment about Andy and cottaging, so I tapped him on the arm and put my finger to my lips. We needed Andy to tell us what he knew of this unknown guy without interruptions.

"Yeah," Andy continued, "our friend Mark was besotted with him. He followed him around hoping for a fling, but for some reason it never happened. Now what did he do? Think Andy think.... Oh yeah, I remember he didn't do much because he was a rich boy. He was doing some obscure course that gave him an easy offer, Portuguese or something like that. He had these friends who used to come down from Oxford to try the gay scene in London. I think he fluffed his finals and then disappeared."

"Do you think you would recognise him if you saw him now?" I asked.

"I guess he'd look a lot different now. So, I don't suppose I would recognise him. Hang on though. Yeees, I remember there was something, I remember Mark pointing it out to me, otherwise I wouldn't even have noticed. The end of the little finger on his left hand was missing. He'd lost it in some sort of accident in his teens."

Jazz was onto the case immediately. "We need today's papers," she said. "There's bound to be a photo of him somewhere. Do you have any papers Jonathan? We've got The Times and The Mirror in the car."

Jonathan found The Guardian and The Independent and after a short search, we came up with five photos of the Reverend Tim Harris: no glasses, short dark hair, dark well-cut suit, white double-cuff shirt, open neck, tie-less. Andy did not recognise him, but thought that it could be him if he were to have glasses and long blond hair. We tried putting on glasses and long blond hair, but with no more success, except that we descended into giggles as we remembered our teenage years making news pictures of Mrs Thatcher look like Adolf Hitler. His left hand could not be seen on any of the pictures.

"This is ridiculous," Jonathan said trying to break the impasse. "We have cable TV with a Tivo box, we can just go on and look at this week's news programmes to find a film of him. All we need to do is find one that shows his left hand."

Clearly Jonathan was the gadget man of the house and we were soon looking at the same news broadcast which we had watched last night in our hotel room. Jonathan was clearly an expert on the use of TV related gadgets and as soon as Tim Harris appeared he managed to keep stopping the film until at last we had a still of the reverend gentleman and were able to focus on his left hand.

"There you are!" shouted Jonathan, pointing at the screen. And indeed, there we were: the little finger of his left hand quite clearly had no tip.

Presumably, this was what Mark had seen. He'd been investigating the One Way Group as part of his research into modern religion; no doubt he'd been intrigued by Tim Harris's history stopping in 1985 and then seen that his little finger tip was missing. Since he'd had a crush on Paul Connor, he would have been just the person to tie the two people together, with fatal consequences.

Jazz sought some extra confirmation before we left. "I've been noticing," she said to Andy and Jonathan, "that Tim Harris has many similarities to American evangelists, but, unlike them, he never has his wife with him. Do you think he's still gay?"

They looked at each other before Andy replied, "Oh yes. He could be celibate now, but Paul Connor was not just trying out the gay scene. He was born and bred, and you never lose that. I wonder what happened to make him anti-gay? "

Whilst Andy and Jonathan pondered this, we phoned Pete to let him know what we'd discovered, and he told us to get back quickly to see what the hackers had come up with. We took our leave of Jonathan and Andy with profuse thanks, promises to keep them updated on what transpired and a warning to watch their backs just in case they'd been identified as our contacts.

Back at the Wembley research facility we received a hero's welcome. We'd identified why Mark had been murdered. If he had revealed Tim Harris's origins as the flamboyantly gay Paul Connor, the O2 rally could not have gone ahead and then the whole plan for Watkinson, or Dawlish as he now seemed to be known, to lead a One Way government would have been scuppered. Poor Mark. He was no doubt unaware of the likely consequences of his discovery and thought that confronting them with the truth would be sufficient.

Pete, however, had more discoveries for us. Some more hackers had come in and, working on Paul Connor, had discovered that he was at prep-school with Samuel Watkinson and that their fathers had been involved in joint business ventures. They'd also discovered that Tim Harris had begun his training as a vicar in the same Oxford college where Watkinson was finishing.

As I was coming to expect, Jazz was both the brains and the common sense of our trio, a fact she revealed when she spoke, "We've done really well today. What we discovered from Andy, and what you've found out from the internet, definitely amounts to a smoking gun. But, and that's a really big but, has it given us something we can use to get rid of the threat hanging over us?" she paused and looked around at us before continuing, "I don't think so. Not unless we can give this evidence to someone who can stop what's going on. Someone who has enough political and legal pull. Would the Metropolitan Police be a good bet? I don't really think so. Since Leveson and Jimmy Savile, they're going to be far too cautious. I reckon our best bet would be someone in the Labour party. They must still have some political and legal pull and they'd certainly have the motivation to stop it. But how do we make contact?"
There's one benefit to being a vicar in the Established Church, you make contacts with members of the Establishment. I tried not to sound too much like the eager beaver geek with his hand always up to attract the teacher's attention as I spoke up, but there must have been a note of triumphalism in my voice as I said," I know just the person."

That got everyone's attention. Jazz, Pete and all the hackers looked up and stared at me.

"Alright, mate," Pete said in a joking voice. "You best friends with the bleeding Queen then?"

Jazz, bless her heart, was more supportive, "That's brilliant babe, who is it?"

CHAPTER TWENTY SIX

As vicar of a large parish in his constituency, I had met the M.P. for my area of Leeds on several occasions and we'd got on really well. He was my kind of a guy, ordinary (came into politics through union involvement), intelligent, no airs and graces. The crucial thing about Ray Pearson for our purposes was that he was a Labour MP who had been in both the Blair and Brown cabinets and so was likely to have the influence and contacts we were looking for.

We were debating how to make contact with him without letting the plotters know where we were or what we were doing when Jazz suddenly erupted, "My Mum!"

"What do you mean babe?" I questioned, putting my arm round her to quell the fear I could hear in her voice. "Your Mum 's not involved. She knows nothing about it, does she?"

"No, she doesn't. I've been phoning her to let her know I'm okay, but didn't want to worry her with news of what's been happening. But just because she doesn't know anything about all of this doesn't mean she's not in danger. They kidnapped me to get at you, didn't they? They kidnapped Mrs Greenwood just to stop her speaking to us. They might try to use my Mum to get at me! I've got to phone to check she's okay before we do anything else."

Of course, she was right. I'd never had parents to worry about. Mum and Dad died at the age when they were no doubt worried about me, but at that point I was at the age where you think parents are just there, the perpetual back-up. As I thought of Mum and Dad, I felt my usual twinges of loss and regret, but I also felt happiness that Jazz cared for her mother and worried about her without being as dependent on her mother as Sarah had been with her minimum of four phone calls a day to her mother after we moved to Leeds.

Silence descended as we all listened to Jazz's conversation: "Hi Mum (I was so relieved she didn't say mummy), how are you?"

We assumed that Mrs Baker replied that she was fine and uttered a few more inconsequential pleasantries before Jasmine continued, "Now Mum, I don't want to worry you, but you need to be very careful at the moment."

Clearly Jazz's Mum wanted to know why she had to be careful because Jazz continued, "Why? Because Simon and I have got caught up with some very nasty people and they might try to get at us through you. Yes, I know it sounds very strange, but just do what I say until I get there. Yes, Simon and I are in London. We'll be with you in about half an hour and we'll explain everything then and take you to stay with Jane till this is all over. No, you can't go on your own. Look Mum, I know this sounds ridiculous, but it's true: these are very dangerous people. Just make sure the doors are locked and then wait till we get there. I'll phone you when we're outside. Now check that front door!"

Next thing we all heard a loud shriek come down Jazz's phone and then Jazz shouted, "Mum shut the door. Get the fire extinguisher from the kitchen and if you can't put it out, call the fire brigade. We're on our way."

Jazz pushed her phone in her pocket and grabbed my hand. "Come on Simon!" she called. "We've got to get to Brentford quick. It sounds like someone's pushed a petrol bomb through Mum's door. She needs us."

I became caught up in her panic and followed Jazz in her rush to the door, but Pete's voice pulled us up sharp, "Hold it a minute! Don't you think we should call the fire brigade first? And don't you think you're doing just what they bloody well want? This is just a bleeding ploy to get us into the open. They are quite bloody literally smoking us out!"

Jazz took no notice of Pete's last comment, but had dialled 999 and was speaking to the emergency services as she went out of the door, and we were in the car driving back onto the North Circular by the time she'd been put through to the fire brigade and given them her mother's address. We were on the North Circular when Pete managed to get through to us. Jazz put her phone on speaker so we could both talk to him and his voice exploded into the car.

"What a bloody nightmare! I'm sure you're desperate to check on your Mum, but it's bleeding stupid to just burst in there and not only let the buggers see you, but also let them see what fucking car you're driving (Pete's language got more colourful the more emotional he was, so I knew he was now very worried). I don't know how we're going to stop the bastards from getting you! Why the bleeding hell didn't you wait and work out a plan of action?"

I put my hand on Jazz's knee to tell her to calm down, I didn't want to have to deal with verbal fireworks in the car whilst negotiating the nightmare that is the Hanger Lane Gyratory, so I spoke before Jazz had a chance to, "I know what you mean mate, but this is Jazz's Mum we're talking about, and she's far more precious than one of your computers. Our first priority is to make sure that she's okay. Then we need to sort out her house, and then, and only, then will we think about how to deal with these stupid bloody people who've not only ruined our lives, but are now threatening the lives of Jazz's family."

The words just flowed without me thinking about them, and I suddenly realised that this was what being in love meant. You identified with the person you loved and hence with their family, friends and emotions.

Jazz now spoke up, "That goes for me too Pete. My prime concern is my Mum. I can't think of anything else till I know she's safe and out of all this."

"Bugger me Jasmine, that is the whole bloody point! If you just bloody well drive up there and let them bloody well see you, they'll have the chance to grab you and Si and your Mum and there'll be bugger all we can do about it!"

I could almost feel Jazz's brain whirling as she took in what Pete was saying. He was certainly making me think about our headlong flight to Brentford. Were we really just playing into the hands of these people who meant us, and, I was coming to see, the whole country harm? A little more calmness and consideration might be no bad thing. The fire brigade would be there before us and no one was going to attack Jazz's Mum whilst they were there. We really did have just a small window of opportunity to get things right.

"I see what you mean Pete," I interjected before Jazz could say anything. "Jazz can phone her Mum and check she's alright and if she is, we'll rendezvous with you to plan the next move rather than just barging in. OK?"

Now Jazz burst in, she'd clearly been thinking quickly, "I can go with that Pete. I'm going to phone my Mum now. We won't do anything till we've phoned you back."

Jazz switched off the speaker phone and phoned her Mum, as I successfully negotiated the gyratory, then the Chiswick roundabout before turning off at Kew Bridge onto Brentford High Street where I spotted a McDonald's and pulled into the car park.

"Mum's alright, but the fire brigade won't be there long, Mum's no sweet little old lady, she'd put the fire out before they arrived. Now they're just checking to make sure everything's safe. But, of course, they've called the police and the firemen are going to wait till the police arrive. The senior fireman has told Mum the police will be there quite a while. Apparently, we're talking about a very serious criminal offence. At the least they'll treat it as arson, but more likely as attempted murder. And of course, being my Mum, they'll be treating it as racially aggravated!"

"So, the police are going to be there for quite a while, meaning sufficient time for us to plan how to get your Mum to somewhere safe without us showing ourselves," I replied. "We need to phone

Pete and tell him to meet us here and we can make our plans over a cup of coffee."

Pete arrived a few minutes later with two of the hackers from Wembley: one was the thirtyish woman, who was still looking as if she had walked out of a Next catalogue, the other was the handsome smart black man in his late twenties. Pete had chosen them, so he told us, because of their martial arts skills as well as their computer skills, just in case things turned nasty and physical. He'd also chosen them because they could act as a couple or as singles to keep an eye on proceedings without attracting attention. They had also seen photos of most of the plotters in their computer searches and so would be able to identify any of the opposition engaged in similar observation tactics. We immediately sent them round to Brook Road, where Jasmine's Mum lived, to keep an eye on proceedings whilst we formulated a plan.

Jazz and I sat at a table with our coffees as Pete waited for his order of Big Mac and large fries, he didn't get to be such a big lad on Ryvita and cottage cheese. When Pete came over with his food, the appetising aroma hit us, and we realised that we hadn't eaten since breakfast. It didn't take much persuading from Jazz to send me back to the counter for a quarter pounder each with a hot apple pie to follow. Somehow eating at McDonald's made me feel younger and more adventurous, perhaps because the first ones came to England in my teens when only the really cool people used McDonald's!

We were not feeling like cool people as we debated what to do: more like the class thickies, since ideas seemed to be few and far between. We just couldn't find any answers to the problem of how to reach Jazz's Mum without revealing ourselves, and then if we managed that, how on earth could we get her Mum to a place of safety without them being able to follow?

The few ideas we came up with were batted about the table until a major problem revealed itself and then it was back to the drawing board, or more accurately the thinking board. Of course, it was Jazz who came up with the decisive idea, "We've got two people there already who aren't known to the plotters, why don't we use them to get Mum out? If they take her to somewhere with a front and back entrance and drop her off at the front entrance, we can wait at the back and get her away. What do you think?"

Pete and I agreed enthusiastically and Pete said, "I know just the place, it's just down the road. But Lindsay and Darren have no transport, how are we going to get round that?"

Before either of us could answer, Peter's phone rang. It was Lindsay telling us that someone had just arrived at Jazz's Mum's and they'd recognised him from some of the stuff they'd studied with Pete. It was 'that dodgy police bloke who tricked Simon and Jasmine' and he'd flashed some sort of ID when he was let in by the uniformed PC standing outside the house. Pete told Lindsay to come back to McDonald's for further instructions.

"What the hell is Byrom doing entering my Mum's home?" Jazz exclaimed. "He has no right to be down here and he's far too dangerous to be anywhere near my Mum!"

I felt for her, but this was no time to let emotion cloud judgement. This was a situation which had to be dealt with, and swiftly. "Babe he's here because he's been sent by powerful and influential people who want to silence us. They know we're in the area and they need someone from the police on their side. I bet they flew him down from Leeds/Bradford as soon as they discovered we were down here. He'll have told some sort of cock and bull story about this being connected to a case he's working on, probably mentioned Blenkinsop's name, and he was in. What we have to do is get your Mum out of there!"

Suddenly my brain was in overdrive. I knew what to do and began issuing instructions like a PE teacher on speed.

"Pete, tell Lindsay and Darren to get round here as quickly as they can to pick your car up. Then Lindsay can go back to Brook Road and pretend to be a friend of Jazz's come to pick her Mum up and take her to see Jazz as soon as the police are finished. She's to tell them Jazz is ill in the Premier Inn down the road and can't get to her Mum's. Jazz, you phone your Mum and let her know what's going to happen. Try to keep it comparatively vague because what you say might be overheard by Byrom. Jazz and I will go to the hotel's underground car park in our car and I'll wait in the car beside the hotel exit. Pete you'll wait here and Lindsay will pick you up as soon as she's dropped Jasmine's Mum off. Jazz you'll go into the hotel and wait near the reception, hidden from the road. As soon as your Mum comes in, you wave her over, rush her down to the car park and we're off with you and your Mum crouched down so you can't be seen. We'll take your Mum to your sister's then we'll rendezvous with Pete at the London Gateway Services at the start of the M1. I think we need to be getting out of London!"

Jazz and Pete looked at me with a mixture of disbelief and admiration, and I must admit I was rather amazed at myself. I was not aware I had such powers of planning and quick thinking. Perhaps it came from dealing with some very hairy Parish Council meetings!

"Sounds good to me," Pete said, and phoned Lindsay to tell her and Darren to come back to McDonald's.

Jazz simply smiled at me, a special lover's smile that made my heart leap, and phoned her Mum, "Hi Mum, it's me again. Now listen carefully. That policeman who's just come in.. Yes, the one from the North. Now try not to say anything when I tell you what I know about him because we've got to make sure you get away from him without him knowing what's happening. You see he's connected with the people who put the firebomb through the letter box. You need to tell the police that I've been taken ill at the Premier Inn and that my friend is coming to pick you up when they've finished questioning you... They've finished have they. It's just Inspector Byrom who has more questions? ... Well tell him Lindsay, my friend, will take you to meet him at Brentford Police Station, after you've seen me... Yes, Mum it's desperately important that we get you out of Byrom's clutches. I know I can trust you, you're still the same sassy woman from Kingston that Dad married. You can deal with a bent copper. I'll make sure Lindsay is there in a couple of minutes so that you can come out with the local police and they'll then be witnesses to anything Byrom does. Okay Mum?"

Jazz switched off her phone and turned to us, "Right, let's go. There's Lindsay and Darren. Get them off in your car straight away Pete. They need to be at Mum's before the Met police leave!"

We left with Pete, because with a little more thought I decided that rather than letting Pete get in his car with Lindsay and Darren, he should come in the car with me and Jazz. Somehow, I couldn't imagine Byrom just letting Mrs Baker go into the hotel on her own, so I wanted Pete and me to be with Jaz and her Mum to deal with any tricks he might try to play.

CHAPTER TWENTY SEVEN

Denise Baker put down the phone and looked at the man who had introduced himself as Inspector Dave Byrom. She had always prided herself on being a good judge of character, and what she had just heard from her daughter merely confirmed what she had already assumed about this tall fair-haired man. Experience had taught her that any man who was immaculately dressed, and more especially as immaculately coiffured as Inspector Byrom, could not be trusted. Any normal man always had at least a few hairs out of place, a scuffed shoe and a tie, if he had to wear one, slightly askew. Byrom, however, had everything perfect, and so Denise was more than ready to believe what her daughter had told her. The difficult job would be controlling, or more particularly hiding, her true feelings about the man.

Denise spoke to the room as a whole rather than just to Byrom, "That was my daughter on the phone. She's been taken ill and wants me to go and see her at her hotel. Her friend's coming round to give me a lift, so as soon as you're finished here, I'd like to go."

"No problem madam," announced the plain clothes officer who had introduced himself to her earlier as the officer in charge of the local CSI. "We all want our mother when we're feeling under the weather don't we lads?" He looked round his squad and received a number of nods and grunts of approval, but not from Inspector Byrom who was looking decidedly uneasy.
"In fact, we've got all the stuff we need in terms of evidence. You've already given us your statement so we'll be off. But I'm going to be leaving a uniformed constable on patrol outside. We're certain this was a racially aggravated arson attack, which could have had nasty consequences if you hadn't been so on the ball. Do you think you could stay at the hotel with your daughter for a couple of

days, we wouldn't really recommend you staying here on your own when there might be another attack?"

The longer the detective spoke, the longer Byrom's face grew and by the time the detective finished, Byrom was looking distinctly like a bloodhound. However, he managed to pull himself together when the detective continued, "Right lads, if you've got everything, we'll be on our way. Are you coming down to the station with us Inspector Byrom, to compare notes about the two cases?"

"Er... I'll come down a bit later, if you don't mind. I'd just like to tie up a few loose ends with Mrs Baker first," said Byrom in a tone of voice and a facial expression which could only be described as oleaginous.

Denise was not taken in by his seemingly innocuous words. She had detected an underlying steeliness to them, a feeling confirmed when he grasped her arm and said, "Tell you what Mrs Baker, why don't I take you to see your daughter in my car and we can tie up the loose ends on the way?"

At that moment the doorbell rang. 'My God,' she thought," I never imagined in a million years that someone like me would ever be saved by the bell.' Then she wrenched her arm out of Byrom's grasp, to his obvious annoyance, and opened the door.

"Hello darling," she welcomed the newcomer in tones loud enough to carry to all the police, not just Byrom. "You must be Jasmine's friend Lindsay. Come in. Did you hear about the fire? Well the police have just finished their investigations and they're about to leave. Will you help me clear up and get an overnight bag together before we go to see Jasmine?"

With these words, Denise shepherded Lindsay into the house and, very politely, began the process of shepherding the police out of her house. She was rather less polite when Inspector Byrom showed no sign of joining the general exodus."I thought you were going," she said brusquely. "I'm going to see my daughter and I would like you to leave my house. I've told you that I will come to the police station to help you when I've sorted my daughter out. Can I make it any clearer than that?"

Byrom looked somewhat non-plussed. No doubt he was not used to being talked to in such a way, nevertheless, he did not give up without a fight. "But Mrs Baker," he said in the smarmiest way possible, "my car's outside. If you come with me now, we could get it all over with before you go to see your daughter, and you wouldn't need to bother your daughter's friend."

His manner rather than persuading Denise simply confirmed to her, if any confirmation were needed, that her daughter's assessment of this creep had been totally correct.

"No Mr Byrom," Denise deliberately replaced Inspector with Mr to indicate to Byrom that he was losing ground fast. "I've made my decision; will you please leave?"

Denise was only five feet two and Byrom towered over her, but she was a strong lady used to running a family and a doctor's reception. Her tone of voice and her belligerent stance intimidated Byrom, and when Lindsay took out a notebook and said, "Do you want me to keep a record of this police harassment Mrs Baker?" he gave in and left.

*   *   *   *   *   *   *

The three of us drove round to the car park of the hotel and sussed out the situation. There was good news and bad news for us. The bad news was that it being four o'clock on a Friday, the car park was full, but that could be dealt with. We weren't leaving the car so with someone in the driving seat, we could double park. The good news was that the barriers weren't operating so we would be able to make a quick exit. Unfortunately, there was more bad news. It was a long time since I'd stayed in the hotel and they'd introduced card keys which you needed to operate the locks on the doors from the car park.

As was becoming usual, it was Jazz who came up with a solution for this. When she saw someone going into the hotel, she leapt out of the car and pretended to be going into the hotel. They held the door open for her and she found a wedge, no doubt used for the laundry deliveries, and propped the door open. Pete now got into the driving seat and waited with the engine running. Jazz and I walked down a long corridor to the door to reception. It had a card key lock, but only on the reception side, so I held it open for Jazz to walk through to reception and stayed holding it open so she could bring her Mum straight out to the car.

Reception was quite busy with people queuing up to sign in. There were wheelie cases and hold-alls all over the place. It looked a one hundred percent perfect obstacle course, just as if it had been specially designed to prevent anyone from chasing Jazz's Mum. Then, as if on cue, Mrs Baker appeared through the front door, escorted by Darren. Given the shocks she must have received from the fire and then the police and then Jazz's phone call, she was looking good and very on-the-ball. I hadn't seen her for twenty years, but she was still the smart and sophisticated black lady she had been then. Maybe there was a little less spring in the step and a few more wrinkles, but no grey in her short Afro hair (of course that could have been courtesy of the dye bottle).

Jazz rushed over to hug her mother, and, before I needed to indicate the need for haste, after a brief embrace they moved speedily through the door. As they passed me, Byrom came hurtling into the hotel and fell headlong over the case that Darren had judiciously placed in his path. I managed a brief chuckle then shut the door, hence locking him out, and hurried down the corridor after Jazz and her Mum. We piled into the car and Pete shot off towards the exit.

As we came up the narrow access road and stopped to pull onto Brentford High Street, I looked for Byrom's car to see which direction it was facing. Pete and I had already decided that if we could go in the opposite direction to what he was facing, it could give us more of an opportunity to get away whilst he tried to turn round. Perhaps his sense of police infallibility was his undoing. He was parked on double yellow right outside the hotel and so was very easy to spot, and, luckily for us, was facing in the opposite direction to the North Circular.

We turned right from the hotel, and headed for the North Circular. Jazz's younger sister, Jane, lived in High Wycombe so we were actually going to turn onto Western Avenue at Hanger Lane and then up the M40 to High Wycombe. We were driving past the iconic Hoover/Tesco building when Pete's phone rang. He handed it to me so he could continue driving, I looked at the caller ID and saw it was Darren.

"Hi Darren, what's up?"

Darren's reply was a bit like a slap with a cold flannel after the euphoria induced by our successful escape from Byrom. "Is that Si? (presumably this was to be my name for all Pete's acquaintances as well). Word of warning for Pete. We've just found a magnetic tracker on Pete's car which was not there before we arrived at Mrs Baker's. We've removed it, but Lindsay thought they might have attached one to Mrs B herself. Can you check and make sure you're not being followed?"

"Oh shit!" was my immediate answer, then I assured Darren that we would check Mrs Baker, and check for any following vehicles. I put Pete's phone down and reported the gist of Darren's message.

Jazz began to panic, but Denise Baker displayed all the sangfroid and common sense of an SAS member. "All we need do is check my outer garments, I don't need to strip off in public. Unfortunately, none of those nice young men saw me without clothes, so if they attached a device to me, it must have been on the outside," she said.

Her joke may have been a bit feeble, but it lightened the atmosphere, and we all calmed down a bit. Pete was first off the mark in deciding what to do, "This time of day on a Friday, we don't really want to come off this road. The slip roads off here will be jammed solid, and, if anyone is tracking us, the last thing we need is to be stuck in a traffic jam. We would be sitting ducks. Jasmine can you check the outside of your Mum's clothing for a tracker device?"

"I can check the outside of her clothes, but I have no idea what a tracking device looks like. Have any of you?"

I was back to feeling like I had in Aberdeen. The thought of being tracked and spied on all the time was terrifying, but, like Jazz, I had no idea what a tracking device would look like. "Can you help us here Pete?" I asked.

"From the fact that Lindsay and Darren found the device on the car so easily, I guess it will be comparatively large. I guess they've bought them from somewhere like Spy Equipment UK or Tracker Shop where it's easy to buy on-line, but the devices are not top of the range," Pete replied.

At that moment Denise Baker yelled, "Got it! It was in my coat pocket!" She produced a small slim rectangular black box and passed it over to me. "This shouldn't be in my pocket, so I assume it's a tracker."

I held it up for Pete to see and he confirmed that it was indeed a tracking device. I'd read enough thrillers to know that I shouldn't just throw it out of the car. We could use it to deceive the trackers, but I wasn't too sure how we could do that on the A40 approaching the M40, but I was thinking fast. I was thinking that if Mrs Baker was to be safe, she had to go to High Wycombe in a different car not only because of the tracking device, but also because it was possible that they had seen our car when we left the hotel in Brentford. I was also thinking Luton Airport, a place where there were bound to be several car rental places open late on a Friday night.

Another thought came to me as we overtook a pickup truck, if we could toss the device onto the back of such a vehicle, we could really confuse the opposition.

My Luton Airport plan was given a cautious approval, though my planned use of the device received a five-star rating. Pete spotted another pickup ahead indicating to go off down the Uxbridge slip road. It was full of builders' equipment which would conceal the tracker. Pete speeded up, then slowed down to drive alongside it. I wound down my window and threw the device hoping the slipstream would take it and then the mixers and ladders would trap it in the pickup.

"Bingo!" shouted Jazz. "It's on the pickup. Part one accomplished. What's next?"

"Next is to join the M25 and head for the M1 and Luton Airport," I replied. "With all of us keeping our eyes peeled to see if we're being followed. Let's hope they were relying on the tracker!"

"Slightly different route!" Pete interjected. "If you lived down here you'd know that the M25 at tea-time on Friday is just a gigantic car park! Don't worry, I know a backwoods route that will get us to Luton Airport using only a bit of motorway and giving us a good chance to check whether anything's following us."

With these words, Pete took us off a slip road just as the A40 became the M40, and we went across country via Amersham, Chesham and Berkhamsted to join the M1 at Hemel Hempstead. As Pete had predicted, the twists and turns and thirty miles an hour zones through towns and villages gave me ample opportunity to check for following vehicles. I was rather worried by a black BMW which followed us closely for the first part of the route. It could have been Byrom's car and it kept behind us through all the twists and turns of the country roads. Then I got a good view of the driver and saw it was a blonde-haired woman, and when she turned off into the drive of a luxurious barn conversion, I knew I had been mistaken.

Jazz had been comforting her mother whilst this was going on, though comforting was the wrong word. It was what Jazz had been intending to do, but her Mum was made of stronger stuff than that, in fact she seemed to be rather enjoying herself. As I was checking on the BMW and Pete was concentrating on his tortuous route to Luton, I listened to the mother/daughter conversation, glad to be involved with two such feisty women.

"Are you OK Mum?" Jazz began.

"What's not to be okay about?" Denise replied. "I haven't had so much excitement in a long time."

"But Mum, you've had a firebomb pushed through your door! You've had the fire brigade and the police at the house. You've been smuggled through a hotel to avoid pursuers. You've even had a tracking device planted on you. Aren't you a bit upset?"

"Look my girl! I'm a seventy-five-year-old widow whose highlight of the week is a church lunch club held in a Pentecostal church whose beliefs I totally disagree with. My husband, your father, has been dead five years. The adrenaline surge from all of this has been wonderful. I've loved it, especially that smuggling through the hotel with that smarmy policeman being tripped up. But now I would like to know what it's all about. You've told me about your relationship with Simon and I have to say how relieved I am that he's no longer a vicar in the Church of England. That Church was responsible for some awful bad times for our ancestors on the plantations! But what have you done that's gotten you into such a den of thieves that I'm being attacked by policemen?"

Jazz gave a brief, but very lucid, account of our finding Mark's body and all that had transpired since. The clarity of her explanation made me realise what a good teacher she must be, and also of the need for us to find a way out of the trap we seemed to be in. A thought echoed by Denise as she said, "How the hell are you going to get yourselves out of this? You can't keep travelling the country in hire cars and staying in hotels!"

"Simon's trying to sort it out Mum," Jazz answered on my behalf.

It was true. I was trying, but were my plans going to be enough? And, more worryingly, were they going to be achievable? The presence of Inspector Byrom had worried me more than I'd let on to Jazz. People with powerful police, political and underworld (I shuddered as I thought of birdman and what he was likely to do if he caught up with me again) contacts were not just chasing us, they wanted to silence us, most likely forever. Was my plan to enlist the help of a Labour politician just a form of whistling in the wind? Did it have about as much chance of success as Spurs did of winning the Premiership?

I debated what to say to the woman I hoped was to become my mother-in-law. A woman I wanted to give a good impression to because she seemed to be a wonderful prospective mother-in-law. A sudden recollection about Ray Pearson gave me a bit more hope for our future and for polishing my image with Mrs Baker. "We're going to get the help of someone important I know in Leeds, Mrs Baker. Someone with connections that might be stronger than those of this this One Way Group."

"Not so much of the Mrs Baker. It makes me sound like an old woman!! Please call me Denise," Jazz's Mum replied. "Anyway, from the way you two seem to be with each other, I reckon you've become part of the family!"

Pete could not stop himself from sniggering at this, and I tried to cover his reaction up by continuing, "Thanks Denise. Anyway, I think Ray Pearson might be able to help because he was Home Secretary in the last Labour government so he must know who to go to, and how to get to them. He's the one who might be able to put an end to this conspiracy and give us back our freedom."

"Do you really know Ray Pearson?" Denise exclaimed. "You might have disappointed me in being a vicar, Simon, but if you know Ray Pearson, you can't be all bad!"

She turned to Jazz and continued, "Jasmine why didn't you tell me he was a proper man, a Labour man?"

Luckily all four of us had similar ideas about politics and we had a good discussion about the benefits of Labour and the deficiencies of the Tories until Pete pulled into the huge car park at Luton airport.

CHAPTER TWENTY EIGHT

It didn't take us long to reorganise the cars and say goodbye to Pete and Denise (as I was getting used to calling Mrs Baker). We could see it was quiet going south on the M1 so they set off for High Wycombe via the M25 whilst we joined the queue to get onto the northbound M1, heading for Leeds in a new black Astra, which would hopefully lead us to a way out from the unholy mess we were in.

Jazz switched on the radio and searched for a news channel, ending up on Radio 5 Live which was, of course, devoting itself to the political developments whilst also keeping up to date with the long-running debate about Arsene Wenger's future at Arsenal. The first story to catch our attention, however, was religious, well religiousish!

'William Hill has just announced that it has closed the betting on the Right Reverend James Scott-Philips becoming the next Archbishop of Canterbury. Apparently, a number of significant bets from new accounts led the betting firm to conclude that a decision had already been taken and the choice had been leaked. At lunch-time today James Scott-Philips was the odds-on favourite at 1:2. James Scott-Philips is the current Bishop of Ripon and Leeds and was educated at Eton and Oxford. He was unavailable for comment.'

I couldn't stop myself from exclaiming, "I don't believe it!"

Laughter bubbled up beside me as Jazz commented, "Oh babe, you sounded just like Victor Meldrew! Come on let's have a good old moan then."

"But, but he's such a, such a," I tried to think of another word, but really there was only one word that described him adequately, "but babe he's such a wanker!"

Jazz laughed again as she said, "I'll take your word for it, but if you mean it literally, it's just too much information."

I laughed with her and at myself. What a wonderful woman she was. She could lighten the most horrific of situations. I turned to look at her and was sorely tempted to pull into the services we were approaching at Milton Keynes, book a room and give into the lust with which she consumed me.

Such thoughts quickly disappeared at the next announcement: *'Reports suggest that Prime Minister Stuart Fairhurst is likely to lose the confidence vote due on Monday. It is felt that the revelations in "Where It's At" magazine have fatally weakened the Prime Minister's authority. Apparently, a growing number of Conservative MPs are supporting Lord Dawlish's campaign for Jemimah Percy-Gilbert to become leader of the Conservatives and lead the party into some sort of association with Tim Harris and the One Way Group. Lord Dawlish claimed that such an association would strengthen both the party and the country. When questioned by a BBC reporter he said, "We all need that strong moral fibre and sense of individual responsibility that religion can bring if we are to overcome the huge economic crisis bequeathed to us by the last spendthrift, unprincipled Labour Government. Christian principles will help us work together to live within our means and remove the deficit which is crippling our economy." The government is already in crisis and most political commentators believe it will fall if the Prime Minister loses the confidence vote. There is no precedent for knowing what would happen then.'*

Jazz was first to react, "This is looking really bad Simon. I reckon these plotters know exactly what they're doing. The right-wing Tories are going to have a free run at joining with Harris without the bother of trying to win an election. And.."

"And," I continued for her, "if One Way can take over the Tory party, they'll be running the fucking country! "

"Oh my God!" Jazz exclaimed. At first I thought she was exclaiming at my use of four letter swear words, but I realised that, unlike Sarah would have been, she had hardly noticed as she continued, "We really are in the middle of bloody cesspool! Watkinson will have gone from running a homeless men's hostel to running the country in little more than a week. The people we saw meeting in Ripon last Thursday are about to become the next government of the United Kingdom, and we're the only people who know what's happening, which, of course, means we're the only ones who can stop them. Even worse than that, they know that we're the only people who can bring an end to all their plans, plans they probably believe have been made by God. We're totally fucked Simon, aren't we?"

The intelligence and perspicacity of my beloved continued to astound me. She was right. I could not fault her reasoning, but I could differ from her conclusion and responded with a positivity I had not really felt before. "No, we are not babe. Far from it! This Yorkshire Tea Party cum Eton Mess isn't going to hurt us anymore, and we're certainly not going to let it take over the country. It might seem like they're holding all the cards, babe, but we have the joker in the pack. Ray Pearson was Home Secretary. He must have loads of contacts in M15, the British equivalent of Homeland Security. Contacts whose job is to stop plots like this and get rid of the perpetrators, and when they do that my darling, we'll be able to go home and lead a normal life."

"I'm not thick Simon, darling. I don't need a cheap American television show to explain to me what MI5 is!"

"Sorry babe," I burbled apologies, and after some deliberation decided to tell the truth. "To be perfectly honest, I keep forgetting that I'm in love with a woman who's far more intelligent than I am because I spent twenty years living with a woman who not only had to have an explanation of why the Tea Party is called the Tea Party, but then needed an explanation of why Britain isn't still ruling the Americas!"

"Oh Simon," Jazz replied in a tone that made me glad I'd decided to tell the truth. "I'm no superbrain, but I am better than that super bitch! Now I'm going to switch the news off and find Classic FM so we can have a peaceful drive back up north."

The peace and quiet lasted for ten minutes or so as we listened to 'The scene by the brook' from Beethoven's Pastoral Symphony. Then we needed to talk. We were newly in love and we wanted to find out things about each other.

" You've been inside religion, babe; I've only studied it from the outside, so I'm finding it hard to understand how my friend found religion and then helped to kidnap me! Can you tell me why so many religious people are so nasty? So many born-again people I've met are incredibly awful people. People like your ex-mother-in-law and my ex-colleague Colin. From all my academic knowledge of religion, religious people should be nicer, happier and kinder than the non-religious, so why aren't they?"
That started me thinking, and talking. I had to admit it was something I had thought about many times in the last twenty years. Why did supposedly good Christian people become vitriolic when someone they didn't like, or even worse someone they didn't consider to be as good as them, was elected to the Parish Council? Why did supposedly good Christian people complain so much about how much work they did for the church and then react with

venomous outrage when someone offered to take an onerous task from them? But, of course, these were very minor. Why were people prepared to kill for the sake of religion? Why, for God's sake, had Sarah and her parents been happy to keep Jazz tied up as a kidnap victim? Why had Jazz's best friend been prepared to kidnap her? Why had the leaders of the One Way Group been prepared to kill a lovely man with that stone pediment? That brought me to the beginnings of an answer because all of these questions were really connected.

"I think it's because people don't want to ask questions about religion. They choose, or are born into a religion, and decide it's true because it comes from God. It makes them feel special, and it's a wonderful insurance policy for a life beyond the grave. So, they don't want people questioning it. I'm sure the insurance policy is why people become more religious the nearer the grave they get."

Jazz wasn't prepared to let me lecture her and interjected," But don't some religious people believe they've been chosen by God, even that they have a direct line to God, and that makes them think they're somebody special?"

"They most definitely do, babe," I replied. "Feeling they've been specially chosen by God is what most religions teach their followers, especially the One Way Group, which is a major problem because it makes them think that anyone who disagrees with them about anything is acting against God, and anyone acting against God deserves to be treated badly."

"Yeah," replied Jazz hesitantly, "I can sort of see that from studying fundamentalist terrorist groups, like the Ku Klux Klan and Al-Qaeda, but does it really apply to the nice members of the good old C of E such as you've been dealing with?"

"Indeed, it does. You should have seen some of the arguments I've had to deal with about the flower rota. And the pomposity that people seem to take on with the job when they're made church warden! You know gaining an official role in the Church, even if you're only the person giving out the hymn books, seems to immediately confer an inflated sense of importance and a propensity to use the position to show off that importance. The good thing about religion is that it gives people a sense of self-worth. The bad thing is that self-worth so often becomes self-importance and with that the sense that whatever you do is approved by God and therefore right."

At that moment, I saw a sign for the services at Leicester Forest East, and a voice beside me said, "OK babe, here endeth today's sermon. I think we need a break and a cup of coffee."

I pulled into the services and we walked up the steps hand in hand before separating to go to the loos. Of course, I was out first and stood beside McDonald's to wait for Jazz. It would have been easiest just to have a coffee in McDonald's, but I saw that not only was it packed, but there was a humungous queue waited to be served. So as soon as Jazz re-appeared, I suggested we go up to the eatery that is built on a bridge over the motorway to have access from both sides.

One thing I love about motorway services is a bun they call a Danish pastry but which is more like a Marlborough bun with extra fruit and cherries and covered in lumps of white sugar. I bought us one each to keep up our strength, a latte for Jasmine and a large Americano for me. We walked over to a table next to a window overlooking the southbound carriageway and sat down. Jazz decided we needed a knife and fork each to attack the Danish and went back to get them.

I sat drinking my coffee and watched the people queuing up at the KFC counter. It was almost as busy as the McDonald's had been and I wondered, not for the first time, why American takeaways were so popular in the UK. Watching the people milling around the counter, it was clear that it was connected to age and family. There were lots of people in the Club Med twenty to thirty age range, but even more people with children. And, it was so classless: upper, middle and very working class families seemed equally attracted to the place.

I was just beginning to wonder what so many people were doing travelling the motorway on a term-time Friday night when I felt someone's eyes on me, eyes that seemed to be burning with an uncontrolled ferocity. I looked across to the passageway coming from the southbound stairs and froze. It was my worst nightmare come true. There staring at me with eyes burning with vitriol was my nemesis: birdman.

I wanted to run away, but Jazz was behind me, I had to protect her. I rose slowly from my seat readying myself to fling my coffee cup at him, then grab Jazz and race for the car. But I had no chance for that as with a horrifying howl he launched himself at me leaping high into the air across the table.

I was readying myself to grapple with him as he landed, when someone hit my back and pushed me flat onto the table and I felt Jazz hugging me as birdman literally flew over us and hit the window. There was an almighty crack, and as I looked up the glass buckled, bulged and then flew out. Birdman went with it, hurtling down onto the carriageway. Jazz and I leapt up and looked down in horror as he hit the road and disappeared under a huge pantechnicon. Jazz grabbed my hand and pulled me in a run back across the cafeteria to the stairs. I came out of my shock at the top of the stairs and speeded up as I realised that, although the whole cafeteria was in a frozen tableau of shock, the man I had seen walking in with birdman was now racing after us!

We raced down the stairs and were at a bit of an advantage as we raced through the concourse in that we knew what was there and knew how to get through quickly. Even better, as we got to the doors, what must have been a couple of coach-loads of passengers came in blocking our pursuers exit. We charged to the car, though wise Jazz made me wait a moment whilst she smeared the number plates with mud from the flowerbed behind us. Then we were off and onto the motorway before the police had chance to close it down.

We had a definite lead as birdman had obviously been travelling south so their car was on the other side and would have to go off and turn round at the huge traffic-light controlled M69 roundabout in order to get onto the northbound carriageway. As we looked over, however, we realised that even that would not be possible. The south-bound traffic was completely stationary. Birdman had stopped the traffic.

As we sped northwards, Jazz's phone rang. It was Pete letting us know that Mrs Baker, I still had to get used to her being Denise, had been safely delivered to her other daughter's in High Wycombe, and Pete was on his way back to the hackers' HQ in Wembley. Jazz then gave Pete a brief account of our encounter with birdman and its conclusion. I could hear the gasps and expletives coming down the phone from him and asked Jazz to put the phone onto conference mode so we could both join in the conversation.

"Turn up for the book eh Pete?" I chimed in.

"That you Si, you murdering bugger?" he asked, with a welcome to the conversation which I could have done without.

Had I really murdered birdman? He was certainly dead, but surely only because I got out of his way; or, more accurately, because Jazz got me out of his way, and surely there had been a fault in the glass of the window for it to smash, it must have been specially toughened glass above a motorway? It had all happened so quickly, I hadn't had chance to think about it.

As I did think about it, I realised that, although I hadn't actually thrown birdman through the window, it was my actions which were the immediate cause of his death. I shuddered involuntarily. Birdman had been an evil villain, but the extinguishing anyone's life is cause for regret. Some words of John Donne came unbidden to my mind, "Each man's death diminishes me, For I am involved in mankind."

"That's unkind Pete," Jazz chimed in, "Simon is no murderer. That guy killed himself because he was trying to kill Simon, and a right mess he's made of things by his lack of consideration. He should have known that landing on the motorway would cause a massive amount of upset to a lot of people, especially on a Friday night!"

Jazz's humorous words defused the situation somewhat and began to settle my mind. Sirens and blue flashing lights began to appear on the opposite carriageway as fire engines and police cars headed rapidly down the hard-shoulder to the scene.

"OK Si mate? Sorry if my poor attempt at a joke misfired there. Are you alright? Bloody hell Si there was no need to bring our history lecture on the 1619 defenestration of Prague into the twenty-first century. Though it is a bloody good word isn't it folks? Defenestration! The throwing of a person or object out of a window. Well bloody well done you two, even if you didn't do it deliberately. Good bloody riddance to bad bleedin rubbish with that one. He was one evil, vicious sod you know. Just think of it as doing society a bloody good service Si. Now what about his mate who saw you two?"

Jazz answered for us, "He saw us, Pete, and presumably told his bosses we're heading north, but I'm pretty sure we got away before he saw the car."

"And even if he saw the car, he couldn't get the number because my super intelligent girlfriend thought quickly enough to cover the number plates with soil," I added.

"Just common sense really," Jazz said self-deprecatingly, "though of course that's something in rather short supply among vicars!"
A loud guffaw came down the phone from Pete, "Brilliant Jasmine and so bloody true. I'll tell you what darling, you're such a bleedin improvement on frosty knickers Sarah. You've done well this time Si."

I could feel my face beginning to burn red with embarrassment as my insensitive and undiplomatic friend continued to embarrass me. I needed to say something to halt this conversation, so I quickly chimed in, "Alright, alright Pete that's enough of that. Just cos birdman's dead doesn't mean we're out of the woods. In fact, I think we're probably even deeper in the forest. This is not the Teddy Bears' Picnic we're threatening to break up, it's more like the Gunpowder Plot. These people are only a day or so away from taking over the country, and they need to get rid of us if their years of planning are to come to fruition. We've got to decide how to bring them down."

"I thought we'd already decided!" Jazz and Pete said in unison. "You're going to get this Ray Pearson guy to do it for us."

"Yeah that's the plan," I replied, but Pete's comments about birdman's friend had made me think some more. "But what if they've worked that out too? They know now that we're on our way north. They must know that we need to stop their plan to have a chance of escaping them. They'll also know we're going to need someone with some power and influence to help us do that. So, they're going to be trying to work out who we know north of Leicester who might have that power and influence. And then it won't take them long to discover that Ray is the only person who might fit the bill."

"Don't be so bloody daft mate," Pete replied to this. "they're not going to know anything about that. I didn't know you bloody well knew him."

Pete's response should have acted like a bucket of cold water and roused me from my pessimistic visions of our future, but they didn't. If anything, they made them darker than ever, as I now envisioned us arriving at Ray's house in Headingly only to be shot by a sniper.

Jazz's lovely alto voice brought a bit of comfort, "Simon's right Pete. If you can find out what you have through your internet hackers, finding our contacts will be child's play to the sort of computer experts they're likely to have!

The beginnings of a plan were formulating. The Leeds area was my stomping ground and I could envisage a potential way out of our predicament.

"Pete!" I shouted in the direction of the phone."I want you to come up to Leeds on the first train in the morning. It's going to need all of us without any traceable vehicles if we're going to get out of this mess. Jazz and I are going to keep out of Leeds and stay in a hotel in

Harrogate I know. It's right next to a station on the rail line to Leeds. We'll come by rail and meet your train."

CHAPTER TWENY NINE

I woke up the next morning to a beautiful brown face on the pillow beside me, and a text from Pete to say he was on the seven o'clock train. Despite all the traumas of the last few days, traumas I could never have expected in my wildest nightmares, it had been worth it to be with the woman I love. Looking at Jazz and feeling the warmth of her body beside mine, I could understand how it could be worth giving up a kingdom to be with the woman you loved.

I had planned on being up, dressed and breakfasted by eight o'clock so that we could be in Leeds well before Pete's train arrived, but plans tend to disappear when the woman you love turns over in bed and hugs you with her naked body. So we decided to breakfast on Leeds station as we hurried across the car park to Hornbeam Park Station to catch the 8.17 to Leeds.

Of course, the Northern Rail multiple was packed with commuters wanting to be in Leeds before nine o'clock, and, just as I had hoped, I could see another mixed couple further down the train. Seeing them made me feel free to cuddle up to Jazz – not that I had much choice given the crowded nature of the train – knowing we would not stand out in this cosmopolitan milieu.

Arriving at Leeds a good half hour before Pete's train was due in, we went over to the Upper Crust and bought a breakfast baguette to share and two coffees. We sat at the chrome table and gazed at each other like two star-struck lovers. Well we were, weren't we?!

Jazz broke the mood as she asked, "What's the plan then super sleuth?"

That epithet had a nice ring to it I thought, especially as I did have a plan. I'd phoned Ray Pearson when we arrived at the hotel and arranged to meet him at his home at about ten a.m. He said he was busy until I mentioned that the reason I wanted to see him was to do with foiling the plans of Lord Dawlish and the One Way Group, and then asked him if he had any contacts with MI5 or Special Branch. Then his morning was suddenly free and I knew that he was going to be prepared for at least some of the things I had to tell him.

"OK babe, the plan is fairly fluid, but, as you know from last night, Pearson is expecting us at about ten. My initial scheme is for you to stay here with Pete whilst I get a taxi up to Headingly and check the environs of Pearson's house to see if there's any sign of Byrom or anyone else keeping watch. If all's clear, we'll all go up there in separate taxis for the meet. If not, there's a hotel a couple of miles up the road where we can meet securely."

"Byrom?" Jazz queried, looking worried. "Why would he be up here? Or rather how would he be up here? He's down in London looking for my Mum, isn't he?"

"I don't think so babe. I would guess he was called back up here as soon as they knew we were coming back North, which no doubt happened within minutes of birdman's death. I would also reckon that he's bearing us one massive grudge. We keep foiling his plans, and I don't think he's the sort of person who takes too kindly to those who impede his machinations. My idea is that by going in a taxi alone, I'll arouse no suspicion. He and his minions will be looking for a white man with a black woman driving a car with the description he was no doubt given by birdman's sidekick, not a lone man in a taxi. Plus, everyone accepts that taxis drive slowly down residential streets looking for the number they've to pick up from, so I'll be able to get a good look without arousing lots of suspicion."

"Wow, you really have become the super sleuth babe! Daniel Craig had better watch out," she laughed as she said this, a laugh that could have raised the spirits of even the most depressed man. "But seriously babe, it does sound like a good idea. I think you're absolutely right about Byrom, and I hate his guts. I'll never forget the way he pulled the wool over our eyes when he came up to Stockton. If he hadn't used his position and lies to gain our confidence, they'd never have found out that we knew something that could end their schemes, and we wouldn't be up shit creek without a paddle like we are now!"

I looked up at the arrivals board and saw that the train from London was pulling in three minutes early. Quite common on the old nationalised East Coast, but not Branson's version! I had a sudden picture of Pete getting off the train and gesticulating exuberantly to attract our attention, a ploy that would attract everyone's attention, and make it even easier for anyone looking for us. I quickly phoned him and told him to meet us quietly (I emphasised the adverb!) at McDonald's by following the signs to Aire Street and the car parks.

We walked down through the lovely Thirties architecture of the North Concourse to McDonald's and found a seat from which we could survey the whole area and everyone in it. Jazz didn't even need an explanation of why we were sitting there, paranoid was becoming our middle name.

It wasn't long before Pete walked in, went up to the counter, bought a coffee and double bacon and egg McMuffin and came and sat at a nearby table. I could see that, like us, he was examining the environs to see if anyone was taking an interest in us. Clearly he also decided there was no threat and came over to sit next to us. I outlined my plan to him, he okayed it, and I left them there and went back to the main concourse to find the taxi rank.

There was a fair-sized queue, but I didn't have to wait long as the taxis came in thick and fast. I'd never paid much attention to Leeds taxis as I, being teetotal, I'd never had need to use them. However, as I waited in the queue, I couldn't help noticing that driving taxis in Leeds seemed to be a Muslim occupation, or more accurately an occupation for those of Indian sub-continent ethnic origin. I remembered reading somewhere that taxi driving was an ideal occupation for ethnic Muslims as it gave freedom to break off for prayer times and kept them away from racist employers. My driver was a young man with a strong West Yorkshire accent belying his sub-continental appearance.

We were soon in Headingly and as we turned into the MP's road, the sight of a black BMW caused me to exclaim involuntarily, "Oh shit!"

"What's the matter sir?" asked the driver in his broad Yorkshire tones.

I had to do some quick thinking as to how to ask the driver to take me back to the station without making him totally suspicious. "That Beemer belongs to my girlfriend's husband, so I think my morning of sex is going out of the window!"

A loud guffaw came from the front of the cab, and the driver asked, "Where to then boss?"
The ploy had clearly worked and gave me the opening to ask to be taken back to Leeds station without arousing any suspicion.
I decided against phoning Ray from the taxi after thinking back to the World War II posters we were tested on in O Level History, and deciding that, in our situation, it might be as well to think of walls having ears!

I was soon back at the station McDonald's, giving Jazz a hug whilst asking Pete to get me a coffee to soothe my nerves. I think Jazz must have been able to feel the tension in me because she immediately asked, "What's up babe?"

I answered in language reminiscent of Pete, "My suspicions were bloody well correct. That fucking bastard Byrom is there in his sodding black Beemer keeping watch. I don't know if there are any more crooked police officers, bent politicians, corrupt bleeding bishops or anyone else there, but there's one thing for sure, we need to keep well clear of Pearson's house!"

"It's alright Simon, calm down. We knew this might happen, didn't we? That's why you went to do a recce. It's no big deal babe," Jazz spoke soothingly, and my anger began to dissipate.

"I know Jazz, but it's that slimy excuse for a police officer, Byrom. It's all down to him. If he hadn't pretended to be our friend, they'd never have known that we knew about Mark, and we wouldn't have to be hiding away, looking over our shoulders all the time!" I ended my outburst feeling rather better to have got it all off my chest.

"True enough babe," she replied. "Even so, you need to get on the phone to Ray Pearson pdq and sort out a meeting somewhere else. With his help, Byrom's not going to be a problem for much longer. And don't forget babe, we have the upper hand now. We know where Byrom is, but he doesn't know where we are!"

Just her presence was enough to calm me down and cheer me up, but her words did even more, convincing me, as Pete arrived with the coffee, that we were still in the driving seat!

Interestingly, Pete's reaction was more like Jazz's than mine, "Look Si. They're bound to be bleedin wetting themselves at the moment. All this soddin planning, you have to admit it's a bloody clever scheme which must have taken bloody ages to plan, and if what we know gets out, it's all been a bloody waste of time! That's why PC Plod, your bent constabulary friend, is lurking outside Pearson's house. They must be abso – bloody - lutely desperate to find us and stop us! Now get on that bleedin phone to Pearson and let's get it sorted out!"

I phoned and explained the situation. Pearson's response was intriguing, "Did you say Byrom? Inspector Byrom from the North Yorkshire CID?"

When I replied in the affirmative, Pearson responded, "A dangerous man Simon, you definitely need to keep out of his way. I'm looking forward to you giving us some evidence against him. Do you know the Weetwood Hall Hotel on Otley Road? I'm sure they'll have a meeting room for us, I often use it for small meetings."

"Yes, I know the Weetwood Hall. We're all at the station, so it'll probably take us about 30 minutes to get there."

"Right Simon. I'll give them a ring now. Just ask at reception for Mr Pearson's meeting."

I rang off and we finished our coffees, then made our way to the taxi rank at the front of the station. Jazz suggested it might be safer if we each went in a separate cab to avoid looking like the group of three they might be on the look-out for, so it was a good thirty minutes before we arrived at the hotel.

Leaving Leeds for Otley takes you out into beautiful countryside on the edge of Wharfedale. As I sat on my own in the back of a different taxi, I suddenly realised that the past week had been so hectic that I had had no chance to appreciate the beauty that is early June in the UK. Nowhere was this more evident than in the grounds surrounding the hotel. As we came up the drive the trees were approaching full leaf with a vast array of fresh spring colours, from yellow, through lime and chartreuse to the vivid reds of the acers. Then we came to the original seventeenth century house with the massive additions built on by the hotel so sympathetically that it was hard to tell which bits were original. I paid off the taxi and went into the elegant reception where Jazz and Pete were waiting for me.

We followed the receptionist's directions and found ourselves in Headingly 1, a well-appointed meeting room too large for our needs, but probably it was not economic for them to have rooms that would not accommodate at least fifteen people. As we were deciding which of the tables to use, Ray Pearson and two companions walked in, closely followed by a trolley with two flasks of coffee, cups and saucers and rather up-market home-made biscuits.

Unlike many politicians who become government ministers, Ray had neither put on weight, nor become grey. He was about six feet tall and very fit looking for a man in his early fifties. He was plainly ready for a meeting in his dark suit with faint stripe, white shirt and Labour red tie. To my, admittedly untrained, eye, his suit looked much more Marks and Spencer than Savile Row bespoke, just as his accent was still very much West Yorkshire as he introduced his companions.

"Hello Simon. Can I introduce two people who're very interested in what you've managed to find out about this One Way lot? This is Chief Superintendent Bexley from Special Branch," he said pointing to a smart looking fortyish lady in a black trouser suit. "And this is a gentleman whose name you really don't need to know, but he's responsible for the internal security of the UK with MI5," he continued pointing to a surprisingly anonymous-looking chap of about Ray's age.

I greeted them both and then introduced the three of them to Jazz and Pete. It still felt good, and also gave me a refreshing feeling of youth, to introduce Jazz as my girl-friend. After getting ourselves another coffee, we sat round one of the tables and Ray asked me to outline everything that had happened.

"Well, it all began with us finding a dead body at the Old Deanery Hotel in Ripon. Do you remember the case?"

Ray nodded as he replied, "Yes wasn't it two gays in a lovers' tiff, one murdering the other and then topping himself?"

"That's what they wanted everyone to think," Jazz said as she took over the tale, "but unfortunately for them, and us, I recognised the murder victim. It took me a bit to sort it out, but he was not the person the police said he was. He was an academic from Aberdeen University, Mark Greenwood, who was gay, but was not the Paul Williams identified by Samuel Watkinson, warden of the homeless men's hostel in Ripon."
"Was that the Samuel Watkinson who's now known as Lord Dawlish?" asked the man from MI5.

"The very same," I replied "and we were foolish enough to contact Inspector Byrom and tell him what we now knew about the misidentification. And that was the beginning of the nightmare. We'd seen some Tory MPs at the Old Deanery who seemed to be having a meeting at the cathedral with Tim Harris and the bishop."

"Can you identify who was there?" Chief Superintendent Bexley, who was taking notes, asked.

"Oh, yes," I replied. "We identified Tim Harris, Bishop Jim Scott-Philips, George Blenkinsop, Sir Henry Smythe and Jemimah Percy-Gilbert, but there might have been more. From what we've discovered since, we reckon that Mark had turned up and threatened to expose Tim Harris as Paul Connor a leader of the gay community at King's College London in the early Eighties."

"What?!" chorused, Ray, the Chief Superintendent and the man from MI5 in unison. "Did you say 'leader of the gay community'?"

"I did, and that's what caused the problem we think. We only found out yesterday that the Reverend Timothy Harris, leader of the anti-gay One Way Group, actually began life as Paul Connor and when he was a student at King's, he was a leader of the gay students. Then, for some reason we don't yet know, he changed his name by deed poll to Timothy Harris, trained as an Anglican priest and started off the One Way Group through the financial backing of Samuel Watkinson. Now whilst he was at King's, Connor had a brief affair with Mark Greenwood whose job at Aberdeen was researching new religious groups, and we reckon that through his research, Mark discovered that Tim Harris was the same guy he'd had an affair with as Paul Connor. Anyway, when Jazz and I told Byrom about the body being Mark Greenwood not Paul Williams, he told us there'd been a police cover-up and asked us to help him to expose it."

At this point Jazz took over again, "I was determined to get justice for Mark, so of course I agreed, and Simon went down to London to try to find the Samuel Watkinson who'd misidentified Mark's body, and Simon saw Watkinson with the Bishop of Ripon at the One Way Group publishers."

"That was when we realised Watkinson was not just the warden of a homeless men's hostel," I continued. "It was also when I realised I was being followed and Pete warned me that the man I'd seen following me was very dangerous."

"From what I'd discovered about Watkinson," said Pete, speaking for the first time. "That guy has fingers in so many pies. Lots of money and few scruples, despite his dog collar. You see he owns several companies and it was his Head of Internal Security, Wayne Jackson, who was following Si. He's a seriously dangerous man who's served two prison terms for gbh. Si identifying him gave us a connection between Byrom and Watkinson because only Byrom knew that Si was going to London."

"Then I discovered another link with Byrom," said Jazz joining in once more. "I saw him at Simon's in-laws' house in Redcar. I'd been to see his wife's solicitors for threatening me." Jazz then saw the expressions on her listeners' faces and continued, "You don't need to know about that, but you do need to know that Byrom was closely involved with the One Way Group in the North."

"To cut a long story short," I interrupted, not wanting to lose them in the detail of what had happened, "We felt under threat. We went by hire car to Aberdeen to check on Mark to see if we could discover why he'd been killed and talked to a Church of Scotland minister who knew, but was killed before he could tell us more than to find Mark's mother."

"Was that Alastair Cameron?" asked Superintendent Bexley, and when I nodded, she continued. "He contacted Special Branch in Aberdeen just before he died, but we couldn't work out what Mark Greenwood had to do with anything. Do you have any evidence of who killed him?"

"No, we never saw them, but we think they hoped to kill us with the same pediment stone. We do have evidence connecting Byrom to the kidnapping of Jazz, and that evidence connects the One Way Group to the kidnap as well. Also, when we freed Jazz – don't ask how because its legality maybe questionable – Wayne Jackson tried to kill her, and me, at her flat and we do have evidence of that."

"So, was all this going on whilst they were speaking to the press and having their O2 shindig?" Ray asked.

"It was indeed, which was why they seemed to become more and more desperate. As soon as they discovered Mrs Greenwood's whereabouts they attempted to kidnap her, but we arrived as it was happening and managed to release her and get her to a place of safety. Then they firebombed Jazz's mother, no doubt you know about that?" I asked and Superintendent Bexley nodded, whilst poor Ray Pearson was by this time looking totally stunned, if not fundamentally gobsmacked – he'd clearly had no idea what we'd been through. I finished the tale off as quickly as I could, "So we got her Mum to a place of safety as well and came up here to see you to see if you could do something to sort this mess out, and let us get on with our lives."

The man from MI5 was made of sterner stuff than Ray, or more probably had more idea what was going on and what these people were capable of. He was straight in with questions.

"Have you found any connections with Smythe, Blenkinsop and Percy-Gilbert?" he asked.

Pete fielded this as he'd been in charge of the hackers who'd found most of the information. "Oh yes. I'll tell you what though, this lot are bloody devious and they're sodding well brilliant at muddying IT waters," He began making a valiant but ever-failing attempt to moderate his language. "Anyway, Watkinson's a major shareholder in, and non-executive director of, 'Where It's At' magazine which, of course, make him close to Sir Henry Smythe. He's also the executor of the blind trust which was set up to look after Jemimah Percy-Gilbert's assets when she became a government minister. George Blenkinsop as well as being ex-Chair of North Yorkshire Police Authority and Chair of the 1922 Committee, is a non-executive director of the Fisherman's Group and on the advisory board of Saviour's Hostel Ripon both of which were closely involved with Watkinson, and with Mark's murder."

MI5's next question went in a different direction. "If this first murder victim was actually Mark Greenwood, do you have any idea how they managed to substitute another victim and a murderer?"

This was one for me to answer I thought and I replied, "Well we know for sure that Michael Brown was Mark Greenwood's lover and had come up to meet Mark in Ripon for something that Mark described as 'serious'. We reckon that Byrom did some dirty work to hang him and make it look like a suicide. He was investigating it and possibly Blenkinsop has a mate who did the post-mortem and didn't look for anything other than the obvious. As far as Paul Williams is concerned, we reckon he was someone who appeared at the hostel with no friends or relatives so that if he was named as the murder victim, no questions would be asked. We reckon Watkinson selected him and Byrom got rid of him somehow."

"So, there might be a body somewhere?" Chief Superintendent Bexley asked.

"Well there's a spare body isn't there!" said Jazz injecting a little macabre humour into the conversation.

There'd been a lot to take in and Ray had given all some thought before he asked, "And what do you think it's all been about?"

Schoolteacher Jazz was the one to give a clear and reasoned surmise, so Pete and I let her be our spokesperson. "Samuel Watkinson and Paul Connor/Tim Harris were at prep-school together and we reckon they stayed friends. Someone who was in the London gay scene at the time thinks he remembers Watkinson coming down from Oxford to stay with Connor/Harris. Whether it was Watkinson who helped with the name change and becoming a vicar, we don't know. But we do know Watkinson was very bitter about his family forcing him into the Church, and that might have set him out on this plan. We reckon," she looked round at Pete and I as she said this, "Watkinson and Harris set up the One Way Group as a way of using religion to get power. Having got the Group thriving, they could then form a cabal with their old school buddies – Blenkinsop, Smythe, Scott-Philips – to take over the government."

"That's going a bit far isn't it lass?" Ray said, his Yorkshire working-class roots coming out under pressure, "I might not like public school Tories, but I never thought they were that bad."

"You maybe be right," responded Jazz. "My idea is only guesswork, but we're pretty sure they had a plan which involved forcing the Tory vote on the Prime Minister, then the O2 shindig starting off a One Way Christian charm offensive on the country, then the publication of Smythe's sting on the Tory Remainers. We reckon that they've engineered it so the Prime Minister will lose the vote, Jemimah Percy-Gilbert will be elected party leader and therefore Prime Minister, their friend Jim Scott-Philips will be appointed Archbishop of Canterbury and Watkinson, as Lord Dawlish, will get a senior government post. What will happen then, we don't know except that we'll have to leave the country or we'll be dead. They can't let anyone else know what we know."

Wow, what a woman! Jazz had put it all so well and now Pearson and the police and MI5 went into a huddle for a few minutes before Ray said, "You won't need to leave the country! Thanks so much for what you've done and for putting us in the picture. We knew, or suspected, much of it, but you've given us the final pieces. Keep yourselves out of the way, and out of their way, for twenty-four hours. Listen to the news and you'll be aware of when you can go back home in safety. The country owes you three. Now we three need to get on with preventing the English Tea Party coup! "

CHAPTER THIRTY

Special Branch officers must have been watching the hotel because the Chief Superintendent was able to check on her mobile that no one was watching and we were safe to go back to Leeds station in one taxi, so that's what we did.

Then, of course, we had to decide where to go, and who to go with. I didn't want to have to tell Pete we didn't want him with us, but twenty-four hours in a hotel room alone with Jazz was looking decidedly attractive. Indeed, it looked far more tempting than having to entertain Pete for twenty-four hours!

I had a feeling that Jazz might protest if I told Pete we didn't want him with us. So, I tried to put the onus on him by giving him a couple of signs that his presence might be superfluous to requirements. Firstly, I put my arm round Jazz, then gave her a big hug. Secondly, I gave her a fairly abstemious, but still far from chaste, kiss.

Luckily, Pete read the signs and said, "OK you two, I think I'll push off back to the smoke. A cockney boy can only take so much bleeding northern air you know. I'll keep a bloody close eye on the buggers through the hackers, and I'll keep in touch. Thanks for everything and Jasmine thank you for bringing some bleeding joy into this miserable bugger's life."

Jazz disengaged herself from me and flung her arms round Pete, thanking him for all his help to me since my parents' death and particularly for the last week. He looked particularly pleased and embarrassed as we walked him over to the London train before going to wait for our geriatric diesel multiple back to Harrogate to pick up the car.

We couldn't continue our stay at Harrogate as the hotel had told us they were fully booked, as, apparently, they almost always were on Saturdays. We decided that our best bet was to go back to the hotel in Newcastle where we'd spent our first night together and stay there until things sorted themselves out. Then we could pick up Jazz's car from the airport, return the hire car and get back to a normal life.

The drive up was uneventful. We had Radio 5 on all the time in case of any news, but there was nothing to do with us, just the usual sacking of a Premiership manager, a Hamas attack on Israeli troops on the Gaza border and some nutty tweets from Trump.

It was about three o'clock by the time we checked into the Newcastle hotel, and when we switched on the TV and went to BBC 24-hour news, we saw that things had changed in a big way: *"News is just coming in, "said the announcer, "of surprising developments in the Conservative Party confidence vote on the Prime Minister. We're going straight over to our political correspondent who is outside Conservative Campaign Headquarters in Matthew Parker Street. The picture changed and focussed on the BBC political correspondent standing outside the building housing Tory headquarters as he spoke, "There have been sensational developments here today. The result of the confidence vote was not expected until tomorrow evening, but it has just been announced by the Conservative Party Chairman. The Prime Minister achieved a massive majority backing by the Tory MP's with only five MP's voting against him. George Blenkinsop, the organiser of the vote and Chairman of the 1922 Committee of Conservative MPs, seems to have disappeared and there are strong rumours that he has resigned."*

We jumped up and down on the bed at this news. Ray and his friends from Special Branch and MI5 had clearly delivered, but it seemed as if it was going to be a very low-key response with no mention of any plots. We had called in the Establishment and they were going to clear up the mess in the Establishment's way - without letting the plebs know that anything had happened. It would not do to disturb their faith in the powers that be!

We had just stopped bouncing and were hugging each other in our joy when another news item came on: "The person who placed a £100 bet at 100:1 on the Bishop of Liverpool becoming the new Archbishop of Canterbury is £10,000 better off this afternoon as it has just been announced from Downing Street that the Bishop of Liverpool, the Right Reverend John Sanderson, from the liberal wing of the Church, has been appointed the next leader of the Church of England. Bishop Sanderson has often aroused controversy over his support for gay marriage in church, women bishops and closer ties with other faiths. The bookies favourite, Bishop James Scott-Philips, was unavailable for comment."

There had been no mention of either Tim Harris or Lord Dawlish, but there didn't really need to be. With the Prime Minister still in office, a liberal Archbishop and Blenkinsop resigned, we had to be safe. It was over, we were free and as we happened to be lying on the bed at the time, there only seemed to be one appropriate way to celebrate!

EPILOGUE

Here we are three months later sitting in an office with a discreet sign outside informing the world that these are the premises of Baker and Keep, Private Investigators.

Jazz never did go back to her job at the school. Although the Head had been told that her unauthorised absence had been due to 'affairs of state', he still told Jazz he regarded it as unacceptable for one of his Heads of Department to absent themselves just before major exams. He had also somehow discovered a connection between Jazz and the unexplained disappearance from his staff of Emma Davies and Colin Taylor. Certainly, he chose the wrong moment to try to blame Jazz for their disappearance, and, after she had told him in very explicit language that he could stick his job in a place where the sun doesn't shine and had gone into graphic details about his character and personality failings, we decided that it would be impossible for her ever to work for him again and she resigned.

It was a wise decision. We are now living together in Jazz's flat, and our office is just a short walk away on the High Street above a coffee shop. Business is booming, I have to admit I had no idea there were so many people wanting to check on marriage partners, find out details about children's boyfriends/girlfriends, check on business partners, or find missing relatives. We haven't been working long, but we both love it and Jazz's expertise in Islam is proving very useful for the large business there seems to be in checking out proposed Muslim marriage partners.

Of course, we have a much closer relationship with Pete than I had when I was married to the ice maiden. We're in London quite often courtesy of Grand Central Railway, but we both prefer the bookshop to the hackers' hideaway in Wembley which has too many bad memories for us.

The ice maiden is truly such now as the Thompson family has migrated to Alaska at the invitation of a Christian group with connections to the Tea Party Movement and Tim Harris. It was all done extremely quickly, no doubt to escape the possibility of criminal charges over Jasmine's kidnapping. In the interests of their escape, and the government being able to keep everything under wraps, I was given all the documentation I need for a no questions divorce, and access to all the money which had been in our joint accounts. All she asked in return was documentation absolving the Thompsons of any involvement in Jazz's kidnap!

Sir Henry Smythe's 'Where It's At' magazine published a huge front page apology for fabricating the report on the Tory Remainers receiving illegal funding from Arabs, and paid them an undisclosed sum in compensation. Although Smythe blamed the fabrication on his underlings, Sir Henry was forced to accept overall responsibility and, as a result, has retired from public life. Jemimah Percy-Gilbert remains a Conservative MP, but is persona non-grata in the party and is keeping a very low profile.

George Blenkinsop resigned all his public offices and his parliamentary constituency citing health problems. He has retired to the Bahamas, no doubt to be joined to his off-shore assets. His police crony, Dave Byrom, has, one might say, been hoist with his own petard. He was found hanged in the same wood where Michael Brown was found. Whether he actually committed suicide, or his suicide was as faked as Michael's we will never know. The fact that a public trial would have brought everything into the open, does lead to certain suspicions.

The establishment excelled itself with the two main players. Samuel Watkinson, aka Lord Dawlish, simply disappeared in a boating accident off Cowes. The inquest recorded a death by misadventure verdict and so no enquiries had to be made. Just afterwards, there was an announcement that Tim Harris had lost his faith and was resigning as leader of the One Way Group. He then simply disappeared from sight and no one seems to know what has happened to him. Without his leadership and Watkinson's financial support, the One Way group appears to be disintegrating.

Of course, the establishment has been helped by the press's fear of the Leveson Report and its aftermath, consequently there has been no investigative journalism of these affairs and it has been easy for them to keep things under wraps.

I was feeling a bit sorry for Jim Scott-Philips who allegedly received a call to serve in a less fortunate part of the Anglican Communion and moved from being Bishop of Ripon to becoming Bishop of Popondota in Papua New Guinea. But that was before I received a letter from him apologising for 'any inconvenience you might have been put to', and ending with these words, 'I'm sure that one day you'll realise we were right. It was the only way.'

33631993R00162

Printed in Great Britain
by Amazon